EQUALLY PAINFUL CONSEQUENCES

by

ALISON NORTH

Author's Introduction

Nearly every young wife, happily married or not, is prepared to grant someone else an occasional share of the sexy little bottom she's supposed to keep only unto her husband. It's just a case of basic instinct temporarily gaining the upper hand. But sometimes the consequences for the aforementioned bottom can be painful in the extreme. Believe me, because I know only too well. So here are some further examples of how I and some of my girlfriends have been made to suffer for our indiscretions. But remember, all you husbands, on the vast majority of occasions our naughtiness remains totally unsuspected. So John, Richard, Graham, Peter, Julian, David, Barry, Mike, Tony, and the rest of all you cuckolds out there, is your wife really at home alone while you're attending the football match tonight...?

Young wives with other guys on the back seat of the car,
  Young wives with sexy sighs as those guys probe so far,
  Young wives with widespread thighs, their bodies smooth and slim,
  Young wives with practised lies to hide what they've let in,
  Young wives with troubled eyes explain where they've been that night,
  Young wives, false alibis, and tiny knickers damp and tight.

Alison North, 20 January 2014.

Prologue

The taxi dropped Jayne outside her large detached house in the suburbs. As she closed the front door behind her she adjusted the superbly filled seat of her full-length evening gown and glanced at her watch. It was nearly one o'clock in the morning, but fortunately Martin's car was not in the drive. Now to remove and then conceal the incriminating evidence...

She walked through the kitchen to the utility room and dropped her semen-soaked thong into the washing machine. It would be perfectly safe in there. Martin didn't even know how to open the door...

Oh, dear! She was starting to feel guilty, now that the champagne was wearing off. She supposed she should never have done it. In fact, she *knew* she should never have done it. It wasn't poor Martin's fault that he worked such long hours. He was only doing what he thought was best for the two of them. She should never have given in to the yearning she'd felt in her loins. A yearning that, over the past few months, had grown and grown and grown. Now it was out of all proportion. And out of control, as well. As witness the events of the evening...

Yes, her conscience was really starting to play up. How could she have acted like that? Like the very worst sort of whore?

But she had to admit how greatly she'd enjoyed herself. The sex had been absolutely phenomenal. She'd never known anything like it. And, apart from her guilty conscience, she was feeling better than she'd felt for ages. She was feeling incredibly uplifted. Just as if she'd taken some sort of drug. And her pussy! It was positively purring with happy contentment. It was positively radiating fulfilment and joy.

How sexy it had felt, being sorted out by Peter over that table, with both Emma and John standing there watching intently! She had to confess it had been fun. Embarrassing to start with, but fun throughout. Great fun, in fact. Her insides had been in turmoil at the way she was being serviced so well under the close scrutiny of two observers.

But how different it had been for poor Jillie Jackson, two years ago last January at the office! Being closely observed on the job, she meant. Jillie Jackson, that lovely blonde girl with the really sexy wiggle that even the women found appealing. Jillie Jackson, who'd been humbled and humiliated by her head of department, George Franks. Humbled and humiliated by being made to lie, face down, across one of the tall computer stands in the IT room - the top half of her body lying flat on the surface of the stand, her legs dangling down at right angles, and her toes only just touching the floor. Humbled and humiliated by being made to lie across the stand in that manner and let him screw her from behind - in full view of the four other men from their department! Humbled and humiliated by being made to let him screw her and pump her full of his seed, while their four other colleagues from sales watched in fascination. It hadn't been any fun at all for her. Jillie hated every second. It might have been okay if she and George had been alone. In fact, she'd admitted that she'd probably have enjoyed housing his grossly overgrown weapon if they'd been by themselves and he'd promised to keep quiet about it - particularly as her lack of say in the matter would have stopped her feeling guilty afterwards. But having to take him in front of four other co-workers, all of whom were bound to talk, had been way, way too much. Her face had been scarlet with the shame of having to lie there - her bare bottom tilted up in the air - while everyone watched George stretching and straining her insides much further than they'd comfortably go. Scarlet with the shame of having to let everyone watch every tiny detail of the way he was cramming himself right up inside her until she was full to the brim, and beyond. And she'd felt even more wretched when the sperm eventually started to fly, burying her face in her hands in dismay as one long, fierce spurt after another jetted powerfully into her womb.

After George had finally finished with her she'd tugged up her skimpy knickers and tottered out of the room, feeling as fucked as it was possible to be, and wishing she could simply vanish from the face of the earth forever. Thank heavens her husband, Tommy, never got to hear anything about it! Everyone else had.

Jillie had told her everything later that day. She'd told her how George had confronted her with the photographs on his mobile phone. The ones he'd secretly taken of her having it off with Jim Browne from marketing the evening before. She'd told her how George had made her lie across the computer stand before slowly baring her bottom in front of everyone. To begin with the hem at the back of her expensively cut designer dress had been carefully turned up to her shoulder blades - leaving her lying there wearing nothing below the waist other than high heels and the very tiniest pair of tight pink panties. After a pause for dramatic effect, and to enable everyone's anticipation to grow, George had reached out with both hands and slid the pretty pink garment all the way down to her ankles. Jillie held her breath and screwed up her eyes in horror, but had been unable to close her ears to the collective sigh of approval.

George began to stroke her bottom. 'Just look at the state of this!' he gloated. 'Just think of the fun that Lucky Jim has been having with it! Isn't it a sight to behold?' Everyone had concurred. 'And the texture,' he enthused. 'It's as smooth as buttered silk. How many times has Jim had more than his fair share of it?' he asked her.

'I'm not going to say,' she replied, blushing wildly as she stared down at the metal surface of the computer stand directly under her nose.

He gripped both cheeks in one hand and squeezed, making her wince. 'How many others have had a slice of it since you've been married to Tommy?'

'I'm not going to say,' she repeated.

'So there have been others apart from Jim?'

'I'm not going to say...'

At length George had unzipped, thereby revealing the enormity of his designs upon her. Jillie had been unable to prevent herself darting a quick look back at him over her shoulder, through a swathe of long blonde hair, and then groaning inwardly at the size of the problem confronting her. The faint hopes she'd harboured of some sort of erectile dysfunction had instantly evaporated.

Slowly, but very surely, he started to plunder her - gripping her firmly round the waist and making her gasp, lift her head, and contort her face in shame and anguish at the intolerable invasiveness of each massive forward push. Then after a while making her gasp and contort even more as he began to hammer into her at speed. Although she kept her eyes tightly shut throughout her ordeal, Jillie had been able to sense that the onlookers were studying her facial reactions to the iniquitous pillaging of pussy just as closely as the sight of George's huge, gleaming-wet penis slithering back and forth between the cheeks of her upturned bottom.

The rest of the afternoon had been a nightmare for her. George implanted her so prodigiously that the residue had still been trickling stickily into her knicker-crotch when five o'clock at last arrived. And every time she'd been obliged to get up from her desk - wet and throbbing at the join of her legs - she felt the gaze of the other departmental members all over the well filled seat of her figure-hugging dress. She knew that they knew that she knew exactly what they were pondering...

'Are you sitting comfortably, Mrs Jackson?' the seventeen-year-old post boy had asked with a cheeky grin. 'I hear you had something rather filling at lunchtime.' She blushed fiercely, wishing she could expire there and then. Even such a junior employee had heard of her disgrace!

4

'I suppose him cumming was the worst bit,' Jillie had confided to her, wriggling her hips uncomfortably as the two of them sat in the wine bar after work that day. 'I mean, it was all horrible, but I think that was probably the worst. You know, all those people standing there and that colossal column of cock jammed right up inside me, swamping me with load after load of his cum. It seemed to go on forever, Jayne. And all the time those people knowing just what he was pumping into me. It was so degrading. How can I ever look any of them in the eye again? I still feel as bad about it as ever. Maybe even worse, the more I think about it. Those people standing there watching him giving me the father of all fuckings!'

'You should have told him to stuff his dirty photos where it hurts.'

'How could I? He was going to e-mail them to Tommy unless I did exactly as he said. What would you have done, Jayne?'

'I'm not sure.'

'Wouldn't you have done the same as me?' Jillie asked, sounding anxious.

Jayne decided to speak the truth. 'I think I'd probably have called his bluff,' she replied as gently as she could.

'Oh dear. I suppose that's what I should have done. He probably wouldn't have sent them to Tommy, would he?'

'Probably not. But you couldn't have been certain, could you? You didn't want to take the risk. Everyone knows what a rat he is. He just might have done such a thing.'

'That's what I thought. Oh, how could I have been so stupid as to let Jim shag me on George Frank's desk last night? We all know what a real sod George is. I thought everyone had gone home. I'd no idea George was there behind one of the screens, taking photos of us with his mobile. Why didn't I make Jim wait until we got to the top floor and found a nice empty room with a lock? That's what we usually do. And what on earth is he going to think of me when he hears what George has just done?'

'I'm sure he'll still fancy you.'

'What? When he hears that all the men in my department have spent almost half an hour watching George Franks fucking me every which way but loose?'

'Well...'

'I've been so weak,' Jillie groaned miserably. 'I should have told George to go and fuck himself, not me.'

'It wasn't your fault. Not really.'

Jillie looked thoughtful. 'I wonder whether it would help if I were to offer to let Jim spank me. If I were to ask him to put me over his knee and slap me as hard as he likes? I wonder if that would do any good. I wonder if it might help him feel a bit better about things. Most men seem to be interested in doing that to a girl, don't they? It's the very last thing I want to happen, but if there's no other choice...'

'You'd have to keep the telltale signs away from Tommy. You know how long it takes for Leanne's cheeks to recover after Terry's dealt with her that way. Look how red she was at the squash club last year.'

'That's not a problem. Tommy's off on a seminar to Birmingham for four nights after tonight. I wonder if I should ask Jim whether he wants to come round tomorrow evening and really hurt my bottom? After all, I guess I probably deserve it, don't I? Maybe, afterwards, he'd want to make things up in bed? Just like Tommy did when he found out I'd been lying to him about Jonathan Crowe.'

'Are you sure it'll all be worthwhile? After all, you're in love with Tommy - not Jim.'

'I know, Jayne. But having it off with Jim every day before I go home is just so much fun. It's something to look forward to all afternoon.'

'Okay...'

'Oh, Jesus! Talking of Tommy, suppose he was to hear about all this? Suppose my lovely Tommy was somehow to discover that everyone at work knows how I had to let my whole department watch me being fucked by George, because of the way he found me screwing Jim the night before? How bad would that be?'

'Tommy won't find out,' Jayne reassured her. 'He doesn't know anyone from work apart from Jim. And he's not likely to tell him, is he?'

'I suppose not. Oh, Lord! I'm going to have to buy a fresh pair of knickers. I really can't go home in these. They're getting wetter and wetter.'

CHAPTER ONE - A TALE OF TWO WIVES
Part One - Confessions of a Not-So-Private Secretary

Leanne Howlet knew she was in dire trouble. Carelessly, she'd chosen the wrong excuse for being over an hour and a half late home on that dark wet evening in early January. 'So you've been working late at the office for Tommy?' her husband, Terry, had asked her to confirm, some two minutes earlier.

'Yes, that's right. I had to finish typing a report to be e-mailed off tonight. We've been working on it solidly since four o'clock. It was a rushed job and Tommy's typing skills just weren't up to it.'

'He was there with you, was he? Tommy Jackson?'

'Yes. He dictated the report as I keyed it in to the computer.'

'All the time since four o'clock?'

'Yes.'

'And then he gave you a lift home in his new car?'

'That's right.'

'He was there with you all the time you were working on the report?'

'Yes.'

'From four o'clock until just now?'

'Yes. He had to check and then edit the whole thing before it could be sent. It was very important.'

'Then he drove you straight home? Just now?'

'Yes. What's the problem?'

'You know what I think about you and Tommy bloody Jackson!'

'I've told you a hundred times, there's nothing between us.'

'Liar!'

'I'm not.'

'Do you think I'm daft, Leanne?'

'On that issue, yes.'

'You've been shagging him again tonight. In his car.'

'I told you, we were working together at the office.'

'All the time from four o'clock until he dropped you home just now? He was with you all that time? In your room while you were typing?'

'Yes.'

'Then you got into his car at the office car park a few minutes ago and he drove you straight here? Without stopping anywhere?'

Unfortunately for her, Leanne had failed to see or suspect the trap. 'Yes, of course.'

Terry's eyes gleamed in triumph. 'Now I know you're lying.'

'Don't be stupid.'

'If you got into his car at the office car park and then drove straight here, how come his car wasn't in the car park at five to five, when you say the two of you were busily working together inside the building? It only takes ten minutes to drive here, not an hour and a half.'

It was then that Leanne realised how grossly negligent she'd been regarding her choice of an excuse, and how she'd landed herself in trouble so needlessly. Why hadn't she said she'd popped in to see her mother? Or had a quick drink with Jayne or Tracie or Alison after work? Or missed her bus? 'Wh-what do you mean?' she stammered, although knowing only too well.

'By sheer coincidence I was up your end of town just before five and was surprised to notice that Tommy's flashy new car was nowhere to be seen. The reason being, I now realise, that he'd already driven you off to a quiet spot somewhere so you could get out of your knickers for him. Again'

'That's not true.'

Terry knew she was lying, but decided to keep the facts to himself and play cat and mouse with her for a while longer. 'So how is it that his car wasn't there at five to five, but was when you say you got into it only ten minutes ago? Answer me that.'

'I don't know...'

'Yes you do. It wasn't there at five to five because the two of you had already headed off in it, seeking a secluded place to park.'

'We hadn't. He must have left it somewhere else during the day and then gone off to get it after five to five...'

'But you just told me he was with you all the time you were working on the report. From four o'clock until ten minutes or so ago. Three times you told me that.'

'Not all the time...'

'Well, that's exactly what you said.'

'Well, I didn't mean *all* the time...'

'How long was he missing for then?' Terry asked with patient persistence.

'I don't know. I was busy doing his typing.'

'You mean he was busy doing his typist!'

'It's not true.'

'You've spent most of the last ninety minutes letting him fuck you in his car.'

'I haven't. I don't know where his car was when you were outside the office car park.'

'Why should he have left it somewhere else earlier?'

'I don't know.'

'If he had done so, why should he nip out and get it, instead of walking to it with you when the typing was finished?'

'I don't know.'

'Why did you tell me he was with you all the time you were working late, if that wasn't true?'

'I don't know. I suppose I didn't think it was important...'

'Well, it is.'

'Yes, I know that now...'

'I bet you do. You remember what I said I'd do to you if I ever found out for sure that you'd been screwing your sodding boss?'

'But I haven't...'

'Just answer the question!' he snapped angrily. 'I'll explain later why I know for sure. In the meantime, do you remember what I said I'd do to you?'

'Yes, of course,' she gulped, feeling her legs go weak at the knees at the thought of what lay ahead. The same way in which they always went weak whenever she realised Tommy was proposing to upend her - but for rather different reasons.

Terry had been jealous and suspicious of his sexy young wife ever since he'd been eighteen and she'd been his sexy girlfriend. Seven years earlier, when she'd been twenty and promoted to the position of Tommy's private secretary, his suspicions had become even greater. He'd been convinced she was having it away with her new boss, the good-looking and charismatic Tommy Jackson, head of a thriving law firm he'd built up from scratch. In fact this hadn't been true until some considerable while later, when Terry's constant accusations finally drove her to entertain Tommy between her legs.

Over the years her attitude had gradually hardened. If Terry was so convinced she was at it, then at it she might as well be, she'd eventually decided. And at it she and Tommy had been about twice a month over the course of the preceding year. 'Just a bit of harmless fun,' she'd always told herself. And, also, something that Terry's endless and unjustified allegations had rendered inevitable. She'd never been unfaithful with anyone else, even though Terry had spent the past twelve years suspecting she had. And she'd found, much to her relief, that her occasional out-of-knicker experiences with Tommy didn't lead her to love Terry any the less. Somewhat the opposite, in fact.

When they were teenagers Terry had lost his temper with her. She'd been far too friendly and chatty with a notorious Jack-the-Lad from his football team, he decided, possibly correctly. She was wanting the so-and-so to get inside her knickers, he further concluded, this time quite wrongly. So, later that night, when they'd had his parents' house to themselves, he put her over his knee and spanked her bare buttocks for half an hour or more, making them glow with pain. Hurting the rounded cheeks of her incredibly sexy young bottom had been the most satisfying experience of his life thus far. More satisfying, even, than the occasion on which they'd both lost their virginity together, some two months earlier. And, much as she'd struggled, sobbed and protested, he'd found - during the subsequent love-making - that the punishment had made her as wet as a rainy weekend in Wales. He also noticed that her general attitude towards him significantly improved. For several months thereafter she paid him considerably more respect and attention than before. Consequently, when that respect and attention eventually started to wane, back she'd gone over his lap for another sound spanking. With the result that two or three times a year from then onwards, the normal colour of her plump bottom had been transformed to a glorious shade of red. A glorious shade of angry red that always took the best part of twenty-four hours before it even began to turn to a sullen pink.

During the very first spanking session he learnt he could minimise her protests and struggles by setting a time limit for the ordeal, and then threatening to add a further five minutes for every time she tried to resist the next series of stinging slaps. As a result, from then on, whenever it was once again time for her to be chastened and chastised, she laid passively over his knee, weeping and sobbing profusely but meekly accepting her fate.

As for Leanne, she'd long since discovered that her naturally submissive personality helped her to endure the pain and humiliation and concentrate, instead, on the sex that she hoped would follow.

Why did she still love him? She'd asked herself umpteen times. It was a question that continued to baffle her, as well as all her friends. But love him she did, despite his jealous possessiveness and the occasional beating of her bottom.

While Terry was biding his time in the living room, Leanne was lying face-down on the antique desk in his study, her feet resting on the floor behind her, her arms spread wide, and her hands tightly gripping either side of the desk in apprehension of what was to come. The top half of her body was completely prostrated as she waited fearfully for Terry to impose his will upon her howsoever he chose. Because of the enticingly uptilted stance of her bottom, the hem of her navy-blue miniskirt - the one of which Terry so strongly disapproved and on which Tommy was always so keen - was fractionally above the line of the delightful little crease that separated buttocks from thighs, thus revealing just the merest hint of tight white knickers and creamy-pink cheeks. The tableau was completed by the knee-length boots she liked to wear with that particularly sexy little skirt. She felt they complemented the way in which the skirt fitted snugly across the cheekiest part of her bottom. Tommy liked the way in which the bouncy little skirt enabled him to slip a hand up inside the seat as he passed behind her and take a generous handful of warm, lightly-knickered bottom.

Terry's views on the garment were very different. She was encouraging men to want to fuck her, he felt. Indeed, the skirt had provoked a hard hand spanking only the previous month, after she'd ignored his wishes and worn it to the office three days in a row. In a rare show of defiance she'd worn it to work again the next day. That was the only occasion on which a sorely blistered bottom had failed to produce the results desired by her husband. Unknown to Terry, of course, she'd told Tommy of the punishment, and allowed him to inspect the aftermath. The effect had been instantaneous. The sight of those poor, sore cheeks provoked him to bend her over the nearest available surface and take her from behind, pausing only to flick down the switch which activated the red *Do Not Disturb* sign outside his office door. Then there'd been a repeat performance later in the day.

On her return home from work, her bold act of rebellion earned her a second painful spanking on top of the one she'd received twenty-four hours earlier, but she felt that the two bonus fucks from Tommy had made everything more than worthwhile.

Leanne groaned to herself in despair. She knew Terry well enough to realise that he meant every word of the threat he'd made one evening, six months earlier. The threat he'd made when she returned home very late from an office function at the King Harold. Once again he'd accused her of fucking Tommy. And once again it had been true...

Not that Terry had always been right, of course. For years he'd wrongly suspected and accused her of cheating on him with Tommy. So, eventually, she had. Just every now and then, and just for fun. Partially because it seemed a good way of getting her own back for her husband's constant accusations. And partially too, of course, because she fancied the boxer shorts off her sexy young boss. She had to accept that fact...

'Never admit anything,' Tommy had warned her, when the first fuck was at long last achieved. 'Whatever Terry says or does, never admit a thing. Deny it all, however suspicious everything might seem. That way he can never know for sure.'

It had been good advice. Despite endless questions and cross-examinations, she'd stuck to her guns and refused to admit any impropriety, even though she'd stepped happily out of her knickers for Tommy more than twenty times since then. They'd done it in his car, in Terry's car, in bed at her Mother's house, and of course that day in Tommy's office - the red light on the door being about the same hue as the bruised, sweetly blushing bottom she'd been so readily prepared to offer up to her handsome boss. They'd even done it in a public swimming pool, as well as on the floor of a deserted squash court...

Leanne sighed heavily. She supposed she'd thoroughly earned all she was undoubtedly about to receive. Much as she still loved and respected her husband, she'd never once had any qualms about being unfaithful with Tommy. It had just been so much fun. So, here she was, here she'd inevitably ended up, face-down on his desk and about to reap her very just rewards...

While Leanne was sprawled forward across the top of Terry's desk, gripping the edges as she fearfully awaited her dues, Tommy Jackson let himself into his house by the side door. Jillie wasn't home. Good. It gave him the chance to reflect further on one of the best fucks he'd ever had...

Leanne had arrived at work that morning wearing the outfit that stirred him the most. The one that made her look like a sexy sixth-form schoolgirl. A white, long-sleeved blouse stretched snugly across the most spectacular pair of breasts that any man could ever wish to lay bare, knee-length leather boots, and that short blue skirt that buttoned up the front. Twice in the past he'd undone it button by button - the undoing of the final one allowing it to slide silently down to the floor in sweet surrender.

'You're looking extra horny today,' he'd finally allowed himself to comment, when the working day was almost at an end. At the time she'd been reaching down, straight-legged, over the lowest drawer of his filing cabinet.

She'd brushed her lustrous brown hair away from her face and looked back at him over her shoulder with the most knowing of knowing grins. 'You mean bending over like this in such a short skirt?'

'Yes, precisely.'

'It gives you ideas?'

'I wouldn't be normal if it didn't.'

'You could give me a lift home tonight, via Denes Park? We haven't been there for a while.'

He'd stared at the outline of her fabulous, bent-over bottom through her skirt, and felt his penis give a violent twitch. 'What a splendid idea,' he replied, relishing the prospect of getting between her shapely thighs once again. Then he studied his watch. 'It's quarter to five. Go and get your things. If we beat the five o'clock exodus we can be there in less than ten minutes. Fuck the rest of the filing.'

'Is there anything else you think ought to be fucked tonight?' she'd asked, as innocently as possible.

He stared again at the shape of her beautifully round bottom, so clearly discernible through the lightweight skirt, and the smooth bare thighs below. 'There certainly is,' he growled.

Denes Park had become their favourite wintertime shagging-field, being dark and deserted by five o'clock from late November through to early February. Just the place on a cold winter's evening to impale and then implant your highly fuckable young secretary on her way home to cook for her husband.

As he'd turned his newly acquired sports coupe into the track that led to the lake, Leanne had begun her standard time-saving preparations. She slipped out of her ankle-length winter coat and tossed it onto the back seat, before sliding her knickers off over her feet. Next she turned her attentions to him, unbuckling and unzipping his trousers, then reaching inside and exposing his rapidly stiffening penis to the cool night air. Still holding him in one hand she reclined

11

the passenger seat as far as it would go. By the time he'd stopped the car on the far side of the lake she was kneeling on the passenger seat in order to lean her head over the central console and take him into her mouth. That was what had made a difference that evening; the high central console in his new sports coupe. It required her to kneel on the seat and then bend right over in order to get her face down to his groin. In his previous saloon she'd been able to reach him with her mouth whilst still sitting down.

He slid his left hand up the back of her tiny skirt... and gasped. The feel of her bare bottom sent a massively enhanced electrical impulse straight to his groin. In that pose, head down and succulent bare bottom on high, he could imagine she was waiting for him to spank her. Whilst holding that delightful thought in mind, it had felt as if every spare drop of blood in his body was being forced into his already over-stretched penis. Never had he experienced a better erection. The only one ever to have equalled it had been twelve months ago, when he'd put Jillie across his knee and spanked her over the bad business of Jonathan Crowe.

So he sat back in the driver's seat, savouring the quality of the very minimal contact between them; just the warm, vibrant smoothness of her buttocks under his left hand, and the glorious wet warmth of her mouth all around his aching dick. He sat back, relishing the thought of the way in which Terry had, on occasions, put her over his knee for half an hour or so, setting those soft cheeks well and truly on fire. What wouldn't he give to do the same thing himself? 'This lovely bare bum to punish,' he said to himself, slowly caressing each buttock in turn, and imagining the pleasure he'd derive from punishing them as severely as Terry sometimes did. The one very minor spanking he'd given her last month was nothing compared to what her husband did to her on a regular basis.

He'd known then, as he continued to fondle her bottom, and as she continued to suck him slowly in and out of her pretty mouth, that it was going to be a fuck to remember...

And he'd been right. Not only had he been significantly longer and thicker than usual, but he'd been so rigid that she'd been unable to move him by even a fraction of an inch. Wriggle her hips though she had, he remained solidly stiff and unmoving inside her, pulling her vagina from side to side as she writhed in delight. And when he pushed all the way forward he'd just known he was stretching her as far as she'd go.

'You feel very good tonight,' she'd murmured appreciatively. 'This is easily the best I've ever been fucked...'

And there was another aspect to porking Leanne, mused Tommy, pouring himself a second glass of red wine. Something that made it doubly enjoyable. Not only was he fucking her in the literal sense of the word, but he was also fucking her miserable little git of a husband in the other sense, as well.

Tommy looked at his watch. Jillie was late back from work once again. It had happened regularly in the past few weeks. Apparently she was working on some new project with Jim Browne from marketing, for their head of department, George someone-or-other. He hoped she wouldn't be much longer. He was

12

feeling particularly horny as a result of his recent coupling with Leanne. He'd shag Jillie within seconds of her coming in the door, he decided. She always appreciated that sort of attention. It demonstrated how special he found her. Then he'd give her another right royal seeing-to when they went to bed. And again in the morning. He needed the sex. And it would help to make up for the fact that after tonight they'd be apart for the first time in their married life. He was off on a course to Birmingham tomorrow evening, commercial property updates, so he needed as much of her as he could get before he had to face sleeping four nights on his own in some lonely hotel bed. Yes, he'd upend her right here on the armchair the very moment she got in. He wouldn't even give her time to get out of her coat. He'd simply whip off her knickers and guide her down onto the chair. She was wearing those tiny pink knickers he'd bought for her last summer in Norwich. His favourite pair. He could remember watching her wriggling into them earlier that morning...

Leanne had been spread out over the desktop for a full thirty minutes before Terry walked back into the study, his right hand clutching the whippy cane he'd bought from a sex shop in Soho some three months earlier. The cane he'd warned her he was buying for just such an eventuality as this. He glared balefully at the superbly filled seat of her miniskirt. The superbly filled seat that was pouting up at him so temptingly.

'Look at me,' he ordered. So she turned her head and stared in despair at the cruel instrument of torture he was holding. She supposed she'd known for the last few months that one day this would happen. But it didn't make matters any easier.

'I haven't done anything wrong,' she insisted, with all the sincerity she could muster.

'Liar! You've been screwing your bloody boss for years and years.'

'I haven't.'

'And you were screwing him just a short while ago, I know.'

'I wasn't. I was working at the office.'

'You were there? He was there? But the car wasn't, until it magically reappeared at six-fifteen so he could drive you home?'

'I told you. He must have slipped out to get it while I was working.'

'Despite the fact you originally told me he was with you all the time?'

'I must have been wrong...'

'You certainly must have been,' he agreed, his voice dripping with sarcasm. 'Or rather, you must have been *doing* wrong.'

'That's not true,' she replied, knowing she simply had to persist with her denials come what may. If she ever admitted even a small part of the truth, he'd be using that evil-looking cane on her buttocks day after day.

Terry glared at the hint of pale pink bottom just visible below the hem of her skirt, and thrilled with anticipation. If he couldn't stop Jackson having her, then at least he could wallow in the revenge he was going to exact. How gratifying this was going to be! But it would be even more gratifying if he could actually get her to admit her guilt. There was a difference between receiving a full-scale confession, and being only ninety-nine point-nine per cent sure of her misbehaviour. Either way, however, this was going to be the most enjoyable night of his life to date - despite the intense jealousy he felt. Or, maybe, because of the intense jealousy he felt...

Yes, *because* of the jealousy he felt. Caning those adulterous buttocks was going to be incredibly enjoyable *because* of the intense frustration and jealousy he felt...

'Where did you park?' he asked coldly, deciding to keep the full extent of his knowledge to himself for a while longer.

'We didn't. I told you, he drove me straight home from the office.'

'Did he fuck you on the passenger seat, or in the back of the car?'

'Neither.'

'Liar!' he repeated. 'You've had the audacity to come home to me tonight shagged silly and brimful of your boss' spunk!'

'I'm not,' she insisted, but unfortunately, she was. She was awash with Tommy's recently sewn seed. Absolutely soaked with it. Tonight he'd seemed to vent even more than ever. Presumably for the same reason his lovely smooth cock had been stretched so unbelievably well. It had felt as if he'd been impaling her all the way up to her tonsils. 'You feel very good tonight,' she'd whispered happily while he was poking her so tantalisingly slowly. 'It's your bare bottom,' he explained. 'Fondling it when it was bent right over like that has made me incredibly big. I can understand why Terry likes to put it over his knee and roast it alive.'

She'd giggled, and then thrust her groin hard against him. 'In that case it's getting its revenge on him right now. I've never been poked so deeply in my life. You're starting to make me come all over again...'

Terry decided it was time to start. 'Listen, Leanne, and don't interrupt. In fact, don't speak at all unless I ask you a question. I know you've been fucking that bastard boss of yours tonight, so don't make me any angrier than I already am by denying it further. It will only make matters worse for you. So just keep quiet. Do you understand me? Don't say anything until I ask you. Okay?'

'Yes,' she whispered, gripping the edges of the desk even more tightly.

'Good. Now, get yourself ready for me.'

Leanne reached back and, as demurely as circumstances would permit, turned up the seat of her miniskirt, before sliding her tiny pair of white cotton knickers a couple of inches down. Now they were strung tautly across the tops of her thighs. Would Terry be able to detect the not-insignificant amount of semen that had already dribbled into the crotch? She must remember to keep her legs pressed tightly together.

Leanne blushed as she felt a cool draught from the door against her naked bottom. Then she took a deep breath and resumed her grip on the desk, as firmly as before. How open and exposed she felt. How open, exposed, and vulnerable! Far more than she'd ever felt in the past, because this time he was intending to hurt her with something much, much worse than his hand. That long, wicked cane was going to inflict untold agonies on the bouncy cheeks of her bottom. She knew from past experience that she couldn't hold out any hope that Terry would be the least bit gentle with her.

Terry stared down at the breathtakingly beautiful cheeks he'd spanked so many times in the past twelve years. He was absolutely certain that those very same cheeks had been just as bare as this when they'd been in Jackson's car one hour ago. He was absolutely certain they'd been bare and merrily misconducting themselves some sixty minutes before. And very soon he'd reveal to her the reason why he was so certain...

Terry continued to glare at the shapely bare bottom that had previously caused him so much pain. Over the years the thought of what it was probably getting up to with Jackson had always been anathema. The thought of Leanne baring those bountiful buttocks for her boss had at times driven him to the brink. He'd taken revenge on them in the past, of course. Twice he'd taken revenge with his hand when he'd been given cause to suspect their felonious conduct. But that revenge would pale into insignificance when compared to the way he was going to scourge them tonight. That revenge was going to pale into insignificance now he had proof of their infidelity, as opposed to strong suspicion. Proof, the nature of which she was soon about to learn.

Just think about it, he said to himself. Just think about the way she'd failed to keep her wedding vows. Just think about the way that juicy-ripe bottom had been bounced up and down in Jackson's car tonight. Just think about the way Jackson had been poking and probing inside her, such a very short while ago. Just think about the way he'd pumped her full of sperm and then returned her home so she could continue to spew forth more of her unending lies. Just think about the way that lewdly exposed bottom deserved everything that was coming to it, and much more beside. Just think of the mental anguish it had inflicted on him over the years. Just think about the way it would shortly be starting to repay part of the debt it owed him. Just think about the pain it was going to experience when the cane started to rise and fall with all his might. Perhaps, when all was over and done, she'd be a little less keen on shedding her knickers whenever her employer decided to click his fingers. Perhaps she wouldn't be quite so ready to bare herself below the waist whenever Jackson took it in mind to steal a slice of this mischievous little bottom. This mischievous little bottom that was supposed to keep itself only unto her lawful wedded husband. Well, now it was time to start. Time to impart the full extent of his knowledge to her, before the punishment began...

Terry began to tap the cane against the fulsome cheeks, making them joggle in a most intriguing way, and making her shiver with fright. Then he pressed it firmly across the fleshiest part of her upturned bottom. 'One final point,' he said coldly, admiring the pretty indentation it made along the line of the intended cut. 'One final point before I begin. A rather important one, actually.'

Leanne felt a sense of impending disaster. 'What is it?' she asked, not daring to turn her head back towards him.

'Perhaps you ought to know that I decided to drive into Denes Park on my way home from work tonight. And then along the track that runs round the lake. Just out of interest. Or, more accurately, just on some inexplicable hunch. And what do you think I saw there?'

There followed an extremely uncomfortable silence.

'Who's car do you think I saw parked on the grass by the bushes on the far side of the lake? The place we used to call "Copulation Copse"?'

More uncomfortable silence.

'Tommy's brand new flash-mobile, of course. The one in which - on your own admission - he's just driven you home.'

An even more uncomfortable silence.

'I'm sure you can remember a set of headlights driving slowly along the track behind his car? At about ten to six?'

She could.

'I imagine you were a trifle alarmed, being well and truly on the job by then? Being bare-arsed and securely nailed to the passenger seat while someone drives past you, no more than a few feet away?'

She had indeed been alarmed... and also well and truly on the job, in the exact manner described.

'His personalised number plate stood out a mile and a half,' added Terry. 'Obviously I suspected it might be you on the passenger seat with him, but I couldn't be sure until you admitted that he'd driven you home.'

Leanne groaned inwardly. The policy had always been to deny everything, no matter what. But this simply wasn't deniable. At the very best she could admit that she'd been on the point of letting Tommy have it, but claim he never actually managed to get it up because of the scare with the passing car. But that would be almost as bad as admitting the truth. In fact, come to think of it, it would be far worse because Terry would never believe her, and that would simply make him angrier still. No, her best course of action was to tell him the truth. To tell him the truth about everything, and hope he'd eventually learn how to forgive and forget. Oh God, why hadn't she used a better excuse?

'I'm sorry...' she whispered at length. 'I really am...'

Terry was surprised to feel his penis starting to stiffen at her long awaited admission of guilt. At the sure and certain knowledge that he'd been right all along. 'You're going to be a great deal sorrier before the evening is through. A very great deal sorrier.'

Leanne stared at the highly polished desktop just a couple of inches below her nose. 'It'll never happen again...'

'I'm sure it won't. Not after I've finished with you tonight.'

'I won't go back to work for him again. I'll start looking for a new job tomorrow...'

'That might be rather sensible... if you want to avoid a repeat of what you're shortly going to have to endure. Which I'm sure you will want to avoid. Now then, how long has this affair been going on?'

Leanne made a quick mental calculation, having already decided not to lie any further. 'Twelve months.'

'Not longer?'

'No, I swear not longer.'

'And how often have you done it with him? How many times?'

'About twice a month, I should think. I don't know how many times, because sometimes we did it more than once.'

'How often did that happen?'

'Several times. About six or seven, I imagine.'

Terry cut the cane viciously through the air, the evil hiss making her wince. 'Well then, twelve strokes of the cane for the number of months, and twenty-four more for the number of occasions, making a rather convenient total of thirty-six. To be delivered in sixes, with all the power at my disposal. Without any mercy at all. Six sets of six of the best.'

'Oh,' she gulped unhappily.

'I shall ask you questions after each set of six. You'd be well advised to answer them truthfully. I want you to tell me the full story, not some watered-down version of what you've been doing with him.'

Leanne decided that the best method - indeed the only method - of pacifying him would be to convince him she was telling the truth, the whole truth, and nothing but the truth. And she realised she could only do that by holding absolutely nothing back from him. By telling him everything she'd been up to with Tommy, warts and all. 'Yes, I promise I won't keep anything from you. I promise I'll tell you the truth about Tommy...'

Terry raised the cane high above his head, carefully taking aim. 'That would be a very welcome change,' he muttered grimly. 'Let's see if - for once in your life - this helps you to do just that.'

The cane fell six times in rapid succession, cracking down noisily across fleshy bare cheeks, and making her writhe her hips and howl up at the ceiling in pain and outraged indignation whilst tears leaked out of her eyes. Terry gazed with delight at the thick red welts that had been raised, as if by magic, right across the widest part of her invitingly upturned bottom. Each welt positively burst with colour and life. Each was well over a quarter of an inch in height and so suffused that there was no mistaking the agony they were causing. The cane had risen and fallen with so little effort, he thought to himself, yet in a space of a mere six seconds or so her cheating bare bottom had already been taught a most excruciating lesson. Already it was ablaze. Wriggle her sorely wounded cheeks from side to side as she might, there was no way in the world she was going to be able to cool them. Never could he have achieved a greater sense of euphoria. There was his bare-bottomed wife, spread over the desk in front of him, freshly fucked by her employer, and now in the throes of bitterly regretting that fact. Now in the throes of bitterly regretting every slippery push and prod, every fierce spurt into her womb. There was his wife, howling her eyes out, writhing her bottom in pain, and fervently wishing she'd kept her tight little knickers safely in place throughout her journey home. Yes, there was his bare-bottomed wife, stickily adulterated and fervently wishing she could reverse the process by turning back the clock. There she was, red-faced and red-bottomed after having been caught, red-handed, with another man's sperm still warm inside her. Would he ever, anywhere, experience anything as gratifying as this totally justified act of revenge?

Teardrops splashed onto the desktop as Terry continued to study his handiwork with ever mounting approval. 'Ohhhhhh!' she sobbed uncontrollably, twisting her head back and forth. 'Oh God, that hurts! That really, *really* hurts! You can't believe how much...'

'I think I can,' he retorted, before slapping the palm of his hand across the centre of the severely afflicted area as hard as he could.

'Owwwwww!' she screamed in shocked surprise, jerking back her head and howling up at the ceiling once again. 'Oh God! Oh, please don't do that...!'

He slapped her three times more. 'That's to remind you that you're only to speak when I ask you a question. Not otherwise. I've told you that already.'

'I'm sorry...'

Slap! Slap! Slap! 'Only when I ask you a question,' he snapped. 'Unless you want a few dozen more of the same. Like this, and this, and this!'

It felt so rewarding that Terry decided to continue with the use of his hand for a while. No one could deny the justice of the punishment he was meting out to his wayward young wife. Not even Leanne.

Leanne clenched her teeth and gripped the sides of the desk with all her strength as the tears continued to pour out of her eyes. Oh God! Each slap of his hand felt like a further six strokes from the cane...

Terry waited until the heavy sobbing had slowly begun to subside. 'When was the last time he screwed you before tonight?' he asked, making her twitch in fear as he tapped the cane against the mass of seething welts.

Her knuckles were white because of the way she was still gripping the desk so tightly. 'About a month ago,' she whispered nervously, tears trickling down her face onto the desk.

'Tell me about it.'

'It was in his office. The day after you spanked me for wearing this skirt.'

'Which day? I spanked you two evenings running for wearing it.'

'After the first time.'

'Go on.'

'I told him what you'd done.'

'And?'

'And he wanted to see the results for himself, so I showed him, just for a giggle. It made him want to have me there and then...'

'So he did?'

'Yes.'

'From behind, I assume?'

'Yes, bent over the top of a filing cabinet.'

'Just the once?'

'No. Once in the morning, and then again when it was time to leave off...'

'So, the last time I spanked this randy little arse it had been on the job with

Tommy just a few minutes beforehand. And also a few hours before that. Just as it was on the job with him less than an hour ago.'

'Yes. I'm really sorry, Terry.'

Terry continued to glare down at the beautifully sculpted cheeks across the fleshiest part of which the cane had so cruelly left its mark, and experienced a strange mixture of emotions - anger combined with intense sexual arousal. He stared at the six hot welts he'd raised so easily. Why on earth did the knowledge of her infidelity give him this weird sense of excitement? This twisted sort of pleasure? Was it some form of masochistic delight derived from a wounded pride of possession?

Well, whatever the reason, this unfaithful bare bottom was going to be far more sorely wounded than his pride of possession could ever be. Far, far more sorely wounded. As she was just about to discover...

Six more strokes followed, laid with all his strength, cracking down across the ripeness of her buttocks in only a matter of seconds, making her shriek and wail just as before. Now her whole bottom was prettily decorated with raised welts. Thick welts that started exactly along the line of the sweet little crease that demarked buttocks from thighs and then ran all the way up to the top of each cheek. White goose bumps adorned each pulsating welt, a testament to the heat the cane had engendered. Across the high point of each cheek three strokes had been laid slap-bang on top of each other, causing a hugely enhanced swelling that Terry found a joy to behold.

Terry rested the cane lightly across the fleshy fullness of her bottom and continued to stare at the succulent cheeks of which he'd always been so proud, yet so jealous and suspicious. Jealous and suspicious with just cause, he'd now at long last discovered. Suspicion was one thing, but knowing for certain of their wanton misbehaviour, that was quite another.

It was incredibly rewarding to see how well he'd already imposed his vengeance upon the cheeks of her cheating bottom. Cheeks so steeped in recent adultery that its stigma was almost a physical thing. Now they were far from their former selves. Their impertinent perfection was already a thing of the past. Now, as they trembled and shook in fear and pain, each cheek bore the most magnificent hallmark of his retribution right across it. And the hallmark was going to grow. It was going to treble in intensity. Twenty-four more lines were going to be added. Twenty-four more intolerably hot, painful lines, most of which would crisscross one or more of the others, thereby doubling or tripling the effect. Twenty-four more lines that would emphasise to her the nature and extent of his authority and his conjugal rights. Twenty-four lines that would emphasise the nature and extent of his ownership of those parts he was now putting to the torch so effectively.

Yes, when it was over it would be a sight that would remain with him for the rest of his life. This pert bottom bare and burnt alive before his eyes. This pert bottom - which during twelve years of courtship and marriage had tormented his soul through his constant fear of its infidelity - squirming in agony at the way in which it had been so extensively, and justifiably, blistered by the cane.

But at the moment it was time for several more hard slaps, in order to emphasise to her the hurt the cane had already inflicted...

The hand spanking was over, Leanne was weeping in silence, and Terry was once again holding the cane across the fullest part of her brightly striped cheeks. 'So, last month he had you twice in one day at the office?'

'Yes...' she only just managed to sniff.

'After studying what I'd done to you the night before?'

'Yes...'

'When you told him your bottom had been spanked, did you guess he'd want to see the results?'

'Yes...'

'And you knew what that would make him want to do to you?'

'Yes...'

'So you decided to get your own back on me by ensuring that Tommy would want to fuck you. Is that right?'

Leanne took a deep breath. Now was the time to start showing him she was prepared to hold nothing back. 'Yes, but there's a bit more to it than that.'

'Go on.'

'I told Tommy I'd also be suffering the same fate again later that evening, for daring to wear this skirt yet again. I said that I must be entitled to at least two good stiff dickings from him in order to compensate, and he agreed with me. Then he gave them to me, one in the morning and one when it was time to go home. It was fun. You know how a sore bottom always makes me feel extra randy. I hope you can see that I'm trying to be completely honest with you, Terry?'

'Is that why you wore this skirt for the fourth day running, even though you knew you'd get another walloping if I found out? You wanted to get Tommy to give you two helpings of cock, not just one?'

'Yes, I'm afraid that's right. Actually, I hoped I'd be able to get home before you and pretend I'd worn something else. But Tommy kept me busy much longer than I'd expected. He was very worked up...'

Terry began to stroke the cane back and forth over the contusions he'd raised across each pouting cheek, causing her to shudder and wince. He was taking his time and relishing the thought that so far he'd scarcely started. So far he'd only administered two of the six of the six of the best. A further twenty-four searing strokes were still to come.

Six more fleshy cracks, like shots from a rifle, accompanied by tears and screeches of pain and outrage. And six more scorching welts to add to the existing twelve. Three of the new ones had been added to the engorged swellings he'd previously raised across her bottom, so that these giant blemishes were now the product of six strokes on top of each other.

Leanne gritted her teeth and gripped the sides of the desk with all her might. Oh God! She was well and truly ablaze! She was really, really on fire. Her poor bottom was a raging inferno. He'd poured petrol all over it and set it alight with a match. It throbbed and burned in a manner she'd never thought possible. And there were still eighteen more strokes to follow! How was she ever going to get through it?

'Tell me about the first time,' Terry insisted, once the blubbering had become more muted.

'It just happened,' she snuffled unhappily.

'How? Where? When?'

'At his squash club. We'd been playing there one lunchtime...'

'Yes?'

'At the end of the game he gave me a hug because I'd played really well... and it just happened...'

'What, at the squash club?'

'Yes, on the floor at the back of the court. There was no one else in the building. He gave me a big hug, and it just happened... twelve months ago...'

'He gave you a big hug, and a few seconds later you were at it on the floor together?'

'Yes, just like that. He hugged me, and I could feel myself melting all the way into his body. The next thing I knew I was flat on my back, minus my knickers, and he was already probing deep inside me. It happened exactly like that. I never meant it to... and it didn't mean anything to me, apart from a bit of harmless fun. It's never meant anything more than that.'

'I knew I should never have let you play squash with that so-and-so.'

'I'm sorry.'

'Yes, I can see that much for myself,' he grunted, staring angrily at her striped buttocks. 'I can see how sorry you are - very clearly indeed. But I think you mean you're sorry you've finally been caught out and caned.'

'It was never anything serious. Just a bit of fun, like I said. I never wanted you to get hurt.'

'Are you sure it didn't happen any earlier?'

'Yes. I swear it. I know you've always thought he was screwing me, but it didn't happen until just over a year ago, I swear.'

'You've been swearing to me that it's never happened at all, until I found you out tonight.'

'I know.'

'So why should I believe what you're telling me now?'

'I can't answer that. But I swear I am telling the truth.'

'Suppose I promised to stop the punishment if you admit it's been going on for years?'

'But it wouldn't be true.'

'So you say.'

'If it was true I'd say so, and avoid the rest of the strokes.'

'Hmm, maybe,' he mused, deep in thought. Then, after a lengthy pause, 'What about that time last summer you were so late back from the office party at the King Harold? You swore blind you hadn't been shagging him. Were you lying?'

'Yes. I took all my clothes off and we did it on the back seat of your car. Twice in a row.'

'You cheating little witch!' he muttered, but his penis seemed to stretch even more at the thought of her infidelity. Why was that? Why, in God's name, was he fascinated by the knowledge that she'd been so unfaithful to him? But fascinated he surely was, even though he was angrier than he'd ever been in his life. On the one hand he was fuming with rage, yet on the other he was sexually excited at the thought of how outrageously this plump little bottom had behaved. This pretty, plump little bottom that was supposed to keep itself only unto him, but with which her employer had been allowed to make so free. Well, now it was well and truly paying the price for its previous misdemeanours.

'How many times did you do it tonight?'

'Just the once.'

'On the passenger seat?'

'Yes.'

'Was it quick?'

'No.'

'How long did it last?'

'A long time. About three-quarters of an hour, I should think.'

'Tell me more about it.'

Leanne remembered her earlier resolve to tell him all the details, warts included.

'He was really big tonight. Really, *really* big. He'd been feeling my bottom for ages before we started, and that made him incredibly hard. So we did it long and slow, to make it last as long as possible. I've never known him so huge. I've never known him come so much, either. I thought he was never going to stop...'

'Did you come too?'

'Yes. Three times. He was stretching me so tightly. In all directions. It hurt, but it felt lovely.'

Terry began to visualise the scene in the car, and felt his sense of intrigue expand even further. At the same time his sense of indignation seemed to ease. Why on earth was that? Why was he actually starting to enjoy the idea of Leanne being shafted by another man? But he was, whatever the reason. He could visualise the scene so clearly. He could visualise her lying back on the reclined passenger seat, her blouse and front-loader bra pulled open in order to expose her magnificent breasts, her knickers round one ankle and her skirt around her waist. He could see her legs wide apart and the man's wet penis sliding slowly back and forth, his hands underneath the cheeks of her bottom as he pushed deeply in and then pulled slowly all the way out. He could see the look of ecstasy on her face as her insides were plumbed and probed as far as they'd go. He could see and hear her climaxing...

His own erection felt bigger than ever at the thought of her adultery. Adultery from which she was still stickily implanted. For some unfathomable reason the knowledge of that adultery, combined with the knowledge of her earlier misbehaviour, was making him fancy her more than ever. Somehow, in some peculiar way, it seemed to make her even more... *interesting*... than ever. Yes, interesting, that was the right word. And as he stared at the welted, perfectly shaped bottom of which her boss had so recently taken his fill, his feelings of pride and sexual arousal were escalating by the second. They were starting to overwhelm him...

'When was the second time you did it?' asked Terry, having to make an effort not to croak.

'About three weeks after the first. It was dark by five o'clock, so one Wednesday evening Tommy drove me to the park and we did it in his car.'

'Yes, go on?'

'I reclined the passenger seat and then knelt on it facing the back, because he wanted to have it from behind. Then he turned on the interior lights so he could watch his groin slapping into my bottom and his dick working in and out between my cheeks. Unfortunately, when we finished we realised there was someone standing in the bushes just outside the passenger window, watching us. It was Paul, one of the juniors from the office. He'd spotted Tommy driving me into Denes Park, and followed us on his bike. He must have seen everything we were doing.'

'What did you do about it?'

'Tommy wound down the window and told him to fuck off. He also told him he'd cut his balls off if he ever breathed a word to anyone else.'

'Did he keep quiet about it?'

'No, I don't think so. I'm pretty sure he told the other two office juniors what he'd seen, because the three of them have kept giving me all sorts of smirks and knowing looks ever since. It's been a bit awkward, really.'

Terry's erection had started to throb even more. 'So one of the youngsters from work has actually watched you getting yourself shagged? And the others know all about it?'

'Yes, that's right.'

'How long did it last for?'

'A long time, actually. He must have got quite an eyeful. Tommy was being really vigorous with me. You know, pulling his prick all the way out, and then slamming it back into me as hard as he could. On and on like that, for ages. I asked him if he was trying to wear me away, and he laughed and said there was no harm in trying. Even though I was nice and wet I was still a bit tender afterwards.'

This was all part of the 'warts and all' process, Leanne said to herself.

Terry felt a sharp shaft of pain, which almost instantly converted itself into a surge of pleasure that shot straight to his loins once again. 'Were your boobs on show?' he asked, no longer able to hide the croakiness in his voice. 'As well as your bum?'

Leanne pressed on with her honesty policy, unsure of the exact effect it was having on her husband. 'Yes. Tommy can't wait to get them out as soon as he's up inside me.'

'Is that why you've been wearing front-loading bras every day for the last year and a bit? For the times when he decides he wants to have every last inch of you?'

'Yes.'

Terry tried to analyse how he felt about the latest revelations, but found he couldn't.

Eventually the cane began to beat down again, and the yelling and yelping was rekindled with a vengeance. Terry's eyes were glued to the grievously stricken orbs of which he'd always been so jealously proud. The grievously stricken orbs that were now covered in a glorious array of scarlet welts on scarlet welts on scarlet welts. Well, he said to himself, she'd been having her fun with her boss, so now he was having his with her. Now he was exacting more than adequate retribution for the way this unfaithful bare bottom had so disgracefully misconducted itself in the past. 'Still twelve more to go,' he said, when she'd regained a little composure.

'Yes,' she sniffed. 'Oh God, I'm on fire,' she gasped, before bursting into a fresh paroxysm of sobs and tears.

'Have there been any other men?' he asked.

Leanne blushed when she thought of the young lads in the swimming pool, but decided to keep that to herself for a while. 'No, only Tommy,' she snuffled. 'There's never been anyone but you and Tommy,' she added, not exactly speaking the truth. Well, she comforted herself, he hadn't really been referring to the sort of thing she and Tommy had let the young lads do to her. He'd been wanting to know whether anyone else had ever got up her fanny, which no one had. Nevertheless, she'd make sure she told him later about what happened in the pool. It would help him to realise that she was being completely honest with him.

'Where else have you two done it?'

'In Mum's and Dad's house.'

'When?'

'Last September, while they were away on holiday. We went to bed one afternoon when we were supposedly out on an appointment together.'

'For the whole afternoon?'

'Yes. For over four hours.'

'How many times did you do it?'

'Three and a half.'

'Three and a half? How do you mean?'

'Well he got it up for a fourth time, but found he was a bit short of juice because he'd already pumped so much into me. In the end it was getting so late that I had to get up and dash home before he was able to finish me off properly. Mind you, I could hardly complain, could I? Not after all he'd already done for me. It was the most cock I've had since that time you gave it to me all night long at Emma's flat, after my eighteenth birthday party.'

Terry was surprised to discover there was something he urgently needed to know. 'Did you shag me that same evening? After you'd spent the afternoon in bed with Tommy?'

'Yes. As soon as I got home, actually. On the sofa. Then later when we went to bed.'

'I can remember it well. You were as horny as hell. You couldn't wait to get out of your knickers the moment you got in the door.'

For some obscure cause, which he still couldn't comprehend, he found the thought enthralling. He actually found himself enthralled by the knowledge that he'd been making love to his wife when she'd still been wet and warm from an illicit encounter with someone else. And what a marathon encounter it must have been!

'I'm sorry. Having it off with Tommy always makes me want to do it with you afterwards. I haven't told him that.'

'Lust, or guilty conscience?'

'Both, I suppose.'

'How long was it between him pulling his dick out of you and you jamming mine in?'

'Um, not very long at all.'

'How long?' he insisted, desperate to know.

'Well, less than twenty minutes, I suppose.'

Terry felt another shaft of painful pleasure surge through him. He slapped the mass of multi-welts, making her shriek. 'I think you've earned a good deal more of this,' he said thickly, his hand starting to crack down across the multitude of blood-red swellings with all his force.

'I know...' she gasped, screwing up her eyes in pain and gritting her teeth as the spanking proceeded at pace.

After several long minutes the relentless application of his hand finally came to an end, and he retrieved the cane from its resting place on the desk. 'And so for the penultimate six,' he said quietly.

She kept her eyes tightly shut and gripped despairingly at the edges of the desk, awaiting the next rapid tattoo from the cane. It was delivered just as efficiently as before, and with the same highly satisfying results so far as her spouse was concerned.

'Where else have you done it?' asked Terry, when she'd had time to get over some of her latest distress.

'Mainly in his car after work...'

'But anywhere else?'

She blushed, and decided to tell him the whole sad story. Perhaps he'd respect her for her candour and realise she wasn't trying to conceal anything she'd done. 'In the public swimming pool last summer. Standing up by the 1.5 meter mark while you were practising your lengths in the swimming club lane on the other side.'

'I can remember that as well. I can remember you spending a lot of time in the water with him. Did you just bump into him in the pool, or did you arrange it beforehand?'

'We arranged it. Tommy wanted to do something a bit different.' She giggled unsurely. 'He said he wanted to give me a few good lengths while you were getting your own in.'

'You were standing in front of him for ages. Almost half an hour. I thought you were just talking. Was his cock inside you all that time?'

'Yes, most of the time.'

'How did you manage it?'

'Tommy leant his shoulders back against the side of the pool so it wouldn't look to you as if we were standing too close together. Then I straddled him, pulled my bikini crotch to one side, and let him in. That way he could keep an eye on you to make sure you didn't swim over to us.'

'The pool was almost deserted, but there were three or four youngsters around you for quite a lot of the time. You know, those cheeky young buggers we see at the pool most weeks. The ones who've taken to whistling at you in your bikini. Didn't any of them see what you were up to?'

Despite her unfortunate circumstances, Leanne smiled secretly to herself at the memory. 'Well, yes, actually they did. They were swimming underwater close by and noticed what we were doing. They asked if they could have a go, just jokingly. Then we couldn't get rid of them. They kept diving under to watch. Because of what we were doing neither of us could really chase them off, could we? Not that we were too bothered anyway. After a while Tommy told them they could slip a hand inside my bikini and hold my bottom until we were through.'

'What, all of them?'

'Yes, all of them. There was just about enough to go round. What we hadn't expected was that one saucy devil would start to frig a finger in and out in time with what Tommy was doing to me.'

Terry gasped in disbelief. He was mesmerised at the thought of what Tommy and the four youngsters had been doing to his own wife just a couple of dozen yards away from where he'd been swimming. 'You mean to tell me that while I was ploughing up and down the pool, Tommy was shagging you underwater and some youngster was finger-fucking your bum? And that three others were groping it?'

'Yes.'

'You didn't object?'

'You know what I'm like when it comes to spanking or sex. I do as I'm told. Actually, it made me come almost as soon as he started to use his finger...'

'Words fail me.'

'I'm afraid there's more to come, Terry...'

'Go on then,' he sighed, excited nevertheless.

'Well I was feeling really randy by then, so I started to give a hand job to the lad who was fingering me. Then somehow, and I've no idea how, he managed to get his dick right up where his finger had been.'

'What, right up your bum?'

'Yes.'

'All of it up, you mean?'

'Yes, I think so. He was very hard and insistent, so I'm pretty sure he got all of it inside me. He was a really tight fit.'

'So the two of them were fucking you together?'

'Yes, but it didn't last very long. It brought the lad off in just a few seconds. And having him come in my bottom like that brought me off all over again. Really strongly.'

'Jesus!' gasped Terry, his penis stretching up past his navel. 'I can't believe what I'm hearing.'

'Then the three others had a go.'

'What?'

'The other three did the same. Shot in my bottom, I mean.'

'You're kidding me?'

'No. They all did it. One after the other. It was just for a laugh, Terry. Just a bit of fun. Nothing serious. It didn't mean anything. It didn't mean I loved you any the less. I was just very worked up by what was happening to me. You know how I can get...'

'All four of them fucked your bum?'

'Yes. Just very quickly, though. It didn't take them long at all. Not as much as a minute for any of them, I'd guess. Because it was so tight for them, I suppose. And it was much easier for the other three to get it up - after what the first one had done, I mean. After he'd stretched me and lubricated me. Plus, I helped to guide them in. I could feel them so well in there. Every lump and bump of their dicks. Each time one of them came it made me come too, because I could feel everything so exactly. Every single squirt.'

'What did Tommy do while all this was going on?'

'He thought it was really funny. He kept screwing me until the last lad was finished, then he shot his lot too.'

'Good God alive!' Terry breathed in disbelief. 'Hellfire and brimstone!'

'It was just a bit of fun, Terry. Nothing else. But I'm glad I've been able to tell you about it. Truly I am.'

'Jesus!' he said, wondering if it was all a dream.

'It was rather embarrassing afterwards, though. Having all four lads staring at my bottom once I'd got out of the pool. Knowing they were all staring at it and thinking about what they'd just done to it, and about what Tommy had just planted inside me. You're always complaining about that bikini being far too small. For once I thoroughly agreed with you.'

'I can remember seeing you get out of the water. I can remember you looking back over your shoulder and blushing furiously while you fiddled with that tiny triangle of bikini seat. I never dreamt of the reason why!'

Terry was thrilled by the sudden realisation that he'd been admiring the shape of his wife's semi-naked bottom just moments after it had been misbehaving so appallingly. Just moments after four lads had taken turns to pump it full of semen. Just moments after they'd taken turns to pump it full of semen, with her boss' penis jammed right up her cunt! Why he felt like that he still had no idea. But thrilled and exhilarated he certainly was. For years the idea of her being touched by another man had been sheer poison to him. Now it was sheer fascination instead...

Leanne decided to plough on. Perhaps he'd be able to see she was telling him everything, if she finished the story. 'Then Tommy and I did it again in his car in the car park while you were playing badminton and I was supposed to be working out in the gym. He told the lads they could stand outside and watch through the window. He made me lie on top of him so they could have a good look at the bare bottom they'd all been shagging. Then he wound down the window so they could grope it. It felt so sexy it made me come so hard it hurt. You said how red-faced I looked when you saw me a short while later, but that was because of all the sex, not the workout I never had.'

Terry was overcome at the thought of what her boss and the four lads had done to his wife, almost in his own presence. 'You unfaithful little minx!' he murmured, but his voice didn't display any real trace of venom. 'Now I understand why they've started whistling at you behind your back.' He squeezed his wife's buttocks in one hand. 'All four of them have fucked this beautiful bottom. One after the other. Turn and turn about. All of them have shot it full of spunk...'

'You could do it to me, Terry. I'm sure you'd enjoy it. I know I would. It's fun.'

'Perhaps I will.'

'All you need is a bit of lubrication to get started. Lord knows how that first one managed it. Maybe the fingering and the fact that my bottom was underwater was some sort of a help.'

'I guess it must have been.'

Leanne was relieved; he didn't sound nearly as angry as when he'd started. Why should that be? It was almost as if he enjoyed hearing about what she'd been up to. Could that really be the case? Or was he just pleased that she was being so frank with him at last? Pleased that she was obviously not hiding anything from him?

'How many times has Tommy had you at the office?'

'Only that time last month, when the sight of my spanked cheeks inflamed him to do it twice in one day. Before he did it for the second time, when it was almost five o'clock, he wanted to add a few hard slaps of his own. Just to freshen up all your good work, he said. So I had to let him. It hurt quite a lot. Then you put me over your knee again when I got back, as I knew you would, because I was still wearing this skirt. You said I was redder than you'd expected when you pulled down my knickers. That was why; Tommy had smacked me about twenty times on each side, quite hard. Enough to make me cry. And enough to make me feel sexier than ever... Then you took me to bed and fucked me while I was still full of Tommy. I really enjoyed that. Having you fuck me so hard, I mean. I really, really enjoyed it. Partly because of all that had gone before, I suppose. I'm being as honest as I can with you, Terry. I'm not holding anything back at all...'

Terry stood stock still, absorbing everything he'd been told and everything he felt. 'Well, here come the final six,' he said at length. 'And hugely deserved they are, too.'

'Yes, I know. I'm sorry I've been such a bad wife.'

Leanne closed her eyes and tightened her grip on the desk as the cane hissed viciously through the air on its downward journey towards her already over-punished cheeks. The cane bit home just as savagely as each of the thirty preceding cuts. 'Owwwww!' she wailed pitifully, whilst her husband savoured the pleasure of delivering the first of the last of the six of the six of the best.

'You can stand up now,' Terry announced some five minutes later, the tears having at last begun to abate.

'Terry,' she sniffed. 'There's something I want to tell you before I do. I want to tell you because it's important that you believe I've been speaking the whole truth about everything I've done.'

'What is it?'

'I told you about the day he shagged me twice at the office, and also slapped my bottom. But I've also sucked him off and swallowed him. In his room at work, I mean. With the red light switched on. I've done that three or four times during the past twelve months. Just very quickly, because there's always a load of work to get through. You haven't asked about that sort of thing, so I thought I ought to tell you. I think maybe you should add a few extra strokes because of that. Then perhaps we can go to bed and start to make up...'

Terry felt a sudden wave of compassion welling up inside him as he continued to gaze down at her lacerated buttocks. Compassion, combined with his earlier sense of overwhelming sexual excitement at what she'd been doing behind his back. All feelings of outrage had evaporated entirely. Now he was simply intrigued by the details she'd confessed. Now he saw his sexy young wife in another dimension completely. Her ultra-saucy misconduct had somehow added to her allure. He felt so proud of what she'd done. It had made her even more precious...

'I don't think any extra strokes are necessary, Leanne,' he said after a pause, surprising her with the unexpected softness of his tone. 'I think thirty-six is more than enough. You're going to be as sore as hell for days, as it is. Let's go upstairs, as you said.'

Two hours later Terry was a different man to the one who'd confronted his wife on her return from work. While Leanne stood with her back to the full-length bedroom mirror, craning her neck to study the cruel marks of the cane, Terry lay on the bed, still fiercely erect despite the furious bouts of lovemaking that had preceded. 'Leanne,' he said, his eyes also fixed on the cheeks of her multi-welted bottom, 'I've been thinking. I've been thinking very carefully, and my attitude towards you and other men has changed completely. I feel proud at the thought of you pleasuring them. Proud of the fact that my wife is able to provide such enjoyment. So, please listen to what I have to say. I don't want you to give up your job. I want you to go back to work tomorrow. I want you to tell Tommy what I've done to you and show him the results. But you're not to tell him why. He's not to know that I know you were screwing him tonight, or any other time. Make something up. I want you to get him to fuck you again tomorrow. I'm sure the sight of the caning will inspire him to want to do that. From now on I want you to do it with him whenever you like. The more times the merrier. From now on you can be as late home from work as you like as often as you like, provided you tell me all about it afterwards. That way there'll be no more secrets between us. In fact the only secret will be ours, because he's not to know that I know anything at all about the two of you. It will make our marriage stronger, I'm sure. The only other proviso is that, every now and then, you accept a few more strokes from the cane. Not as many as tonight. Maybe six or ten, at the most. Just so you understand to whom you owe your allegiance. Just to remind you of that fact. Will you do all this for me, please?'

She turned her face towards him, her eyes shining with a look of adoration he'd never quite seen before. 'I'll do anything that makes you happy,' she whispered. 'Anything at all.'

'You know how much Jim Browne fancies you?'

'Yes,' she giggled.

'I might want you to let him fuck you as well.'

'Okay.'

'There might be others.'

'All right.'

'I might want to take part myself. A threesome. Two of us piling into you together. Or one immediately after the other. That sort of thing. I might even ask those lads from the pool if they'd care to come back here and help me get you fucked in the more usual way. And maybe those three office juniors would also like to have a go at you?'

'I'm going to be busy,' she sighed.

Epilogue Part One

The four cheeky lads turned their heads and stared back at Leanne as she stood by the edge of the swimming pool in her teeny bikini. 'You're kidding,' two of them gasped together. 'Surely you are?'

'No, I'm serious,' replied Terry, gesturing to his wife to go to the female changing rooms. As she complied with his instructions five pairs of eyes were glued hungrily to the delightful sway of bouncy, almost bare buttocks. The last remaining marks of the cane were still discernible to Terry, but only because he knew what he was looking for.

'Fuckable, isn't she?' Terry remarked casually.

'Yeah,' they breathed in reply. 'Very...'

Ninety minutes later Leanne was lying on her back on the matrimonial bed, Terry clasping her hand with husbandly pride as the fourth and final young man suddenly started to empty himself inside her.

'Okay, guys,' said Terry, when the lad had eventually finished. 'I think she's had enough foreplay. You can all buzz off now and let me spend the rest of the evening sorting her out for real.'

Epilogue Part Two

The following day, after work, Leanne was in the stockroom at the office, having only recently regained her minuscule black knickers after yet another close encounter with Tommy - but she had no intention that they should stay in place for long. Paul stood in front of her, using both hands to paw greedily at the superbly outthrust breasts he'd had no trouble at all stripping bare. The two other office juniors stood on either side of her, their hands thrust up the back of her new miniskirt and then inside her panties, gripping and groping satin-smooth buttocks with equal enthusiasm.

'You mean we can all do it to you, Mrs Howlet?' asked one of them, unable to believe his luck.

'Yes, if you want to,' confirmed Leanne, tightening the two-handed grip she'd taken on Paul's stiff penis.

'Right here and now? One after the other?'

Leanne could feel Tommy's juices starting to ooze out of her. 'Yes. Provided you lock the door first, and don't say anything to Mr Jackson. He might not be best pleased with any of us.'

'Are there any other provisos?' asked the one standing on her other side.

'Yes,' she replied, turning her head to look back at him. 'As a matter of fact, there are. You can pick up the skirt you've just yanked off me, and fold it neatly over that box of envelopes. It's part of an expensive set of six short skirts my husband was kind enough to buy for me last week, because he's now decided he likes my body to be on show.'

'Sorry...'

She looked at the other junior behind her. 'And you,' she added, 'you can stop tearing at my knickers like that. They're silk, and part of a set of six that exactly match each of the skirts. Another gift from my husband. Just slide them down gently so I can step out of them, please. There's no need to try to rip them off me.'

'Sorry, Mrs Howlet. I just got carried away at the sight of them stretched so tightly across your fabulous bum...'

She leant back so that her shoulders were resting against the wall. 'Now then, Paul,' she said, cocking her right leg over his left hip and making final adjustments to the angle of the penis she now held in only one hand; her other arm being wrapped around his neck for extra balance. 'Push forward slowly. You'll find I'm more than ready for you.'

'Jesus, Mrs Howlet! I can't believe I'm really doing this to you...'

'Well, I can guarantee that you are,' she breathed, closing her eyes as she felt him slide all the way up inside her, opening her as wide as she could have wished. 'And you two others, you can clamp your hands back round my bottom, if you want. I love being held like that when I'm on the job with someone else.'

They did as she suggested, exchanging looks of startled surprise. 'Is that all right, Mrs Howlet?'

'Yes, fine,' she replied dreamily, gently wriggling her hips against the groping hands. 'Now you can feel free to be as bold as you like.'

Leanne sighed to herself; oh dear, three office juniors with raging hormones and hard-ons! And no husband to shoo them away, like last night... How long was it going to take to satisfy them all? And how long would Terry take to satiate himself on her after she'd finished telling him about everything she'd been up to? And about everything that had been up her...?

Meanwhile, back home, Terry was watching TV and patiently waiting to hear all about her day at work. To his delight it was almost nine o'clock when she finally tottered through the front door - worn, weary, tired-eyed and ready to confess all.

'How many?' asked Terry.

'Four.'

'Four times?'

'No, four dicks. About fourteen times, I should think...'

'That's just about acceptable,' he laughed.

'Those three youngsters simply couldn't get enough,' she giggled. 'They just wouldn't leave me alone. I thought they'd never let me go. The moment one was finished there were two others fighting to take his place. "I'm sorry but I'm going to have to bone you again, Mrs Howlet", they kept on saying. In the end I had to double them up. You know, bend over and use my mouth on one while another did me from behind. It was the only way. Otherwise I'd have been there all night. Even so, it was still quite a job to get away. There was always someone ready for another go - usually the third one who'd been squeezing my boobs while I was dealing with the two inside me. Eventually I just told them flatly that I was going home, even though Paul was rock hard and desperate for yet more. If I'd stayed to sort him out the other two would have been stiff again by the time I'd finished. And so it would have gone on...'

Terry smiled happily. 'I can picture the scene very well.'

'I'll tell you all about it in a minute. Right now I need to visit the bathroom and then put my skirt and knickers in the washing machine. I was so wet and uncomfortable sitting on that bus seat for almost half an hour.'

'Okay. Then come back here and sit on my cock instead of the bus seat. You'll find it's very up for it.'

Leanne sighed wearily. Terry's weapon had always been reasonably substantial, but ever since the caning it had seemed almost twice it's normal size - she was totally delighted to say...

Part Two - The Admonishing of a Far-Too-Personal Assistant
Prologue

George Franks, head of sales, as well as marketing and technical servicing - and known to almost all of the company's twenty-nine female employees as King Rat - was the only person who knew why he'd called a lunchtime meeting of his sales department behind the locked doors of the IT room. Jillie Jackson - tall, blonde, and as drop-dead gorgeous as the polar day is long - grew more and more red in the face as he carefully detailed the gross breach of office discipline he'd witnessed taking place across his very own desk the previous night, and how he was going to redress the sheer effrontery of it all. Whilst her own discomfiture grew, the four men who comprised the rest of the department listened with ever-mounting intrigue.

'The perpetrator needs to learn and inwardly digest the exact reasons why it would be a mistake for such an incident to be repeated,' explained George.

The Redress

Jillie groaned to herself in despair. This was definitely the most hideously horrible day of her entire life! Here she was, in the IT room, bent right forward. Here she was, the top half of her body lying flat on the surface of this tall computer stand, her hands tightly gripping the front edges and her toes only just touching the floor - while that awful George Franks and the four other men in her department stared down at her totally bare bottom! And this was only the beginning. George had clearly stated his intention of fucking her - right here and now. Right here, in full view of everyone else. What a truly ghastly state of affairs!

What on earth was Jim Browne going to think of her when he heard - as he was sure to hear - all about it? It was bound to be the end of their six week fling. Their six weeks of fun and fornication after office hours. How stupid she'd been last night! How stupid to have given in to his urgent desire to screw her there and then in what she'd thought was a deserted sales department, instead of insisting that he should wait a couple more minutes until they were safely behind lock and key in an upstairs office! How stupid to have allowed George Franks the opportunity, albeit unwittingly, to take explicit photos of their coupling from behind a nearby screen! And how stupid to have antagonised him so greatly by letting Jim shag her - bottoms up - across George's very own desk! He might not have been quite so incensed if they'd been doing it on hers...

Lying here, naked from the waist down and being ogled by all five men in her department, was the most mortifying experience imaginable, yet she was so incredibly wet. Why on earth was that? She'd better make sure she continued to keep her thighs pressed tightly together, in order to hide her unhappy condition from everyone else.

Oh, God! Perhaps it was just as well she was so wet. She'd just heard the sound of a zip fastener urgently parting company with itself, and risked a glance back over her shoulder through a mop of curly blonde hair. It was true! It was all true! The various rumours she'd heard about George were all one hundred per cent correct. He was hung like the proverbial donkey! It was easily the biggest weapon she'd ever seen, both in length and girth. Oh Mary, Mother and Father, was there going to be no end to her shame and humiliation? Was she really going to have to accommodate that gigantic dick right here in front of all these men? Oh gosh, she guessed she already knew the answer to that! George had just moved right up behind her and taken a purposeful grip round her waist with both hands... and now she could feel the tip of his hot monstrosity starting to poke insistently against her wide-open lower lips...

Five pairs of eyes watched in fascination as George began to force-feed himself to her. Five pairs of eyes watched George's grossly oversized erection as it began to disappear, slowly but surely, between the cheeks of his personal assistant's beautiful bottom, sinking into her inch by long slow inch, until it was eventually buried right up to the hilt inside her.

Crimson-faced, Jillie lifted her head from the surface of the computer stand and groaned, open-mouthed, with a mixture of discomfort, shame and humiliation. That giant cock was all the way up her tight little channel, stretching and pressing so unbelievably hard, demanding to occupy everything she possessed - and quite a lot more that she didn't! She was packed to full capacity, and beyond. She was bursting at the seams. Already it was starting to hurt. Whatever would it be like when he began to move? And all those others watching! How was she ever going to be able to look any of them in the eye again? How was she ever going to be able to face *anyone* at the office again? Word of her ordeal would spread like wildfire. By five o'clock everyone in the building, including Jim Browne, would know what George had done to her - in full view of her whole department...

As George pushed forcefully against the bounciness of her buttocks in order to penetrate her to the very maximum, making her groan once again, the men raised their gaze and stared at the reflection of her face in the wall mirror in front of her, noting with approval how the features were contorted in anguish - due not only to the immense physical encroachment, but to the shamefulness of her situation as well. Never had she felt so stretched or so wretched. And she could sense the men studying the extent of her plight in her facial expressions.

Sweet revenge, thought George. Sweet revenge for the way this incredibly sexy bottom had spent the past six months wiggling and jiggling its way around his department, clad in the most hip-hugging designer skirts and dresses, teasing and tormenting him as it went, but denying him all access. Sweet revenge for the way the lateral swing of deliciously bouncy buttocks had frustrated and driven him to the brink. Sweet revenge, also, for the way in which those same delightful buttocks had so shamelessly allowed themselves to be bared for the benefit of Jim Browne, his arch rival from marketing, whilst all the time steadfastly refusing to permit George to charm them out of their protective wrappings. Sweet revenge, too, for the way in which his very own desk had been desecrated so shamefully last night. What better means than this to emphasise to his incredibly fuckable personal assistant the gross error of her ways?

And, to add insult to injury, there was going to be something very permanent about fucking this classy blonde beauty whose husband was a prominent, well-heeled lawyer. Once he'd fucked her there was no way in the world she was going to be able to get herself unfucked again. Once he'd had her she was going to be obliged to spend the rest of her life having been had. Two, four, or however many years later, he'd see her in the street with her husband and children, and say to himself that he'd been there, where only poor hubby was supposed to tread. He'd say to himself that he'd had a slice of the action, a slice of her smooth little bum. A slice that had belonged to somebody else. And however hard she might try, there was no possibility of her returning it to its rightful owner. It had gone from dear hubby once and for all, poor chap. George would know it, she'd know it, and both of them would know that the other one knew it. She'd nod politely and say hello, but he'd know that she knew he was recalling that earlier time when she'd had to let him all the way up to the top of her hot little hole. He'd see her blush, ever so slightly, as she walked past, arm in arm with her husband...

George stood stock still, relishing the moment. Relishing the warmth and texture of the smooth, bent-over bottom pressed firmly into his stomach and groin. Relishing, also, the tightness of the hot passage he was stretching much further than it had ever been stretched before. He'd take his time before he started to shaft her. He'd make her wait as long as he could. The delay would embarrass and humiliate her even further. He could see from her reflection in the mirror that she was already in distress. Let her have a little more time to dwell upon her unfortunate predicament, before providing her with even greater cause for shame.

Still gripping her tightly round the waist, George at long last began to move back, just as slowly as when he'd entered her. Jillie gasped as he began to withdraw. It felt as if the huge tip of his enormous appendage was turning her inside out. It felt as if it was drawing her insides out with it, leaving her empty in its wake. Empty and disembowelled. The process of this first withdrawal seemed endless, so much brawn was there for him to remove. She couldn't believe how long he was. She couldn't believe she'd been capable of harbouring something that size, nor that there was still more for him to withdraw. The process had started at a point that had almost seemed to be somewhere in her chest, and she could still feel him retreating, despite the bulk that he'd already pulled out. How on earth had she managed to take him? A vast amount of iron-hard flesh had already slithered out of her, yet he was still powerfully present inside. They were still firmly coupled, even though he was now over halfway out.

Further and further he drew back, continuing to suck out her insides as he went, leaving a throbbing empty void where his oversized organ had been. Never had she been so horrendously filled and then so emptied. At long last only the massive knob was left. It rested just inside her, still stretching her apart.

After a short pause George eventually voided her completely, making her sigh with relief. But she wasn't left in that happy state for long. For the second time that afternoon he sank into the hot wet honeypot he had at his mercy, at about the same pace as the original incursion. Again she groaned with dismay as she felt him opening her all the way up to the top of her vagina. She opened her mouth wide and sucked in her breath, needing all she could get for the ordeal that was already underway. As she felt herself straining to accommodate him she could also hear her juices squelching inside her. Squelching against the mammoth shaft that was once again stretching her painfully in every direction - almost as if her insides were protesting at the scale of the invasion. The truly monstrous invasion of the yielding privacy of her person.

After several more ultra-slow insertions and withdrawals he began to increase the pace a little. Steadily and evenly he began to pole her, using strokes of awesome length and weight, and listening in fascination to the slurping sound inside her as penis parted pussy with contemptuous ease. Listening, and also still savouring the feel of the creamy-smooth bottom pressed firmly against him whenever he was all the way home. Home but far from dry. Still savouring, too, the tight grip of the hot little hole he was opening and stretching much further than it would comfortably go.

Jillie closed her eyes even more tightly in a vain attempt to remove her mind from the reality of her situation. If she could hear her own internal juices squelching against his invasive presence, then so could everyone else. Everyone could hear as well as see the way in which she was being plundered and probed so deeply.

'Hold onto your hat, Mrs Jackson,' he muttered at last, pulling all the way out of her. 'I'm now going to open the throttle wide!'

As indeed he did. Still gripping her around the slimmest part of her waist, he began hammering into her with a savagery she found almost impossible to abide. In and out of her he thrust. All the way in and then all the way out. In and out, in and out, in and out, with a force that none of the onlookers imagined he'd be able to sustain. But sustain it he most certainly did, much to everyone's delight, apart from she who was on the receiving end of the onslaught. The audience marvelled at his stamina as the minutes ticked remorselessly by, yet he continued to shaft her without the slightest relent or respite, opening and stretching her to capacity and ramming against the neck of her womb. Voiding her entirely with each withdrawal, and then jamming himself all the way back at electrifying pace.

Smack... smack... smack... smack... went groin against bouncy buttocks, just as if he was spanking her, as well as plumbing her innermost depths. *Squelch... squelch... squelch...* went her internal juices, as George raced back and forth with glee.

36

'Ohhh!' groaned Jillie, unable to prevent herself lifting her head from the top of the computer stand and twisting her face in discomfort and despair at the way she was being so fearsomely fucked.

Oh *yes*, thought the male observers, their eyes riveted to the intriguing spectacle of wildly plundering penis provoking such deep dismay.

'Take this...' George growled. 'And this, and this, and this!'

The onlookers stared in wonder as he continued to exit her completely, only to re-enter a split second later, forcing himself all the way inside in less time than it takes for an eye to twinkle, before withdrawing once more - and then repeating the process over and over again. And then over and over again and again after that. Jillie could feel him slowly tightening his grip around her waist as the brutal bludgeoning proceeded without abate. She groaned out loud once more. If anything he seemed to be gaining in stature! Surely that couldn't really be the case? Surely no one could be that big...?

Jillie gritted her teeth and strengthened her hold on the stand as one monstrously hard stroke followed another, straining her insides and jarring the whole of her upper body, time after time after time, lifting her momentarily off her toes with the power of each incoming thrust. When was it ever going to finish? How much longer would she have to suffer this unbelievable assault and battery? Was he truly getting bigger and bigger, or did it just seem that way? How was her poor pussy going to cope with the aftermath when he was finally done with it? How sore was it going to be after this merciless pounding from behind? Even the cheeks of her outthrust bottom were starting to feel hot from the constant slapping of hard male groin against them. Thank the Lord she was still sopping wet.

What must this look like to all those other men? What must they be making of the sight and sound of George's groin slapping noisily against her naked bottom, and of his hugely overstretched dick ripping all the way in and all the way out at a truly blistering speed? Piling all the way in and out as if there were no tomorrow? How on earth was she ever going to be able to face anyone at work again? And what, in God's name, was she going to say to Jim Browne?

But all things - good or bad - must come to an end. And at long last George came to the boil. There was a gasp, a moan and a groan, followed by a choking grunt of pleasure, and finally she felt the first scalding ejaculation bursting powerfully into her womb. Spurt after fierce spurt followed at speed, swamping her while she groaned in horror and buried her face in her hands. Being hugely and heavily spunked by that awful George Franks was bad enough, but oh, the shame of all this! The shame and disgrace of having to let the rest of her department stand there and greedily devour every tiny detail of her total degradation.

And still he continued to vent, his groin thrust into the fullness of her bent-over bottom in order that he could penetrate her to the absolute maximum. His penis crammed right up inside her, solid and still, wanting to implant her as deeply as possible. Without even realising it she wriggled her hips and pushed back against him, subconsciously wanting the same. On and on went the invidious insemination, the onlookers gaping in awe as one long forceful emission followed another, with intervals of about a second in between. On and on it went, his juices swirling turbulently around inside her whilst squirt after powerful squirt still jetted into her.

The greatest flood, George said to himself proudly, since Noah took to his Ark...

But eventually George was spent, and withdrew - slowly and very stickily. 'Jesus!' whistled one of the onlookers, eyes glued in disbelief to the round buttocks from which he'd just dismounted, now several shades more colourful than when he'd started to slap himself against them.

'Ditto,' murmured two of the others.

George began drying his gradually wilting organ by wiping it meticulously back and forth across her upturned cheeks. When this was done to his satisfaction, he reached down to his knees and retrieved his displaced garments, leaving Jillie to continue to lie on the stand, face in hands, feeling more fucked than she'd ever felt in her life. She groaned miserably to herself. Not only had she been scoured and reamed out more deeply and more thoroughly than she'd ever imagined possible, but she'd also been pumped full of enough seed to sink a whole flotilla of battleships. And all of this in front of her four colleagues from sales!

'Now then, Mrs Jackson,' growled George, slapping playfully but firmly at the blushing bottom that was still very much under his command. 'Am I to take it that a valuable lesson has been learned?'

Jillie was too exhausted to speak, so he slapped her again. 'I'm waiting for a reply, Mrs Jackson.'

'I don't understand...' she whispered.

Slap! 'I was asking whether there will be any further incidents of fornication with men from marketing?'

She blushed furiously. 'No...' she whispered, even more quietly.

George looked down at his palm, then wiped it across the tops of her thighs in order to remove the mixture of juices it had collected from the slapping.

'No? No what? No, a valuable lesson hasn't been learned? Or no, there won't be any further incidents of copulation between my personal assistant and men from marketing?'

Jillie was even more crimson-faced than before. This was almost as embarrassing as when he'd been fucking her to the full; having to lie here answering questions whilst bare-bottomed and full of his come. Now he'd succeeded in having his way so massively, why couldn't he just let her get up and leave?

Slap! 'Come on, Mrs Jackson. Which one is it?'

'No, there won't be any more incidents...'

George inspected his hand closely and then wiped it across her upper thighs once again. 'A valuable lesson has indeed been learned?' he enquired.

'Yes...'

'You will no longer be entertaining men from marketing on company premises?'

'No...'

Slap! 'No what?'

'No, I won't be entertaining men from marketing...'

'On company premises?'

'On company premises...'

'Obviously what you choose to do elsewhere is a matter that's between you and your husband.'

'Yes...'

'In that case, I think you can go.'

With a sigh of relief Jillie slid backwards off the IT stand and onto her feet, pulling down her dress and then taking a couple of unsteady steps towards the door. She reached out to unlock it, desperately trying to tug her minuscule knickers into place with the other hand. Already she could feel George's fluid starting to seep out of her womb.

'Don't forget I need that report on the Allen account before five o'clock,' George called after her.

The Aftermath

Two and a half hours later Jillie was sitting at her desk staring unseeingly at the computer screen in front of her. Oh God! How embarrassing! She was going to have to make yet another trip to the Ladies. The fourth since she'd made her escape from the IT room. Once again her knickers were full of George Franks! If she waited much longer it would start to soak into her smart new dress. Once again she'd have to endure the stares and the smirks of the five other people in her department, as well as that wretched post boy at his desk in the corridor. Once again she'd be able to feel their gaze all over the snug-fitting seat of her dress. Once again she'd know what they were thinking. Once again she'd know they knew where she was going... and why. How could anyone shoot so much, even with equipment the size of George's?

Why did she always wear dresses and skirts that displayed her bottom so clearly? Well, until now there'd been no reason not to do so, she supposed. She'd always been pleased to show off the cheeks of which her hunky husband, Tommy, was so exceptionally proud. But all that had changed dramatically since she'd been confronted by George Franks in the IT room during the lunch break. Now she hated the thought of all the men being able to stare at the seat of her dress and ogle the shape of the bottom they'd watched being bared and then mounted so massively right before their eyes.

Oh grief! Her knickers were so uncomfortable. Not only were they soaked through, but the tight little things were cutting right into the still puffed-up lips of her wet vagina. She'd never felt so utterly fucked in her life. Having all four other men watching her getting it made her feel as if all four of them had porked her as well. Mind you, due to his size and stamina, the total yardage that George

Franks had been able to pump into her was probably the equivalent of five ordinary bonks anyway. Maybe even more. Thank heavens she'd been so well lubricated! Although she'd hated every moment her poor pussy had been a really good little girl in that respect. But even so, she could tell she was going to be sore. That awful George Franks had stretched her deeper and opened her wider than anyone had ever done in the past. And for such a long time, too. Oh, what a positive disgrace; fucked to a frazzle by her head of department in front of the rest of her department! And with everyone in the building certain to know all about it before it was time to go home!

Well, at least it was highly improbable that her lovely Tommy would ever find out. He only ever came into contact with Jim Browne, and Jim was hardly likely to say anything, was he? But Jim would probably know all about it already. Would he still be so keen to upend her after what George had just done? And after what George had been seen to do? She rather suspected he wouldn't. She rather suspected she'd already lost most of the allure she'd held for him up to now.

And would George keep to his word? Would he delete all the porny photos from his mobile phone, now that she'd obliged him in the way he'd demanded? He'd promised he would, but could she trust that rat to do as he'd said?

What would it have been like if she and George had been on their own and he'd promised to keep quiet about everything? Would her lack of say in the matter - and therefore her lack of guilty conscience - have meant she'd actually have enjoyed taking that enormous tool all the way up inside her? Oh dear! She rather suspected the answer might be in the affirmative.

Well, she supposed she couldn't delay another visit to the loo any longer. For the fourth time that afternoon her pretty pink panties were absolutely awash. She supposed she'd better get up and suffer the humiliation of all those stares and thoughts. And if she tried to curtail her natural wiggle she'd probably end up tripping over and falling flat on her face. Well, one thing was for sure. After today she'd wear much more modest attire to work. She'd make certain she wore a dress or skirt that was loose around the hips. Something that wouldn't display her bottom quite as blatantly as the clothing she'd always worn to date. But on the other hand, if she did that was there a risk that Jim Browne might find her even less alluring?

Oh well, here goes. Stand up and walk through the door - trying to keep your mind completely blank. Trying to forget that everyone knew the stickiness of your predicament. And trying not to look at that cheeky little bugger of a post boy who'd given her such a knowing grin the last time she'd nipped to the toilet. Fancy him telling her earlier that he'd heard she'd had something rather filling at lunchtime! What a diabolical nerve!

'What an arse!' Peter Perkins whistled coarsely, the eyes of all five of Jillie's work colleagues having been avidly glued to the spectacular swell of the shapeliest pair of buttocks any man could ever have wished to watch undulating their way gracefully out of the room. Yes, what an arse, he'd repeated, this time to himself. And what a privilege it had been to observe it on the job. What a privilege to have seen it bared by George Franks, to have seen it fondled so extensively, and then to have watched George's male groin spanking endlessly and remorselessly against it as he poked her all the way up to her throat...

And talking of spanking, had anyone ever done that to her? What a treat it would be to have that beautiful bare bottom resting over your lap and to be able to slap it until it was raw. Until it was bright red and as hot as a furnace, while she sobbed and cried buckets of tears...

The Offer

Later that day, having said goodbye to Jayne at the wine bar, and having visited the Ladies of a store in Oxford Street in order to slip into a minute pair of newly purchased knickers, Jillie spotted Jim Browne standing on the platform at Victoria Station, waiting for the same train as she. 'Hi,' she said, more than a trifle nervously, but still experiencing the twinge of excitement she always felt in her loins whenever she saw him.

'Hello,' he replied, sounding cool and distant, she thought.

She decided to bite the bullet there and then. 'Erm, I suppose you've heard what happened at lunchtime, Jim?'

'Yes,' he said, looking and sounding just as distant.

'He was going to e-mail the photos to Tommy. What else could I have done?'

He shrugged, but said nothing.

'It wasn't any of my seeking.'

'If you say so.'

'It was horrible. No fun at all.'

'Yeah, I guess so.'

He didn't sound too convinced, she gulped to herself.

'It was awful. All those people watching...'

'Yeah...'

'You're a bit upset by it all, aren't you, Jim?'

'You could say that.'

'So you think I should have taken the risk and told George to get lost?'

'Yes, of course I do.'

Jillie groaned inwardly. Oh dear! This wasn't at all promising. She'd have to employ desperation tactics if she wanted their early evening frolics to continue - loath as she was to use them.

She moved up close to him. 'I think I might have earned a spanking,' she whispered, gently squeezing his hand. She noticed the immediate gleam of interest in his eyes, and knew that she was now committed to her last-ditch plan of campaign. 'Putting me over your knee and really hurting my bare bottom might help both of us to feel better about everything. Tommy's away for four nights after tonight. You could come back to my place with me tomorrow after work and give me everything I deserve. What do you say to that?'

'Okay,' he replied - rather quickly and enthusiastically, she noted with mixed feelings. She'd been spanked twice before, very soundly, and didn't in any way relish the prospect of a repeat performance. But it would be worth it, she sighed to herself, if it meant she and Jim could continue with their strictly-for-fun, after hours affair...

The Close Shave

One hour later Jillie was sprawled out on her lounge armchair, fully clothed apart from her knickers. She was still wearing her hat, scarf, gloves, long suede overcoat and knee-length boots, and she was still even clutching her handbag as she grinned sexily up at the overexcited husband who'd just jumped on her and debriefed her within seconds of her arriving home.

But suddenly the grin vanished from her face. 'These aren't the knickers you put on this morning,' said Tommy, staring at the petite powder-blue panties he held in his hand.

'Yes they are...'

'No they're not. I watched you wriggling yourself into those tiny pink ones I bought you in Norwich last July.'

'I, er, changed my mind and swapped them for these a bit later. I know the pink ones are your favourites, so I decided to save them until you get back from Birmingham.'

'Oh.'

She pulled open her coat and parted her legs invitingly, enabling him to see all the way up to the pretty pink lips of the closely shaven pussy that positively gushed with eager anticipation, despite the horrendous mauling it had received at the departmental meeting earlier that day. 'Come down here, Tommy,' she husked. 'Come down here and start giving me what you've got in your own pants.'

As he knelt on the floor between her outstretched legs, struggling with his zip, she dropped the handbag containing the spunk-encrusted pink knickers onto the carpet beside the chair, and sighed with relief.

The Exorcism

Less than twenty-four hours later Jillie settled herself nervously over Jim Browne's lap, wriggling forward daintily until the fleshiest part of her bottom was almost at the apex of her pose. She lay there in an inverted V, her hands and toes touching the floor and her long wavy hair falling in front of her face. Exactly the stance in which Tommy had punished her twelve months earlier after finding out about her all night fling with Jonathan Crowe. She blushed as she felt him starting to pull her short skirt up to her waist, knowing how little cover she had underneath.

Jim gasped at the sight of a black thong pulled tightly into the deep cleft between her bountiful buttocks. He'd never seen anything so pretty. Her bottom was so perfect that, in its current bent-over pose, it simply took his breath away. He felt a physical pang of pain at the thought of how it had been so grossly misused by George Franks, whilst being ogled by the rest of her work department.

He slid his right hand underneath the thong, relishing the honey-smooth texture of the flesh beneath. Slowly he peeled the black satin garment a few inches down towards her knees, leaving it clinging across her uppermost thighs. Then he returned his hand to the luxury of her buttocks, stroking and caressing them tenderly, savouring the vibrant lubricity of each in turn. He drew a deep breath and held it, at the same time raising his hand above his head and staring hard at the immaculate oval cheeks, at their pale pink plumpness and perfect shape. How he longed to imprint them! How he longed to make his mark! Their sauciness was just overwhelming, their recent misconduct at work a shameful disgrace. His head was starting to spin at the prospect of the retribution he was about to inflict upon them...

But with an effort of will he restrained himself and lowered his hand. This was simply too good to rush, he warned himself. He must make her wait a while longer. He must sit still and allow his anger to escalate whilst, at the same time, fully absorbing the moment. He must be patient until the time was right for the punishment to start...

Jim began to recall the first time he'd seen her bottom in all its near-naked splendour. It had been a few weeks earlier. Five or six, he guessed. She'd been working late in Mr Davis-Davies' room, leaning forward over the computer screen to check his appointments for the following day. Playfully he'd slapped the seat of her short skirt, and she'd given him a look of mock reproach. This had become fairly standard procedure over the course of the previous six months. Her rear end was so sexy that he'd always found it very difficult to keep his hands off it, and she'd never appeared to mind too much.

'You feel rather bare under there,' he'd mused.

'I'm perfectly respectable under my skirt,' she'd replied with a grin. 'Perfectly respectable.'

He'd told her he doubted her veracity and challenged her to prove the point. Eventually, after further banter and debate, she'd turned her back to him once again and flipped up the hem of her skirt, thus revealing the sweet little thong she was sporting. He'd stared long and hard at the delightful apparition of pink, all-but-bare buttocks and tight white cotton thong. 'Jesus!' he whistled at last. 'What a glorious sight! I've never seen anything so incredibly horny. I think I'm going to burst my zip.'

She'd blushed prettily, still looking back at him over her shoulder as she continued to hold the skirt up past the small of her back. 'We can't have that,' she giggled. 'What would Lisa think if you returned home with a broken zip? You'd better relieve the pressure at once.'

Seconds later the door had been locked, the thong was round her ankles and she was bending forward with her hands on the desktop allowing him to slap his groin lustily into her lovely bare bottom as he probed her from behind...

And now here was that same bare bottom folded neatly over his knee. But how greatly it had trespassed against him since that first encounter, he pondered, continuing to gaze down with mixed emotions at the smooth cheeks that pouted up at him so provocatively. Round, slippery-smooth cheeks upon which George Franks had been mounted only yesterday - in front of her whole department. This ruttish little bottom, with which George had been allowed to make free, was so infuriatingly attractive. It was so perfectly sculpted and formed that it absolutely screamed out to be put to the torch for the way it had sinned. Those saucy, pearly pink orbs were so immaculately shaped and flawless that they positively pleaded to be abused with all his might. How he yearned to mistreat them. How he yearned to burn them alive. How he craved to watch them discolour while she yipped and yelped with pain! Each heartless blow from his hand would help to produce such a wondrous result. Within just a minute or so the sheer and utter perfection of this naughty bare bottom would be a thing of the past. Within just a minute or so these plump buttocks would be bouncing and starting to blush with pain. And how they'd continue to bounce and blush thereafter! Time and again he'd punish them for yesterday's indiscretion with one fleshy crack after another. One loud, fleshy crack of hard male hand against the fullest part of each impudently upturned cheek. What music that would make! That and the sobs and wails. And how he'd be able to feast his eyes on those reddening twin globes. Globes that were currently gleaming up at him with such impertinent pride.

And now it was time to begin. Now it was time to punish this randy little bottom until it was raw. Now it was time to make her wish she hadn't been so wanton as to let George Franks pillage and plunder everything she owned. Time to emphasise to her how wretched he felt about the way in which she'd accommodated George Franks' hugely overgrown tool in full view of all those men. Oh yes. Now it was time to start burning this beautiful bottom with an intensity she'd find hard to endure. This beautiful bare bottom upon which he was supposed to have second call.

Jillie sighed unhappily, still very red in the face. This was really rather embarrassing. Really rather humiliating. Her totally bare bottom peeping up at him, she meant, literally right under his nose. Okay, he'd had it bare after office hours almost every working day for the last six weeks. But being draped over his lap like this, waiting for him to start spanking her, that was very different. That was definitely more than a trifle embarrassing and humiliating. Not to mention the pain and discomfort she was going to have to suffer. It had been clear from his demeanour that he was thoroughly looking forward to that which she was about to receive, so she couldn't really expect him to show any leniency so far as her poor helpless bum was concerned. She was beginning to wonder whether she'd made the right decision last night at the railway station. Would all this be worth it? Would the prolonging of their five o'clock frolics be worth it? Would the preservation of their five o'clock fun and fornication be worth all that was to come? Well, she supposed it was a bit too late to change her mind now. She supposed she was just going to have to put up with it. In any event, he might even refuse to let her stand up, should she try to call a halt.

How much was he going to hurt her? As much as Tommy had done after the Jonathan Crowe disaster, when he'd put her over his knee and spanked her through her jeans for a good ten minutes, and then on her bare bottom for at least another half an hour?

'I'm sorry about George Franks,' she decided it might help to whisper.

'So am I,' he responded, rather grimly she thought. Perhaps it had been a mistake to mention that name...

'Ouch!' she gasped, as Jim painted the first perfect pink handprint across the centre of her pouting right cheek. He smacked five times more, turning the handprint red and blurring the edges. The process was then repeated on her other cheek, with exactly the same result. Then he slapped six times as hard as he could, across the centre, across the high point of each wildly bouncing cheek. Then he did the same all over again. Very quickly Jim realised that the repeated application of his hand on the same area of flesh caused the greatest dismay. So he slapped twenty times on one cheek, twenty on the other, then twenty across the middle of both. The pain brought tears to her eyes, as well as warm sticky oil into her vagina. Twenty more slaps followed across each side, and twenty more across the middle.

Jim paused and glared down balefully. Yes, just as he'd predicted. In less than a couple of minutes her bottom had been completely and utterly transformed. Its purity and perfection was now a thing of the past. Already it was highly discoloured and pulsing with pain. Already it was paying the price for the way in which it had been mounted so mightily the day before. And there was much more of the same mistreatment to follow. Much, much more of the same to come...

Slap! Slap! Slap! Slap! Slap! Slap! On and on and on. Twenty ringing slaps on one cheek, twenty on the other, then twenty across the high point of each. Over and over again.

Jillie squirmed her hips and screwed up her face in anguish as teardrops squeezed out of her eyes and trickled down her face. Oh! Ouch! Oww! She was on fire! Her poor bottom was being well and truly set alight. She'd forgotten all about the cumulative effect of a hard male hand landing heavily on the same part of the same cheek time after time after time. Each slap seemed to hurt twice as much as the one before, until she felt she simply couldn't take any more. But take it she had to do. There wasn't any option. She just had to lie there, weeping, and accept whatever Jim cared to dish out.

Why did men want to do this to a girl? Where was the fun in inflicting such pain and suffering? For the life of her she couldn't see the pleasure it gave them, although she was well aware that pleasure it gave. And why was her quim so wet? Why on earth was that? She supposed it must have something to do with the way it made her feel so utterly female. So utterly feminine, lying there, helpless, waiting without hope as one stinging blow after another cracked down noisily across her upthrust cheeks...

Half an hour later Jillie stood in the corner of her sitting room, her skirt round her waist and her thong round her thighs as she faced the wall in disgrace. Half an hour later she stood there, tears dripping down onto the supremely filled front of her blouse, one hand cupped gingerly round each blistered cheek. Half an hour later she stood there facing the wall - big, bare, brightly burning buttocks throbbing with an urgency she'd never believed possible. The retribution for her previous misconduct had been administered with a force and determination that had left her sobbing uncontrollably.

Jim lit a cigarette as he studied the hugely satisfying sight of her weeping in the corner of the room, bare-bottomed and in obvious distress, like some naughty teenage schoolgirl. Weeping profusely, whilst tenderly nursing her red-hot cheeks as if she feared they might burst into flames at any moment. His heavy male hand had dealt with her in a way he'd found utterly enthralling. It had splattered those saucy, plump, bouncing cheeks in the most delightful manner imaginable. How rewarding it had been; her ever-increasing discomfort as the pain of the spanking grew and grew and grew. Yes, how rewarding, making her gasp and twist her head this way and that in torment as one hard smack followed another, with intervals of little more than a second in between. And how satisfying, too, exorcising the thought of George Franks in that way. Exorcising the thought of everyone watching his huge cock scouring out her insides, and then pumping her full of sperm.

And then, of course, there'd been the final exorcism. The application of his belt buckle. Six times on each soundly spanked cheek, with all his power. Followed by six more of the same on each, and then another six. How that had made her holler and howl! What music it had been to his ears. What intense gratification it had brought him.

But what a good girl she'd been throughout. She'd never once struggled or protested, not even when the belt had been biting into her bottom. Never once had she tried to break free or begged him to stop. She'd just lain there over his lap, hands and feet on the floor, yelping as she writhed her female bottom from side to side at the intensity of the punishment - yet submitting to it without resistance or complaint.

Oh, yes indeed, the belt. The belt and the welts it had raised all over her beautiful bottom. One after another, time after time, again and again. How deeply it had bitten. How she'd jerked up her head and wailed so pitifully at each cruel caress...

Jillie darted a glance back over her shoulder, through tears and a tangle of hair. 'Keep facing the wall,' Jim ordered. 'I'll tell you when you can turn round.'

'I'm sorry...' she sniffed.

'And take your hands away from your bottom. I want to be able to watch it burn.'

She dropped her hands to her sides. 'Sorry...'

Jillie groaned to herself. She was in agony. Jim's terminology had been spot on; her poor posterior was simply burning away. It had proved quite incapable of being soothed by the gentle ministrations of her hands. It felt as if Jim had set it alight with a blowtorch. And the blotchy swellings his belt had raised all over it! They felt absolutely enormous, especially the ones on the very roundest part of each cheek, where the belt had bitten into her time and time again. Those would be with her for ages. Thank heavens Tommy was in Birmingham for the next four nights. Would she ever be able to sit down again?

And yet she was as randy as hell. She'd even have fucked George Franks, the King Rat himself, if he'd been offering it to her. But how lovely it would be if only she could have either Tommy or Jim.

Her poor, sore little bum. It had simply been roasted alive. And it seemed to be getting hotter and hotter by the moment as she stood staring at this rotten wall. Waves of pain were pulsating through her stricken cheeks. This was a far more severe punishment than the one Tommy had given her last year. Jim hadn't spanked her for quite as long, but the use of his belt had been sheer torture. It had seemed to slice right into her cheeks. Then he'd finished her off with several dozen slaps across each of the two main swellings, making her gush with even more tears than before. Tears that were only now starting to ease.

But at least she was feeling a lot less guilty about the way she'd laid across the computer stand in the IT room and allowed George Franks to take his fill. About the way she'd let her department watch him shag her and then implant her so ferociously. Yes, she was definitely feeling better about that. She'd been telling herself, as Jim had been punishing her bottom, that the beating ought to help to ease her conscience in that regard. And it did seem to have worked. The exceptionally hard spanking had erased a great deal of her former sense of shame.

Perhaps the punishment would also help her to feel easier when she was in the presence of George and the others? Perhaps it would help even more if she got Jim to spread the word about what he'd just done to her? Perhaps it would help if her department was made aware of how she'd asked Jim to make her suffer for her sins?

At last Jim spoke again. 'So then, Mrs Jackson,' he growled, sounding far more his former self, it seemed to Jillie. 'Shall we adjourn upstairs to the matrimonial bedroom?'

She gasped at the sudden rush of lust to her loins, and knew at once that she'd made the right decision twenty-four hours earlier. 'Am I to take it that you're now wanting to administer the rest of what I so richly deserve?' she giggled - much, much, *much* more happily.

CHAPTER TWO - HOUSEWIVES, INC.
Part One

Emma Brampton was perched on a bar stool in the brightly lit cocktail lounge of the London Hilton, her black hair cropped short in a sort of urchin cut that perfectly suited her beautiful, but decidedly mischievous, face. She was elegantly attired in a full-length evening dress that fitted her snugly. 'I'm a bored housewife,' she sighed, only semi-jocularly.

'So am I,' agreed her lifelong best friend, Jayne Jamieson, similarly perched and attired. 'I mean, I do love Martin very much. But I never see him. And he doesn't like the idea of me taking a part-time job. He thinks my place is at home, making everything perfect for the few short hours a week he spends there.'

'Chris is exactly the same. How can I shower him with love and affection when he's always at work?'

'Perhaps we should never have married two such high-powered legal beagles?' mused Jayne. 'Right now a lusty, ever-present milkman would suit me just fine.'

'It's been worse since the two of them were made full equity partners in their law firm,' sighed Emma, gazing aimlessly up at the huge crystal chandelier in the middle of the room.

'Much worse. Martin didn't get home until three o'clock this morning.'

'I know. Neither did Chris. They were both working on the same file, apparently.'

'Yes. Some last minute contract they had to produce for Sir Roland Rayke by eight this morning.'

'Commercial lawyers!' groaned Emma. 'They may earn a fortune, but we never get to enjoy it. Chris says there's no way he'll be able to find time for a proper holiday this year. And probably next year will be out of the question as well. I guess Martin is the same?'

'Yes. Exactly the same. Sir Roland Rayke and his multi-national conglomerates seem to take up every moment of his time.

'And as for our sex lives...'

'You mean the lack of them.'

'How can you make love to a husband who spends all day, seven days a week, and almost every evening, five miles away from the matrimonial bed?'

'With great difficulty.'

'Chris says things will get better in a couple of years. Then they'll both be senior enough to demand a salaried partner to act as personal assistant.'

'I know. But two years of almost total celibacy is rather a long time.'

'It was only a year ago that two days seemed too long.'

Jayne took a sip from her champagne flute and then glanced at her watch. 'They're late again. The ballet will start in less than half an hour.'

At that moment her mobile phone began to ring discreetly, so she plucked it out of her handbag. 'Hello, Martin. Where are you?'

Emma waited while her friend listened to what her husband had to say. 'Okay, darling,' Jayne said at length, before ending the call. 'Can you believe it!' she sighed, shaking her head in sorrow, rather than anger.

'What is it?'

'They're stuck at the office all evening. Sir Roland Bloody Rayke strikes again!'

'There they are,' said John, staring across to the bar counter at which Jayne and Emma were perched so prettily. 'Sitting at the bar in evening dresses. One blonde angel and one raven-haired beauty. Just as Maxine said.'

'Jesus!' whistled Peter. 'Just look at the state of those two! Worth every penny, don't you think?'

'I've never seen two hornier young strumpets. Maxine has certainly done us proud this time.'

'Now that is what I call high class,' breathed Peter. 'Nothing but real genuine, one hundred and ten per cent rock-solid state of the art. They look as if they've just stepped off the front cover of Vogue.'

'Come on. Let's not hang around. Let's introduce ourselves to them.'

'You must be the young ladies from the agency?' Peter enquired with a smile.

Jayne and Emma glanced up in surprise at the two good-looking men in their late thirties who'd just approached them. They could see at a glance that here was breeding, money and charm in ample proportions.

'Must we?' asked Jayne. 'What makes you say that?'

'Well, no one else in here could possibly be.'

The girls looked round the sparsely populated room. 'Couldn't they?' enquired Emma.

Peter laughed unsurely. 'Well, hardly...'

'Why not?'

'Most of them are with their partners...'

'Those three aren't,' said Jayne, nodding to three plump middle-aged women plastered with expensive jewellery.

'No, but they're not, er, exactly the type...'

'And we are?'

'Well, yes, definitely.'

'This agency...' began Emma.

'Yes?'

'Did they give you our names?'

'Well, no. Just, er, um, confirmation that our requirements would be met.'

'And what exactly were your requirements?'

Peter looked uncomfortable. 'Well, come on, girls. You know the sort of thing I mean...'

Emma looked at Jayne. 'And we fulfil them, do we? Your requirements, I mean?'

John spoke for the first time. 'Yes, very much so,' he enthused. 'Why don't we buy you some more champagne? In fact, why don't we buy a magnum for all of us to share?'

'Why don't you?' agreed Emma. 'We'll move to that empty table over there, and you can join us with the booze.'

'They think we're from an escort agency,' Jayne whispered to Emma as the two of them sat down.

'I know,' giggled Emma, looking across to the bar where the men were talking to a waiter. 'I suppose we should take it as a compliment.'

'What are we going to do about it?'

'We could escort them to the ballet, instead of our husbands?'

'I don't think that's quite what they've got in mind.'

'I know it isn't. I also know that what they do have in mind would be much more fun than sitting through even the finest performance of Swan Lake.'

'Emma!'

'I'm only joking. But they do look as if they could be quite good company. Let's have a laugh and a drink with them, and then tell them the truth.'

'What happens if the real escorts turn up?'

'As I said, we tell them the truth.'

Forty minutes later the feel-good effect of champagne was more than evident, a second bottle having been ordered and quickly emptied. But the real escorts still hadn't arrived and the truth still hadn't been imparted.

'Would you girls like to eat now or later?' asked John, draining his glass.

The girls glanced at each other. 'Oh, later, I think,' replied Emma, her dark blue eyes sparkling impishly. 'We never fuck on a full stomach, do we, Jayne?'

'No, never. It's so bad for the digestive system.'

Part Two

The four of them stepped out of the private lift that opened directly into the lounge area of the penthouse suite.

'Wow!' exclaimed Jayne, staring out of the floor-to-ceiling window that ran the whole length of the room 'What a view!'

'You can see right along the river as far as Greenwich,' pointed out Peter.

'How long are you staying here?'

'Just a couple of nights after tonight. Business mixed with pleasure.'

'Business must be good?'

'It is. Exceptionally good. But I think tonight's pleasure will be even better.'

'Let's hope so.'

'How do you want to be treated?'

'Pardon?' both girls asked together.

'Do you want us to treat you like ladies or like hookers? It's totally up to you.'

'Oh, like hookers,' Emma replied at once, feeling a sudden surge of excitement at the prospect. 'After all, that's what we are.'

'Yes, like hookers,' agreed Jayne, slightly less surely. 'Provided you're not too rough with us.'

John laughed. 'You needn't worry about that. It's just handy to know how you'd prefer us to behave, that's all.'

'Well then, as lecherously as possible,' breathed Jayne. 'Deal with us like a couple of whores deserve to be dealt with.'

'You said it,' growled Peter, advancing on Jayne with obvious intent.

Jayne took a deep breath, savouring the delicious thrill of anticipation. God, was she ready for this! Martin hardly spent any time at home these days. And when he did he spent most of it asleep. She knew how wrong this was; Martin was only doing what he thought was best. But that didn't alter the fact that she was as up for it as she'd ever been in her life. What she was about to do wouldn't alter the way she felt about Martin. She was still in love with him - even after five years of marriage, including twelve months of virtually no sex at all. And she still would be, even after Peter had succeeded in having his wicked way.

'Oh!' Jayne squawked in surprise, Peter having spun her round and bent her right forward across the highly polished table in the centre of the dining alcove, thus enabling everyone present to stare in delight at the exquisitely filled seat of her evening dress now tilted up at them so saucily. 'Oh!' she gulped, blushing fiercely as she felt Peter tugging the hem of the dress up from her ankles. It snagged momentarily, across the fullest part of her hips, but with a twist and a pull it was round her waist in no time at all. 'Oh!' she gulped again, her tight black thong having been whipped down to the floor, suddenly and unceremoniously, leaving her bent over the table with nothing below the waist except lace-topped stockings, matching black suspenders and high-heeled shoes.

Now all three of the other persons in the room were able to gaze in approval at the perfectly sculpted cheeks of her bent-over bottom, as bare as Nature had ever intended. Then, behind her back, came the sound of a zip-fastener urgently parting company with itself...

'Ohhh!' she gasped open-mouthed, feeling Peter's monstrously long and thick penis sinking into her all the way up to the hilt. He gripped her tightly round the waist and stood there, motionless, pressing hard into the springiness of her buttocks in order to penetrate her to his absolute maximum.

'Crikey!' murmured Emma, staring at the scene in awe, before feeling John's hand taking a gentle but generous handful of her lightly clad bottom. 'Mmm...' she purred, wriggling her hips luxuriously as he began a slow and very thorough exploration. 'Mmm...' she purred again, his other hand having joined in the caress. 'Doesn't that look so sexy?' she whispered to him over her shoulder, continuing to gaze at Peter and Jayne as they stood in front of them, securely coupled but still unmoving, still savouring the moment. She'd only seen it once before, she said to herself. Another couple on the job, she meant. It had been ten tears ago, after that wild party at Jayne's parents' house, when she and Jayne had both been eighteen. Their friend, Tina, had flounced off home in a strop, so the two of them shared Tina's boyfriend on the back seat of his beaten-up old Ford Granada. Watching Jayne getting it on the seat right beside her had been just as much fun as when the situation was subsequently reversed. Well, almost as much fun, at least...

While Emma was recalling the events of ten years earlier, Jayne groaned with a strange mixture of desire and embarrassment. He was all the way up inside her! All the way up to the very top of her wet channel! Jammed hard and fast against the neck of her womb! And it had all happened in a flash. One moment

51

he'd been standing there in front of her, asking her how she wanted to be treated. A few short moments later he'd been buried in her from behind, as far as he could possibly go! She couldn't believe she'd been breached so quickly. Five years of being faithful to Martin had ended almost before she'd known what was happening. One second everything had been normal and semi-respectable, the next she'd been impaled all the way up to her throat. Skewered from middle to mouth. And all this had taken place in full view of Emma and John! She'd been expecting him to march her through to the privacy of one of the bedrooms before setting about her. And she'd also thought there'd be some sort of foreplay - rather than just straight in and up. Was this really how hookers were treated? She had to admit it was rather exciting...

As Peter began to slide slowly back and forth, using strokes of considerable weight and power, Emma turned towards John. 'Let's watch them for a while. It's making me feel incredibly horny.'

'Okay. I guess I can contain myself a bit longer.'

Emma reached out and playfully tweaked his groin. He felt to be just as sizeable as Peter. She tweaked him again. 'Mind you,' she giggled, 'if it makes you any bigger than this I might live to regret my suggestion.'

'Let's hope you do then.'

Standing side by side they watched and listened as Peter's glistening, over-nourished organ worked steadily in and out between Jayne's upthrust buttocks. Emma squeezed him once again, feeling the heat of his erection through his clothing. 'That's my favourite way of having it,' she murmured. 'From behind. Chris' dick is a really good size, but taking it in like that makes it feel even bigger. Not that I've ever had much choice in the matter. He's always wanted to do it to me that way.'

Peter was still fondling her bottom with both hands. 'I think I know why,' he replied.

'It's the same with Jayne. Martin always gives it to her from behind. Isn't she pretty down there?'

'Really pretty,' John breathed in agreement, watching spellbound as Jayne gently wriggled her hips from side to side against the power of each incoming stroke. 'And I'm fairly confident Peter's feeling the same. Judging by his demeanour.'

Jayne screwed up her eyes and took a deep breath. This was really weird. Standing here like this, she meant. Standing here, bent right forward and gripped round the waist whilst being plugged full of cock in front of two other people. Standing here receiving length after length of Peter's scalding hot weapon, while two other people conducted a running commentary on what was happening to her. Weird, but not totally unpleasant. In fact, come to think of it, not unpleasant at all. Just different, she supposed.

Well, okay, if she had to be brutally honest, it was really arousing. It was making her feel really sexy. Especially now that Emma and John had taken a couple of steps to one side in order to be able to study the look on her face each time Peter forced himself all the way up inside. It would still have been great fun if Emma had been the only observer. She and Emma had watched each other at it once before, and enjoyed it. But having a man she'd never met before standing there staring at every intimate detail of the way she was being so comprehensively reamed and scoured, that was unbelievably exciting. Not to mention Peter, of course. Not to mention the other man she'd never met before! Not to mention the one who was gazing down at the cheekiness of her bare bottom while he did the reaming and scouring.

Oh Mother! The thought of all this extreme naughtiness was starting to make her come...

John turned towards Emma as Peter picked up the tempo in order to increase the strength of his partner's climax. 'That's enough voyeurism,' he said. 'Take off your dress and bend over the other side of the table so you're facing Jayne.'

Emma did as she'd been told, her bare breasts and skimpy pink thong now on prominent display. 'That's right,' he said encouragingly as she began to bend. 'Now lean forward and kiss her with your tongue. And keep on kissing her.'

As the girls rested on their elbows, hands holding each other's faces, kissing sweetly, Emma's thong was slipped down to her silk-stockinged thighs, allowing John to feast his eyes on her beautiful buttocks. And truly beautiful they were, too. Every bit as perfect as Jayne's, and possibly even cheekier. The cleft between each sweetly dimpled cheek was deep. The cheeks themselves resembled an inverted heart. They were plump but firm and pert, full and rounded at the bottom, then tapering upward in perfect proportions as far as the small of her back. And the texture was impeccable; silk and cream combined. Big, bare, beautifully moulded buttocks which, over the years, had provided her husband with unendurable delights - apart from the past twelve months, during which he'd scarcely had time to glimpse them, let alone manhandle them in the way that any husband should.

For many long seconds John gazed down in delight, her naked bottom gleaming proudly back at him as it reflected the overhead light in the centre of each pouting cheek. It really was the most spankable bottom imaginable. How many times, if ever, had it been draped over somebody's knee and set on fire? And had anyone ever shagged it? It was such an inviting shape that he wouldn't be at all surprised to learn that someone had insisted on fucking her in there. Unfortunately the agreement with the agency excluded anything like that. But spanking it? That was a different matter. Thank heavens they'd booked that option...

John cupped a hand round each honey-smooth globe and squeezed firmly. 'Gorgeous,' he murmured with feeling. 'Absolutely gorgeous.'

'Thank you,' whispered Emma, before returning her tongue to the succulence of Jayne's mouth.

Emma sighed with pleasure as John entered her, slowly but powerfully, stretching her and expanding her in the most delightful way. It was more than four weeks since Chris had last been in there, she said to herself, in an attempt to assuage her conscience. And before that time her wifely wares had remained unsampled for almost three months. So she wasn't going to let herself feel bad about what she was doing. She'd just concentrate on having a really good time...

Now both girls - still kissing with increasing passion - were being taken vigorously from behind. Hard male groins smacked noisily and repeatedly against soft, bouncy buttocks. Over-extended penises parted pussy with consummate ease. Despite the feelings of guilt Jayne and Emma were relishing each slippery push and pull. Eventually they were enjoying it to the extent of forgetting the fact of their infidelity and focusing, instead, on the way they were being so fearsomely fucked.

And their long-lasting kiss! Sharing a kiss of genuine passion with each other was something they'd barely thought about, let alone experienced. Jayne had kissed Emma on one occasion before, but those kisses had been ones of compassion, not passion. Their enjoyment of each other's mouths added that final touch of deliciously wild abandon. Pricks pumped relentlessly in and out, but the savouring of each other's female sweetness raised the pleasure platform beyond belief.

'What a fuck!' Emma whispered into Jayne's ear, having temporarily halted their kiss.

'Oh, wow, yes!' sighed Jayne. 'Kiss me again with your tongue. As hard as you can...'

Both men raced in and out at speed. *Slap, slap, slap...* went groin against bouncy bare bottoms. *Squidge, squelch, squidge...* went penis in soaking wet pussy. 'Ohh! Ahh! Ohh!' gasped both the girls.

Then the men swapped positions, Peter thrusting hard into Emma, while John pierced Jayne with all his might. The new partnerships added to the girls' excitement, making them wriggle their hips even harder from side to side, while the men gripped them tightly around the waist and started to rut. The chase was on as before, almost as if the men were in competition with each other.

On and on they raced, pumping lustily into their partners as fast as they could, tearing in and out with gusto while the girls clung to their long, passionate kiss. Then the partners were swapped again. And then again after that. It seemed to add an edge to the men's performance. So they began to swap every couple of minutes or so. Fuck, fuck, fuck into one of the now-not-nearly-so-bored young housewives, then fuck, fuck, fuck into the other.

Emma sighed with pleasure. It was like being made love to three times over. Not only did she have John working away inside her but, as she and Jayne kissed, she could almost feel Peter's penis working away in her friend. Indeed it was almost as if he was inside her, as well as in Jayne.

And the men sensed the same. Every time they pushed forward it seemed they were entering both women. Entering their immediate partner and, at the same time, pushing through her into the other girl.

Emma slightly adjusted her stance, so that each thrust from behind was causing her clitoris to rub against the surface of the table. Jayne realised what was happening and did the same. Within less than a minute both of them were consumed with orgasm.

'Oh, my God!' gasped Jayne, having to break from the kiss in order to fight for breath.

'Oh yes indeed!' groaned Emma, closing her eyes and forcing her bottom into the rampant male groin behind her. Then they were kissing and caressing each other as before.

The lovemaking proceeded at pace, the girls gently savouring each other's mouths whilst relishing the stark contrast between the tenderness of the kiss and the power of the coupling. The contrast became even greater as the men began to pump with all the strength they could muster. In and out ripped hot hard flesh at a truly blistering speed. The girls clung to each other, kissing and petting each other reassuringly, whilst at the same time wriggling against the intruding organs. Now both girls could feel both men; one penetrating directly and one inside her friend.

Inflamed by the sight of the lesbian love, the men gritted their teeth and continued to shaft as fast and as hard as they could. But this only served to make the girls love each other even more.

'Bugger this!' Peter muttered to himself, thrusting brutally into Jayne. 'I'm going to give her the very mother of all fuckings!'

As indeed he did, with John following suit. A seemingly endless pumping of penis into already over-poked pussy. Nevertheless, all good things must come to an end, and eventually the men were exhausted and spent - Peter having heavily implanted Jayne less than a minute before John began shooting his white-hot essence deep into Emma's willing young body.

The men shed all their clothes, except for their boxer shorts. These they retained in order to demonstrate that they were in control. John looked over at the girls, who were still loving each other on the table. 'You can stop that now,' he ordered. 'Stand up and strip each other off to your stockings, suspenders and high heels.'

Standing face to face they did as they'd been bid, slowly and sexily, smiling into each other's faces. Neither girl was wearing a bra so Emma was easy to strip, only requiring her thong to be dropped to the floor. But Jayne's dress had to be pulled down from her waist and unzipped before she could step out of it and reveal her own outthrust breasts to the light of the penthouse suite. Sensing what the men would want, their arms encircled each other and their mouths were eagerly reunited. As they stood there - mouth to mouth, nipple to nipple, hands slowly exploring silky buttocks - the men's seed began its downward journey inside them.

'I do like the feel of your bottom,' breathed Emma, squeezing firmly with both hands as she pushed her groin into Jayne's.

'Ditto,' sighed Jayne, reciprocating in kind, and reflecting on the stark contrast between Emma's smoothly-rounded cheeks and the usual bony male buttocks.

Emma began to rub her clitoris against Jayne's mound, managing to prompt a mini-climax almost at once. 'You do the same,' she giggled softly into the other girl's ear. 'It's amazing how quickly it works when you've just been fucked...'

'Oh!' squealed Jayne, responding instantly. 'Oh, that's lovely...'

'Let's keep doing it together.'

Now both girls were locked even more warmly and tightly together, panting and gasping with pleasure and enjoying the admiring gaze of the men they could both sense upon them.

'Okay, hookers,' John cried at last, both he and Peter starting to slap playfully - but hard - at bouncy bare bottoms, and provoking girlie squeals of laughter and shrieks of protest. 'That's enough of that. Through to my bedroom now. There's more champagne waiting for you in the fridge, by way of refreshment. But before then it's time for your hors d'ouvres.'

'Our *hors d'ouvres?*' asked Jayne, failing to dodge another ringing slap from Peter.

'Yes. Sperm-laced pussy. You're to get on the bed and start to eat. Peter and I will sample some of the vintage while we watch.'

The jumbo-sized bed was eight feet square. Jayne lay across it on her back, legs apart, while Emma's face was buried between silky upper thighs. 'Oh, my God,' moaned Jayne. 'You're making me come all over again...'

John gazed appreciatively at the four pink handprints that had been painted so prettily across the fleshiest part of Emma's mouth-wateringly plump bare buttocks. He was already fully erect once more, and ready for further action. But he'd wait until both girls had eaten their fill. Then, and only then, would it be time to revive the fornication. In the meantime he'd have a cigarette and another glass of wine... and admire the view.

Emma raised her head and smiled at Jayne. 'Your pussy tastes delicious,' she murmured happily. 'Here, let me share it with you.' She kissed the other girl with her tongue and then went back to work, prompting further sighs of sheer delight.

After a while Emma raised her head once again. 'Roll onto your side across the bed,' she said to Jayne. 'I'll show you how Annie taught me to do it in the sixty-nine position.'

So Jayne adjusted herself on the bed and began to learn.

Jayne was now her third female lover, Emma thought to herself, as both girls licked and lapped each other. Annie had been the first. Annie, the beautiful red-haired head girl from boarding school. The eighteen year old from the upper sixth who'd taken a shine to Emma. Annie had first seduced her in the school library, when they'd been sitting side by side at a table behind a high bookshelf. She could clearly recall the thrill of feeling Annie's hand creeping slowly up between her thighs, under her navy-blue gymslip, and then a slim finger being slid all the way inside her.

'You're incredibly wet!' Annie had whispered.

'I know,' she'd replied, red-faced and breathing heavily. Then Annie worked skilfully on her until she brought her off, her mouth buried in her hands in order to stifle the shrieks of delight. Eventually, after many passionate sessions involving fingers and tongues, they'd been found in bed together. Annie had been caned by the Headmistress, and then expelled. Her own bare bottom also received six of the best, but she hadn't been expelled. Where was Annie now?

She still felt a soft spot whenever she thought of her. Yes, there as well...

Now each girl had feasted on the other and the champagne had been consumed. Now the girls were lying side by side on the bed, face up, their bare bottoms being bounced rhythmically up and down by their paying customers. The men were still swapping partners at regular intervals, but both of them were aware that, this time, Peter would wish to spunk Emma, whilst John would want to unburden himself into Jayne's hot little hole. In the meantime, however, they were busily mixing a cocktail of both girls' juices and both men's seed inside each of the girls.

On and on went the shafting; the men possessing even greater stamina now it was their second time around. Emma gasped to herself as Peter suddenly doubled the pace. Good grief! She was getting more cock tonight than Chris had given her during the whole of the past twelve months. Much, much, much more, in fact. She could just about count on the fingers of one hand the number of times they'd made love since he'd started to work so hard at the office. And each of those had been relatively quick. Chris was so tired these days that his performance in bed resembled that of a much older man. She could remember the old days so well. The days when he'd been such a stud. He'd wanted to upend her whenever and wherever he could. Bless his little cotton underthings! It wasn't his fault that he was now always so knackered. But then again, it wasn't her fault either. She'd much prefer him to earn half the money he did, if it meant he'd spend twice as much time with her. The money wasn't important, after all.

Thank heavens her pussy was being such a good little girl! Thank heavens she was lubricating so heavily! Otherwise she might have been a trifle tender in the morning...

Oh! That was nice! John had just swapped with Peter and rolled on top of her, starting to service her so sweetly. He was using long, slow, gentle strokes that glided smoothly up and down the full length of her channel. It was a real contrast to the way Peter had previously been piling into her with such abandon. As a result she was swooning with pleasure. It felt as if he was *floating* his penis in and out. She could feel his hardness well enough. A hardness that filled and stretched. But it was such a sleek, slippery hardness it made her want to cry out with delight as he slid so slowly and sweetly up to the hilt, nestled, and then eased himself all the way out. She could tell the effect it was having inside her. She was becoming wetter and more slippery by the moment. And she'd been really wet already!

And another thing; at this pace she could feel his dick so well. She could feel the bulbous tip and the thick cord of artery that ran all the way down to his balls. It fitted her so perfectly, like a hand in an elasticated glove. It felt as if she could discern every ridge and wrinkle he had. Every lump and bump of his penis as it slithered lazily back and forth...

Emma closed her eyes and moaned softly, luxuriating in the warmth of an orgasm so slow and tender she could hardly believe it was true. The leisurely rhythm of the coitus had brought her to a delightfully different form of climax. One that soothed and pampered, rather than hammered right through her. One that lasted and lasted, bringing tears of joy to her eyes as she squirmed her hips underneath him. Now John was motionless inside her - solid and still inside her, allowing her the freedom to work him just as she chose. 'That's unbelievable!' she gasped, as the waves of pleasure flowed gently up through her body. 'That's really unbelievably good...!'

A few minutes later, when the climax had finally passed, John slipped his hands underneath her bottom and squeezed cheeks so silky and slippery-smooth that they slid straight out of his fingers. So he did it again, with exactly the same result. 'I think it's time to exercise the spanking option,' he told her, unable to wait any longer.

'Pardon?' asked Emma, thinking she must have misheard.

'The spanking option. You must know what I mean?'

'Oh, well, er yes, of course...'

'Maxine did tell you we wanted it?'

'Um, well yes, that's right...'

'We'll pay the extra charge, of course.'

'Extra charge?'

'Yes, the extra charge.'

'Oh, right...'

'Good. I think it's time to exercise it now.'

'The spanking option?'

'Yes, of course.'

'Are you sure?'

'Yes. Completely sure.'

Emma gulped. Surely there was a way out of this, short of confessing all? But if there was it currently eluded her completely. How much did he intend to hurt her? Just a few playful love-pats, or something much more painful? She'd been down that latter road before, and had no wish to travel it again. She supposed that only time would tell what lay in store.

John withdrew from the glorious wet warmth of her vagina and rolled onto his back. 'Get on top of me,' he said. 'Fit me back in, and then lie flat on top of me, legs close together.'

The other couple watched with intrigue as Emma nervously complied, blushing slightly. John was up to the root in her once again, but this time her shapely bottom was on prominent display. Peter could ogle it by turning his head to his left, while John and Jayne had a clear view of it in the ceiling mirror above them. Everyone waited, full of anticipation. Emma closed her eyes and tried to prepare herself for what was to come.

Suddenly, and venomously, John cracked his hand down across the centre of her pouting pink cheeks six times. Emma squealed and jerked, forcing his penis even deeper inside her. 'Ouch!' she yelped, tears already starting to prickle both eyes. 'Oh!' she gasped, as his penis scoured her insides.

John repeated the process. Several times. Loudly and enthusiastically, hammering her harder and harder onto the point of his erection with every stinging slap, making her squeal with pain and gasp with pleasure. Suddenly her climax returned, much more sharply than before. 'Ohhh!' she exclaimed in surprise. 'Oh God, you're making me come...!'

'Perhaps she'll waive the extra charge?' Jayne said dryly, admiring the way in which her friend's pretty bottom was bouncing and reddening so attractively.

Emma writhed in pain as the beating proceeded without relent. Each crack of the hand seemed to drive him even further into her, stretching and making her gasp and squawk with a strange mixture of external discomfort and internal pleasure.

Slap! Slap! Slap! Slap! Slap! Slap!

'Oh! Ohhh! Ouch!' she gasped and then sobbed, tears trickling down her face. 'Oh Jesus! It hurts like hell! But you're making me come so hard!'

'I know. I can feel.'

Very quickly, however, the orgasm passed and the pleasure evaporated completely, leaving nothing but the pain of the spanking, which continued with pace and power. Emma contorted her face and tried to squirm away from him, but found herself held fast by John's other arm - as well as the solidity of the coupling.

Slap, squawk, squirm. Slap, squawk, squirm. Slap, squawk, squirm. On and on and on. Time after time. Again and again and again And then again and again after that.

'Oww! Ouch! Oww...! Ouch! Ouch! Ouch...! Oh, Mother! Oh, Mary! That really hurts! Can't you please stop now?'

'Not a chance,' growled her tormentor, his left arm still wrapped round her in order to curtail her struggles to break free. 'I've only just started on you. Can you feel the effect it's having on my dick?'

Emma could. She closed her eyes and gritted her teeth, realising she had no chance of stopping him, but still trying to get free nevertheless. She'd forgotten about the compounding effect of a hard hand-spanking. Each slap seemed to hurt twice as much as the one before. Each slap seemed to sting more and more, until she felt she simply couldn't stand another. She could feel his penis expanding inside her while it was happening, which was really weird. Really different. But it was in no way compensating for the ever-increasing pain.

'Please!' she gasped breathlessly. 'Please, please stop now! You don't know how much it hurts!'

'No, but I can guess. In the meantime you'll just have to put up with it.' So saying, he increased the speed of the assault on her stricken cheeks.

The struggles and protests finally stopped, because she no longer had the strength to try to resist, and because she knew it was hopeless anyway. She lay there on top of him, tearful and submissive, flinching at every stinging rebuke from the palm of his hand. She could feel the power of his erection, emphasised so succinctly each time his hand landed on target. So she squeezed him with her vaginal muscles, hoping that if she could bring him off her ordeal would end.

But it was not to be. He was not to be brought to the boil in that way. He was having too much fun punishing the naughty bare bottom he held at his mercy. The naughty bare bottom, he said to himself, of another man's wife. The naughty bare bottom that would, in a while, be taking itself home to hearth and hubby. For her sake he hoped she'd keep it well and truly under wraps until it had regained its original hue. Both girls had talked openly about their husbands, so he was well aware of the potential problems they faced later that night. He was delighted they'd been so frank. It was incredibly refreshing to be able to bed a part-time call girl who was also a married woman. For some reason it seemed to give just that extra edge. It was the element of her infidelity that added to the appeal, he supposed. And what value for money the spanking option provided! It was good that several agencies now offered the service.

Emma lay still, sobbing quietly but profusely, trying to focus her mind on something else. Anything else at all. Anything that would distract her from the raging fire being stoked up so surely across her bouncing buttocks. But it wasn't possible. Each ringing slap reminded her so clearly of her current plight. Each ringing slap and each streak of fire ensured she remained fully aware of her highly uncomfortable situation. Perhaps it was no more than she deserved, she wondered haplessly. How much longer was this going to continue? Her poor bottom was so fiercely ablaze. But he didn't seem at all interested in reaching the point of orgasm, only in hurting her more and more.

John gazed up at the image in the ceiling mirror. What a truly wondrous sight! That plump, perfect posterior suffering one heartless smack after another, making it redder and hotter as time ticked slowly by. And the crying; the muted sobs that accompanied the flow of tears. How incredibly rewarding that was. This gorgeous raven-haired beauty subjugated to his will so completely. This gorgeous raven-haired hooker and housewife crammed full of his overstretched penis whilst having no option but to accede to and accept the domination of his right hand against the succulence of her lovely female buttocks. A domination that was making itself felt more and more as he swatted her time after time after time, with all the strength at his disposal.

Emma continued to lie stock still, weeping softly but refusing to complain further, in the hope that her show of total submission might help bring an earlier end to the punishment. But John's heart was hard. No mercy was being shown. No remorse being felt. He closed his eyes to savour the situation. To savour the feel of his erection being battered against the neck of her womb with every blow from his hand.

'I'm sorry,' she whispered tearfully, wondering if that might help to reduce the length of time she'd have to suffer.

'For what?'

'I don't know really,' she admitted, as his hand continued to crack down. 'Just sorry that my poor bottom's suffering so much pain, I suppose.'

But eventually her torment was over, and the gentle sobbing slowly started to cease. She lay on top of him, breathing deeply, her pointed nipples boring into his chest, her tears soaking his neck and left shoulder, and his penis still pressing hard against the top of her vagina. Very slowly, and very gingerly, she began to run a hand over the afflicted cheeks, before realising she was starting to enjoy, once again, the bulkiness of his presence inside her. 'Mmm...' she breathed, almost silently, as she began to wriggle her hips from side to side. She removed her hand from her burning bottom and tried to snuggle even more closely to him. 'Mmm, that feels nice,' she whispered into his ear, wriggling firmly against his rigidity. He was so stiff that she couldn't move him at all, much to her ever increasing delight. Now that the punishment was over she was beginning to feel as randy as before.

Peter pulled out of Jayne with a decided slurp. 'Now then, let's see how this gorgeous young strumpet reacts to the same treatment.'

'Oh, I'm not so sure about that...'

'Hookers who ask to be treated as hookers have to learn to do as they're told.'

Jayne knelt over Peter's groin, gazing down apprehensively at her best friend's blistered buttocks. 'Oh dear,' she sighed unhappily

At long last both spankings were concluded, much to the relief of the phoney call girls. The infliction of pain by the men was over and the gaining of carnal pleasure by the girls was resumed.

Peter was still slotted securely into Jayne from underneath, whilst Emma was on elbows and knees on the bed, like a supplicant before the sultan. John was mounted on her back, his knees straddling hers as he poled her at medium pace. He looked down, watching appreciatively as his wet erection slid back and forth between pouting, red-hot cheeks. She was a fabulous fuck, he thought gleefully. This raven-haired housewife now wriggling enthusiastically against him. A truly fabulous fuck. What a fantastic little honeypot she possessed. As hot as Hades itself. It seemed to be scorching the end of his dick. And it grasped him so wonderfully well. So firmly and tightly, just as if she was squeezing him in the palm of her hand. Yet it was as smooth and slick as could be. Lubricated so beautifully that it seemed to draw him in of its own accord, without any real effort from him, making her impossibly easy to fuck. Making it seem he was sliding his end back and forth through hot, liquid silk.

And what a spectacular pair of buttocks. Just made to be fitted snugly into a rampant male groin, like so. And decorated so appealingly by his own heavy hand. Both cheeks were now crimson as a result of the mistreatment. It seemed as if the pleasure he'd derived from spanking her, and from watching Peter laying into Jayne in exactly the same way, had forced every drop of blood in his body into his bursting, burning erection. He was sure he'd never been this size before. He was sure he'd never had an erection quite like this...

Emma moaned as John picked up speed. It was the seventh or eighth time that evening he'd been inside her, but this session was lasting longer than any of the previous, with the result that her insides were now melting away. Melting away, yet yearning for him to implant her; for him to force-feed her with Nature's own special gruel. And at long last he began to provide. She gasped with excitement as the first fierce squirt erupted inside her. Once again she experienced the sensation of being a complete woman as she felt the long-awaited produce of his loins gushing warmly into her womb. The delicious sensation of being a woman completely at one with the natural world, as she shuddered with pleasure and submitted so willingly to the duty imposed on all womankind at the very dawn of creation. Submitting to it, subservient to it, slavishly accepting the hot male seed, whilst mounted from above and behind in the classical fashion of the animal kingdom.

Part Three

The taxi dropped Jayne outside her large detached house in the suburbs. She glanced at her watch as she opened the front door. It was nearly one o'clock in the morning, but fortunately Martin's car was not in the drive. Time to remove and then conceal the incriminating evidence.

She walked through the kitchen to the utility room and dropped her semen-soaked thong into the washing machine. It would be perfectly safe in there; Martin didn't even know how to open the door! Very ruefully she began to rub the snugly filled seat of her evening dress. Oh! She was as sore as anything. Possibly not quite as sore as poor Emma had been two years earlier, when Chris put her over his knee after her unfortunate little misadventure with Jonathan Crowe. But certainly sore enough. Well, at least she wouldn't have any trouble hiding her soundly spanked bottom away from Martin; he hardly ever came after it these days.

Oh dear. She was starting to feel guilty, now the champagne was wearing off. She supposed she should never have done it. In fact, she knew she should never have done it. It wasn't poor Martin's fault that he worked such long hours. He was only doing what he thought was best for the two of them. She should never have given in to the yearning she'd felt in her loins. A yearning that, over the past few months, had grown and grown and grown. Now it was out of all proportion. And out of control, as well. As witness the events of the evening.

What should she do with the money? Two thousand pounds in cash. Where would be the safest place to hide it? In the boot of her car, she supposed. Then she could bank it when she went shopping in the morning.

Oh crumbs! Her conscience was really starting to play up. How could she have acted like that? Like the very worst sort of whore?

But she had to admit how greatly she'd enjoyed herself, despite the pain of the spanking. The sex had been absolutely phenomenal. She'd never known anything like it. And apart from her guilty conscience, and her grossly overheated bottom, she was feeling better than she'd felt for ages. She was feeling incredibly uplifted. Just as if she'd taken some sort of drug. And her pussy! It was positively purring with contentment. It was positively radiating fulfilment and joy. And leaking sperm, as well...

How sexy it had felt, being sorted out by Peter over that table while both Emma and John stood watching. She had to confess it had been fun. Embarrassing, but fun. Very great fun, in fact. Her insides had been in turmoil at the way she was being serviced so well under the close scrutiny of two observers.

How different it had been for poor Jillie Jackson, two years ago at the office. Being closely observed on the job, she meant. Jillie Jackson, that lovely girl with the really sexy wiggle, who'd been humbled and humiliated by George Franks, her head of department. Humbled and humiliated by being made to bend forward across one of the computer stands in the IT room, the top half of her body lying flat on the surface of the stand, her legs down at right angles, and her toes only just touching the floor. Humbled and humiliated by being made to lie across the stand in that manner, and let him screw her from behind - in full view of the four other men from their department!

Humbled and humiliated by being made to let him screw her and pump her full of his seed, while four of their colleagues from sales watched in fascination. It hadn't been any fun at all for her. Jillie had hated every second. She wouldn't have minded housing George's grossly overgrown weapon if they'd been on their own and he'd promised not to tell anyone. In fact, she admitted she'd have enjoyed it, particularly as her lack of say in the matter would have stopped her feeling guilty. But having to take it in front of those people had been way, way too much. Her face had been scarlet with the shame and humiliation.

For the next ten minutes Jayne remained deep in thought concerning the unfortunate fate of her friend. Suddenly, though, she came back to the present. Oh dear, time was slipping away. Fancy daydreaming about the total humiliation of poor Jillie Jackson two years ago. About the way she'd been forced to participate in a live sex show. She'd better take a bath without any further delay. Martin would be home soon, she suspected. And she was in no fit state to receive him, even if he only went straight to sleep. It just wouldn't be right for her to join him in bed until she'd had a really long hot soak and washed away all the physical aspects of her mega multi-adultery.

Perhaps she could coax him into a spot of lovemaking? That would probably help her feel a bit better about what she'd been up to. Maybe he wouldn't be too tired for a bit of marital nooky? In the old days he'd upended her almost every morning and night. And some lunchtimes, too What a shame he no longer possessed the energy or desire to sort her out in that way. In the way she knew she so desperately needed.

Jayne turned towards Martin as he climbed naked into bed, and reached for his groin.

'I need to sleep,' he muttered tiredly. 'I have to get up in four hours and head back to the office.'

'Just lie back and close your eyes and I'll use my mouth. It'll help to relax you. It doesn't matter if you don't get hard, or if you fall asleep while I'm doing it.' She giggled sexily. 'And if you happen to get hard in your sleep, I'll just kneel over you and help myself.'

'That would be nice, sweetheart...'

'Oh!' Jayne gulped in surprise, some sixty seconds later. Martin had got erect surprisingly quickly, and she'd done as she'd said. She'd knelt over him and helped herself, even though he was still awake. And the second she slotted him inside her she started to come! And of course, she knew the reason why. She was still highly aroused from the events of the evening. She was still really turned on and up for anything. What a disgrace! She was now orgasming like mad with Martin as a direct consequence of the colossal amount of cock on which she'd previously been fed! Thank God he couldn't get into her mind as easily as she'd been able to get him into her heavily lubricating quim. She'd better try to conceal what was happening to her.

Oh well. There was no need to worry too much about that. Martin had fallen asleep almost as soon as she'd put him in. He was lying there on his back, snoring softly while she rode slowly up and down the full length of his stalk. Well, at least it was better than not having him inside her at all. And there was another consolation. She wouldn't have to worry about him wrapping his hands round her bottom and wondering why it was so blazing hot.

Emma lay in bed beside her comatose husband, her bottom also on fire but her groin even hotter. She sighed happily to herself. Sex without involvement, that was the answer. Or rather, sex without involvement, and without a severely spanked backside, that was the answer. Sex without the risk of any emotional baggage. Lots of long, smooth cock, but without having to be in any way involved with the man on the end of that cock. That was what had made the evening so successful. Successful, apart from the pain of the spanking, of course. That was why she now felt so good. That was why she now felt as if a great weight had been lifted from her. She wasn't interested in becoming involved with anyone except Chris. But for the moment he wasn't interested in fucking her. So the answer was clear; for the time being fuck someone else. But someone in whom she could never have any other sort of interest.

It was odd. Tonight was only the second time she'd been unfaithful to Chris, yet on both occasions her bottom had suffered severely as a result. Had tonight been worth it? Yes, there was no doubt that it had.

But it was a bit of a coincidence. Adultery and spanked bottoms. Twice she'd done it and suffered, and now Jayne had done it and was suffering the same. Jayne had never cheated on Martin before tonight yet here she was, her rear end suffering in exactly the same way.

And there were two other strange coincidences. After her schoolgirl affair with Annie had been exposed and then ended in a caning from the headmistress, rumour of her ordeal spread like wildfire. Mike, her boyfriend, had heard of the whole episode that very day. As a result she'd spent a large part of the same afternoon over his knee, bare-bottomed and shrieking and struggling while he spanked the six raised welts with all his might. How her poor teenage bottom had suffered that day! And how enormous her boyfriend's dick had been when he'd finally finished punishing her! Almost twice its normal size. It had taken ages to fit all of it inside her.

Then secondly, there'd been that Christmas Eve at the bank three years ago when she'd been newly married to Chris. It hadn't actually been adultery, but she supposed it had been the next best thing. Or should that be 'next worst'? Her line manager, Lisa Browne, found her giving George Franks a blowjob in the deeds depository. Just for a bit of Christmas fun. Nothing serious, of course. George had wanted to fuck her for Christmas, so she'd offered him a compromise instead.

That was all there'd been to it. But once again she'd ended up sore-bottomed and tearful. Lisa had made her bend over the back of a typist's chair and then walloped her bare buttocks *two hundred* times with a heavy ruler until they were raw. She knew exactly how many times the ruler cracked down across her, because each searing stroke had been counted out loud. She supposed, looking back, it had been Lisa's way of gaining her own bit of Christmas fun. Like so many of her friends, school friends and work colleagues over the years, both male and female, Lisa had never been able to refrain from absentmindedly patting and petting the cheeks of her pouting rear end. She still found that sort of thing rather nice, in a way. Sort of cosy and comforting, despite the events of that Christmas Eve when Lisa finally managed to achieve what she must always have been wanting to do to her.

She supposed, thinking about it further, that most of the others who petted her bottom would also like to do exactly the same thing to it. 'It's so nice I want to hurt it,' an ex-boyfriend had once said, gripping her bottom so hard that the finger marks had lasted for days.

Well, at least she'd been able to finish the process with George, before Lisa summoned her to her office. The lovely salty taste in her mouth helped her through the torment that followed. How embarrassing it had been, going back to work after the Christmas break. Everyone seemed to know about the sucking and consequent spanking. Rather like the way everyone had become aware of her unfortunate episode with Jonathan Crowe, just over a year later...

Well, never mind about coincidences. It couldn't keep on happening. The spanking consequence, she meant. Cock was what was needed. Cock without complications. So then, she must talk to Jayne in the morning...

Part Four

Emma opened the door as soon as Jayne rang the bell.

'What's so urgent?' asked Jayne. 'We're playing squash together after lunch.'

'Come through to the sitting room,' Emma said excitedly. 'There's something I want to show you.'

'What is it?' asked Jayne, intrigued.

'Come and see for yourself. It's over there.' Emma pointed to a table in the corner of the room, on top of which her laptop computer was reposing. 'Come and look what I've surfed up on the Internet.'

Jayne bent forward and peered at the luridly illustrated website displayed on the screen of the PC. 'What on earth is this?'

'Just read it, for God's sake. Then we can talk.'

Jayne sat down on the chair in front of the computer and started to read...

HOUSEWIVES, INC.

Fuck Someone Else's Wife Tonight.

We have dozens of gorgeous young housewives on our books. Genuine young housewives. Dozens of gorgeous, genuine, bored young housewives who - for one reason or another - are not getting enough of what they need at home. Do you want to give it to them? Do you want to help them out? For just one thousand pounds you can spend an hour in bed with the girl of your dreams. She won't be a professional escort. She'll have a husband, and maybe even a family, at home. For only an extra three hundred pounds you can send her back to hearth and home soundly spanked, as well as rogered rigid. (That would remind her of the duty she has to respect her husband and ignore her libidinous cravings, would it not?) Longer bookings can be negotiated. Here are our answers to some of your most frequently asked questions:

Q Where and when will I meet her?

A We will give you full details of the rendezvous, if applicable, and - if necessary - tell you how you will recognise her. Please bear in mind that as your escort has a husband at home to be concerned with, you should be as flexible as possible with the date and time of the meeting. She will have excuses to make and alibis to arrange.

Q Where will I fuck her?

A You must arrange and pay for hotel accommodation, preferably somewhere in central London, and advise us of the details in advance. We can help you here, if you wish. If you want to use a private residential address or other location you must obtain our approval when making the booking. We reserve the right to reject this at our sole discretion. However, rejection is unlikely, particularly if you are already known to us. Office/workplace and outdoor locations are usually acceptable to us. Please read our terms of service regarding taxi fares outside central London etc. before contacting us.

Q How do I choose her?

A E-mail us at the address below with your phone number and we will ring you to discuss your requirements. For our security, you cannot phone us. For your security, we will never e-mail your computer unless you ask us to do so. In the unlikely event that you are not entirely happy when you meet her, then you are under no obligation to proceed further. Equally, our blushing young housewives reserve the right to reject you. In the latter case, the full cost of your hotel accommodation will be refunded to you on the spot.

Q How do I pay for her?

A You pay the young lady in cash before you bed her. You pay nothing to us.

Q What do I get for my three hundred pounds' worth of spanking?

A You can spank her with your hand as hard as you like for a maximum of ten minutes. Please note that this 'extra' must be booked in advance.

In order to whet your appetite, you can now view a selection of our naughty and nubile young housewives. Click on the housewife's name to view everything she owns. Please note, however, that some of her facial features have been altered, in order to protect her identity. We guarantee, however, that in real life she is just as pretty as the image. Click, also, on the 'Doubles' section if you'd like to see what some of them do to each other in order to stop themselves becoming too bored. If you want to 'double date' these girls, either on your own (if you're that greedy) or with a friend, then that's just fine.

New escorts welcome.

For all enquiries, e-mail us.

Jayne stood up, mystified. 'And your point is?' she asked.

'It's perfect. It's absolutely ideal. Do you see how they even have to pre-book the spanking? That must mean we can refuse it. My poor little bott is still incredibly sore. But that bit must mean we can refuse in advance, mustn't it?'

'We? What do you mean *we?*'

'We... you, me, us.'

'What the hell are you talking about?'

'That escort agency. We should apply to join it. To become a pair of escorts. That way we can get all the sex we need without any risk of getting tangled up with another man. Can't you see? It's the answer to our prayers. It's just what we need until our husbands have more free time on their hands. Yard after yard of cock, but nothing else. Nothing on the end of it.'

'I suppose there might be something in what you say,' she mused...

Emma began to key in the e-mail. 'We are Emma and Jayne,' she wrote. 'We're housewives who're gorgeous, young and bored. My mobile number is 077...' Then she clicked on *send.*

'That's not your number, is it?'

'I bought a new phone this morning. Just for this purpose. No one else knows about it. It's that one there.'

'Make sure you keep it well hidden from Chris.'

'Don't worry. I'll make sure he has no idea it exists. We'll just use it for this one thing, and nothing else.'

'You'd better delete that website from history, too.'

'It's done. Not that Chris ever uses my girlie little laptop. It's not nearly macho enough for him. Nowhere near enough mega-giggowossies, or whatever. His study is crammed full of all sorts of bits and pieces of computer kit. I wouldn't know where to start on his contraption.'

Suddenly the brand new mobile started to ring. 'Jesus!' gasped Emma. 'That was quick!'

Private number calling, said the display. Emma pressed the receive button at once. 'Hello,' she said excitedly.

'This is Tracie.'

'Hello, Tracie.'

'Are you Jayne or Emma?'

'Emma. But Jayne's right here with me.'

'Are you serious about this, Emma?

'Yes. Very.'

'We get quite a few prank e-mails, you know. Mostly from men, I have to say.'

'No, this isn't a prank.'

'Have you done this sort of work before?'

'No, never.'

'But you think you'd like to try?'

'Yes definitely.'

'You need the money?'

'Not really...'

'The sex, then?'

'Yes. The sex...'

'Can you get into town this afternoon?'

'Yes. We were going to play squash, but we can cancel that.'

'There's a café/bar near to Covent Garden called The Green Banana. Do you know it?'

'No.'

'It's on your left as you walk down to the market from the tube station.'

'Okay.'

'Can you be there at four o'clock?'

'Yes, I'm sure we can.'

'Sit near the door, both of you wearing white T-shirts and blue denim jeans.'

'Okay.'

'Good. I'll see you there at four. But you'll need to pack a small suitcase. Here's what I want you to bring...'

Chris and Martin were sitting on either side of a large oak desk piled high with paperwork. 'Sir Roland is a cunning so-and-so,' remarked Martin, looking up from the file in front of him.

'Tell me about it. This Pearson contract ties the other poor sods down so tightly they won't be able to draw breath.'

'That's their lookout,' said Chris. 'I have to admire the clever bastard, even though I can't stand him.'

'He's known as London's most lecherous man.'

'I know. And it's true, I'm sure. Last month, at that cocktail party at the Savoy, he spent all his time trying to persuade Emma to spend a weekend with him in New York.'

'Not all his time. He was also trying the same thing on with Jayne.'

'Does he think they won't tell us about it?' asked Chris.

'In my view he doesn't give a toss whether they do or don't. He looks on us, and this firm, as just a bunch of overpaid lackeys. I'm sure he couldn't care less what we think of him. He knows we know on which side our bread is buttered.'

'If he wasn't the best client this firm has ever had I'd tell him to go and stick his head up a dead bear's bum.'

Martin snorted with laughter. 'If you did that you'd probably end up as dead as the dead bear.'

'Don't worry. I know where it's at. He can letch after Emma as much as he wants, and I'll refrain from saying a word.'

'At least the girls told us about it. It would have been a bad sign if they hadn't. At least we know we can trust them. Even with a billionaire.'

'I wonder if it's true what some people say? About the sex parties? I wonder if he really does go in for that sort of thing?'

'It wouldn't surprise me at all,' replied Chris. 'So many people have mentioned it that I have to believe there's some truth in the rumours. Wild sex parties. Group sex, all that sort of thing. As a sweetener for his business associates. As a way of greasing a few palms.'

'A few what? I wouldn't have put it quite that way myself.'

Half a mile across the City of London Sir Roland Rayke's office window looked down upon the River Thames. 'Get Parkinson up here,' he said to the most senior of his personal assistants, staring in disbelief at the computer screen in front of him.

'Yes, Sir Roland.'

'He's offered far too much commission to the Japanese. The profit margin's minuscule for us. He'll have to renegotiate the whole thing before midnight. With all seven parties. Everything has to change. I will not take less than point-four per cent. Otherwise it's a no-deal all round and we'll go back to the Americans. Either way, those bone idle legal beagles will have to redraft the entire contract by morning. I want it signed by ten at the latest. They'll just have to work all night. Like us.'

'Yes, Sir Roland.'

'In fact, you tell Parkinson for me.'

'Yes, Sir Roland.'

'I can't face him. I'll just lose my temper. And that's bad for me.'

'Yes, Sir Roland.'

'Changing the subject completely, has Tracie done anything about next week's corporate entertainment?'

'I'll ring her, Sir Roland. After I've spoken to Parkinson.'

'Remind her how important this one is.'

'Yes, Sir Roland. Of course.'

'Tell her I'm looking for something a little bit different.'

'Yes of course, Sir Roland.'

'Tell her there are plenty of other organisations such as hers I can contact, if she can't come up with something new. And remind her how much money she gets from my patronage.'

'Yes, Sir Roland.'

'And ring the fucking legal beagles and keep them on stand-by again for tonight. If they do well on this one I may even offer them some of the entertainment for themselves.'

'That would be very generous, Sir Roland.'

'Mind you, I'm not sure those two lack-lustres would really be up to the job. But never mind. At least they're both razor sharp when it comes down to their work.'

Jayne giggled as the black cab crawled slowly through one traffic jam after another. 'And then he said - if we couldn't go to New York - why didn't I let him take me to the Paris fashion shows for a couple of days. So I could choose as many outfits as I liked.'

'He never gives up. He rang me at home a couple of days ago with the same very indecent proposal. I told Chris all about it, of course.'

'Yes. I told Martin. He says that sort of thing is quite commonplace. I told him I was very polite about it all. And I got the feeling he was glad about that.'

'Chris was the same. He didn't tell me not to kick the lecherous sod in the bollocks, but I got the impression he'd much rather I didn't.'

'Angela has slept with him, I know. She says his dick's about eighteen inches long.'

'Hmmm... perhaps we should change our minds about Paris...?'

Tracie studied the two pairs of tightly-denimed buttocks and thighs as the would-be escorts chose a table near to the door and sat down. Very promising. And with breasts and faces in keeping. Yes, very, very promising indeed. Two special young housewives to recruit. She must be careful not to scare them away. Here were two young ladies of genuine style and class to add to her very special list. Yes, here was gold dust in its purest form...

Which one was Emma? The raven-haired darling, or the beautiful blonde? Perhaps Jayne - whichever one she was - would be every bit as feisty as Emma had sounded on the phone? The clients liked that sort of thing.

Yes, here was gold dust indeed. Nuggets, in fact. Two incredibly attractive young women who wanted to indulge themselves with complication-free sex. She knew the motivation very well. It had been the starting point of her own career. But then she'd moved on, of course.

It shouldn't prove too difficult to recruit them. These two were obviously after a mile and a half of cock. And they'd do women, as well as men. She could see that in their faces. Okay, they may not have indulged themselves with another girl as yet. But they would. And they'd be good at it, too. And they'd enjoy it. Five years in the trade had taught her a great deal. Here were two horny young housewives who, with the right handling, would vastly swell her bank balance. As well as their own.

It was just a matter of getting it all dead right...

Sir Roland sat in the private bar on the fifth floor of his office building, a tumbler of malt whisky in his hand. He was a virile-looking man in his late forties, with iron-grey hair, cut short, and a trimmed beard to match. Yes, those wishy-washy legal beagles were red-hot when it came to their professional duties. The two best legal brains he'd found in years. But he very much doubted their libidinous abilities. So he probably wouldn't include them in next week's corporate hospitality. Sexual lame ducks were not ideal guest material when it came to that sort of occasion.

How did the legal beagles manage to find - and keep - two such horny wives? Those girls could have anyone they wanted. Why did they choose to stay with - and be faithful to - their half-baked husbands? Why hadn't they shown any interest in his offers to shower them with presents in New York or Paris? It was really extremely galling. He simply wasn't used to rejections of that nature. It wasn't as if their husbands were fabulously wealthy. Okay, they probably earned three to four hundred thousand a year from their law firm. But that was nothing compared to the riches that so many people, such as himself, would be prepared to lavish on them in return for their continuing sexual favours. He supposed they'd claim they were 'in love' with their husbands. But he'd seen far too much of the world to know that such emotions never lasted long. Women were fickle. After a short while they wandered.

So why hadn't those two wandered in his direction? Why had they steadfastly refused his various offers. And why was he so concerned?

He understood his own problem, of course. When fabulously rich, the more difficult it was to have something the more you craved it. And craved it he certainly had. He had to admit he'd been as desperate to fuck those two women as he'd ever been in his life.

Of course, if he ever got the chance he'd make absolutely sure they suffered for their persistent refusals. He'd teach them humility beyond their comprehension. Humility, through the process of intense humiliation... and much, much more beside. There were several fascinating ways in which that could be achieved. He'd just pour himself another drop of this excellent Highland malt, and ponder the various ways and means by which he'd be able to make his extreme displeasure felt. And then felt again. If, as he'd just said, he ever got the chance...

'Bugger!' exclaimed Martin Jamieson, hanging up the phone.

'What is it?' asked Chris.

'We'd better order coffee and sandwiches. Lots of both.'

'Sir Roland?'

Yes. One of his PAs just rang. The Japanese connection is about to go belly-up.'

'No. Surely not? I thought that was rock solid.'

'So did I. But it seems he just pulled out of the deal and is proceeding with the Yanks instead.'

'Fuck it! He'll need a totally new contract by the morning.'

'I know. The Yankee attorneys are e-mailing us their requirements shortly. We'll be lucky to get to bed at all tonight.

'I'm going for a walk,' said Chris. 'You can phone Jayne and tell her about it.

Then she can tell Emma.'

'Thanks pal. Thanks a lot. I was the one who had to phone last night and impart the happy tidings.'

'So you're well practised at it. So you can do it again. Just ask Jayne to tell Emma how sorry I am... and that I'll make it up to her when I can.'

'Which, at this rate, may be never.'

Chris walked briskly along the Embankment, his back to Westminster bridge. He knew he was pushing it a bit too far. Marriage-wise, he meant. All this work, the late nights, the weekend business meetings. And the lack of sex between them - due to a combination of the fact that he was never home, and when he was, the fact that he was always totally knackered. Perhaps he should relent and let Em take another part-time job. After all, it was unlikely the same thing would happen again. Or was it? He knew he wasn't satisfying her in bed, so how could he be sure she wouldn't indulge herself elsewhere? For a second time in their marriage. How could he know she wouldn't take the opportunity of having another bit on the side, if the chance arose? And with a girl with Emma's looks, the chance would certainly arise. He could be sure and certain of that. Some lecherous so-and-so would have a stab at her, if she was working in a large office or organisation. After all, she'd succumbed once before, hadn't she? And on that occasion there'd been no problems at home. No lack of marital sex. Much the opposite, in fact. No excuse at all, apart from feeling a bit too horny after work to keep her knickers in their rightful place.

He could remember the incident as if it had happened yesterday. Even after two years. He could still vividly recall the weird mixture of emotions. The intense jealousy combined with a strange but strong sexual arousal, and then the gratification of meting out a very appropriate punishment to those parts that had sinned.

It had been the one and only time she'd been unfaithful, he felt sure. She wasn't very good at lying to him in response to a direct question, so he was prepared to accept that it hadn't happened before. And he was fairly confident it hadn't happened since.

He'd been working on a file at home. At about seven o'clock the phone rang and it had been Emma, sounding slightly breathless - he'd since decided. 'Hi, Chrissy!' she said, a shade too brightly - he'd also since decided. 'Are you okay?'

'Yes, fine. Where are you?'

'Um, I'm just leaving the office. Jayne's with me. She, erm, called into the office a moment ago. She's suggesting we play squash and then go for a bite to eat. Is that all right with you?'

'Yes, of course. I'll heat something up in the microwave for myself.'

'You're an angel. I'm sorry about this. But Jayne can be rather demanding. And I do quite fancy a, um, bit of exercise.' She'd giggled. A trifle unsurely - he'd once again since decided. 'So I'll be back in a couple of hours or so.'

He'd spent the next two and a bit hours working on the file from the office, and then watching TV with a bowl of chicken curry on his lap. Then the doorbell had rung. Emma must have forgotten her key, he'd decided, standing up. Only it hadn't been Emma on the doorstep. It was Jayne, looking absolutely ravishing.

'Hi, Chris. I was just passing, so I thought I'd pop in to see Em and fix up a game of squash for tomorrow night, or Thursday.'

He stared at her, bewildered. 'Emma's not here,' he said at length.

'Oh, that's a shame. I'm sorry to have disturbed you. Can you ask her to phone me when she gets back?'

'Haven't you seen her earlier tonight?'

'No. Why do you say that?'

'You haven't seen her at all?'

'No. I haven't spoken to her since Monday evening. But I've got a squash court booked for tomorrow, and I thought I'd see whether Em could make it.'

He'd felt a sinking feeling deep inside. 'Come in for a minute, Jayne. I'll see if I can reach her on her mobile.'

But just as they'd walked into the living room he heard Emma's car turning into the drive. 'I think that's her now,' he said, rather grimly. 'I think she might be a trifle surprised to see you here.'

'Why's that?' Jayne asked with a smile. 'I often pop round to see her, don't I? Why should she be surprised?'

'I suggest you wait and see for yourself, Jayne.'

Emma had breezed into the room, bouncy and bubbly and full of smiles. 'Hello, darling...' she'd begun, before spotting Jayne. 'Oh dear...!' she gulped, suddenly very straight-faced and no longer the least bit bubbly. 'Oh dear...' she repeated, turning bright red.

'Jayne came round to see you,' he said. 'Just a minute or so ago. Hoping to arrange a game of squash for tomorrow. Strange that, don't you think?'

Emma shuffled her feet and stared down at the carpet. 'Oh, um...'

He turned towards Jayne to explain. 'You see, a couple of hours ago my dear wife rang me to say she'd be late home.'

'Oh?'

'Yes. She was going to play squash with a girlfriend, I was informed. And then go for a spot of food.'

'Oh?'

'With you, she told me. You'd called into the office to see her. And suggested a game of squash this evening. That's what I was told. I take it she wasn't exactly telling the truth?'

Jayne looked uncomfortable, but said nothing by way of response. So he turned inquisitively to his beetroot-faced wife. But she also appeared totally tongue-tied.

'It was Jonathan Crowe, I assume?' he asked icily, referring to her boss at work. But still there'd been no response; just a heightening of colour and another lowering of the eyes. 'It was Jonathan Crowe?' he barked. 'Wasn't it, Emma? You've been screwing Jonathan Crowe. Haven't you?'

'I'd better leave,' Jayne suggested.

'No, don't...' Emma whispered. 'Please don't go yet, Jayne...'

The guilt had been written all over her face. She hadn't needed to confess. A deep hurt and an even deeper anger started to overwhelm him. That bastard Jonathan Crowe! It wouldn't have been so bad if it had been anyone else. Anyone at all other than that smug, pretentious, worthless son-of-a-bitch!

He'd taken a handful of the short, raven-black hair he loved so greatly and led her to the sofa. Then he sat down, drawing her over his knee. 'Are you going to tell me I'm wrong?' he demanded. 'Are you going to tell me you haven't been screwing him?'

'No...' she whispered, almost inaudibly.

'No, what?'

'No, I'm not going to tell you I haven't been screwing him...'

Emma must have sensed Jayne taking a step towards the door. 'No. Please, Jayne. Don't leave me alone like this.'

'Jayne's not going to be able to save you from what you have in store.'

'I know. But I'd rather she was here. Please, Jayne...'

Jayne knelt on the carpet in front of Emma, looking into her face with concern and compassion. 'Why didn't you ring me?' she asked. 'Why on earth didn't you warn me?'

'I tried. But your mobile didn't respond. After that Jonathan didn't give me much of a chance.'

Thwack! His hand landed with all his force across her pouting right cheek. Her lightweight summer skirt and minuscule knickers afforded her scarcely any protection at all.

Thwack! It landed again. And then several more times after that in rapid succession. At length he turned his attention to the other side of her upturned bottom, spanking that to the same degree. Emma hadn't protested or struggled. She'd just lain there over his knee, weeping softly but profusely as she accepted the inevitability of her fate.

With some difficulty he tugged her short skirt up over the fleshiest part of her hips, and then yanked her filmy knickers down to her knees. The crotch had been noticeably soggy. A fact that had done nothing to improve his mood. Her shapely bottom, revealed in all its splendour, had already coloured nicely. But he'd been intent on colouring it much, much more. Her skirt was around the slimmest part of her waist. So with his left hand tightly gripping the back of the rolled-up material, in order to ensure that she remained compliant, his right hand set to work - without remorse. The crack, crack, crack of hand on bare buttocks began to echo throughout the house. And continued to echo. He soon discovered that the repeated spanking of one cheek at a time caused the greatest distress. So he'd begun cracking his hand down across her right cheek twenty or so times in a row, then twenty or so times across her left, and then the same across the middle of both, time after time after time, again and again, burning and blistering them for all he was worth.

As tears continued to pour forth Jayne had taken Emma's face in both hands, very tenderly, in an effort to soothe and comfort her. 'You should have told me,' she whispered, kissing away the tears, and then kissing Emma on the mouth as well.

'It hurts,' Emma sobbed quietly, prompting Jayne to kiss her once more. 'It hurts a lot...'

'I know, I can tell,' Jayne replied, trying her best to console her closest friend.

He glared down balefully at the sweet bottom that, such a short while earlier, had been misbehaving itself with Jonathan Crowe. The sweet bottom, so steeped in recent adultery that its stigma was almost a physical thing. The same sweet bottom he'd cherished and adored ever since he'd first laid it bare and taken possession five years before. The mixture of feelings had been unbelievable. The immense satisfaction of his heavy male hand impacting noisily on soft pert cheeks, again and again and again, coupled with the painful - yet somehow sexually exciting - knowledge that those self-same cheeks had only just finished cheating on him. And so, with grim determination he slapped and slapped and slapped, turning her bottom an ever-darkening shade of red... while the irrefutable evidence of her adultery started to trickle slowly down her thighs. And while Jayne had continued to cradle Emma's distraught face in her caring hands, kissing away the tears and, occasionally, kissing her lightly on the mouth with her tongue.

'How many times have you done it before?' he demanded after a while.

'I haven't... this was the first time...'

'Why did you do it today?'

'I don't know... it just happened... we were larking about in the photocopying room, and it just happened... I don't know why...'

'And then it just kept on happening? Over a period of more than two hours?'

'Yes... I'm sorry...'

The spanking raged on and on, his wife's lovely bare bottom glowing brightly as it wriggled and writhed in severe discomfort. But still she suffered in semi-silence. The tears continued to flow, but still she suffered her ordeal in semi-silence. And still Jayne tried to console her friend with her hands, lips and tongue.

'Anyone can make a mistake, Chris,' Jayne said after a while. 'Isn't that enough?'

'Not yet,' he replied, beating his palm down across the plumpest part of her bottom with all the power he could muster, causing both cheeks to bounce, colour, and bounce, again and again and again.

'I'm sorry I've got you into trouble,' Jayne whispered sympathetically to Emma. 'I do wish you'd warned me...'

And all the time he found himself fascinated by the thought of her infidelity. A bizarre, twisted sort of fascination. But fascination, and arousal, nevertheless. He'd been unable to stop torturing himself. He'd been unable to prevent himself imagining the other man's hands and eyes all over her beautiful bottom, the other man's wet penis ripping in and out of her tight little cunt, the other man's sperm flooding her womb...

And there was another thing, he said to himself as she'd been lying there over his knee receiving her extremely just desserts. There was another problem with his wife getting herself fucked by someone else. There was something very permanent about it. Once fucked, there was no way in the world she could get herself unfucked again. Once she'd been had by someone else she was obliged to spend the rest of her life having been had. Three, five, or however many years later, this other man would see her in the street and say to himself that he'd been there, where only poor hubby was supposed to tread. He'd say to himself that he'd had a slice of the action, a slice of her sexy bare bottom. A slice that had belonged to somebody else. And he'd know that however hard she might try, there was no possibility of her returning it to its rightful owner. It had gone from him once and for all, poor chap. He'd know it, she'd know it, and both of them would know that the other one knew it...

Oh yes. She could smile sweetly at her one-time seducer in the street, but he'd know that she knew exactly what he was thinking. He'd know that she knew he was recalling that earlier occasion when she'd let him all the way up her cunt. He'd be able to see her blush, ever so slightly, as she walked past, arm in arm with her husband...

And others would know about her inability to return to her former state of grace. Men talk about that sort of thing all the time. From day one the other man's friends and work colleagues would be able to gaze after her with interest, staring at the superbly filled seat of her miniskirt or jeans and speculating with intrigue on exactly how it had been for 'good old Jonathan' that time when he had her all ways up...

All that stuff was pretty much okay, of course, provided you - the husband - were blissfully unaware of the situation. But when you knew only too well what she'd been up to, and who and what had been up her...

These thoughts - as he spanked her, and spanked her, and spanked her - had hardened his heart even further, strengthening his resolve to let justice be done to the full.

Eventually, after more than half an hour, he stopped and told her she could get up from over his knee.

Part Five

When Jayne had finished talking to Martin on her mobile Tracie moved over to their table and sat down. 'So, then. Who's Emma, and who's Jayne?'

The girls looked up at the attractive, slightly older woman who'd just joined them.

'I'm Emma.'

'And I'm Jayne.'

'And I'm Tracie, of course. It's nice to meet you. And I must say at once that you both look entirely suitable.'

'Thank you.'

'You've never done this sort of work before?'

The girls had already decided to discount the events of the previous night. 'No, never,' they said together.

Tracie looked at their wedding fingers. 'And you're both married, yes?'

'Yes.'

'Good. We do try to insist on that. The clients are very keen on it. They love the idea of shagging someone else's wife. A genuine housewife, not an out-and-out hooker. We don't want our girls to appear too professional. So it's a big bonus if you really are genuine housewives.'

'Oh, we are,' replied Emma. 'Very much so. Aren't we, Jayne?'

'Yes. We're very married indeed. With husbands we hardly ever see because of their work commitments.'

'Excellent. You can talk to the clients about all that sort of stuff. It puts them at ease. And that's almost as important as fucking their brains out.'

Emma sighed. 'We're really looking forward to doing that.'

'Yes, we are,' Jayne agreed at once. 'Sex without any involvement, that's what we want.'

'The money isn't important?'

'No. But it will be nice.'

'We can buy things for our husbands,' said Jayne. 'Extra nice birthday presents, and so forth. It'll help to ease our consciences.'

'You'll have to be careful not to appear too flush,' warned Tracie. 'And make sure you keep the money well hidden, too.'

'Yes. We've thought about all that,' replied Jayne. 'Don't worry. We're not stupid.'

'No. I can see that for myself. Now then. As we're talking about money, let me tell you how it works. Everything's split down the middle. We get half and so do you. And the clients always pay you. Never us. You pay us our share within three days.'

'How do you know you can trust us to do that?' asked Emma.

'Oh, we have your e-mail address and mobile phone number. We could find you if we had to. And that would be bad news from your point of view.'

The girls looked at each other. 'She was only joking,' said Jayne. 'We'd never dream of keeping all the cash.'

'I know,' Tracie replied. 'I've had a lot of experience in this business. I can tell the sort of girls you are. I don't have any problems there.'

'Thank you.'

'Now then. Dress. This is important.'

'Yes.'

'For all evening assignments at hotels or private addresses, full-length evening gowns that fit snugly round boobs and bum. Unless the client stipulates something else, of course.'

'Okay.'

'It adds that extra touch of class. The clients like it, and after all, they're paying an awful lot of money for your favours. Never forget that fact.'

'We won't.'

'Also, it makes it easier for them to spot you.'

'Right.'

'The dress must be strappy and low cut, with a zip at the back, not the side.'

'Why's that?'

'It helps to break the ice in the bedroom. You know, that awkward moment when no one's quite sure what to do next. So you smile sweetly, turn your back and ask him to help you unzip. It will help to put both of you at ease. That's important.'

'Yes, got it. Good idea.'

'The dress should also be split at the side all the way up to the top of the thighs. This will enable the client, if he's feeling frisky, to take liberties with you before you get to the bedroom.'

'Liberties?'

'Yes. For example, say you're standing or sitting side by side, and no one's watching too closely. He may want to slip a hand inside the dress and indulge in a little pussy-petting, or bare bottom fondling. Or both. It will help to set the tone for the evening. And that's important, too. You need to ensure that the client feels as horny as hell.'

'Right.'

'You need to be raunchy with him. Not common, just sexy and playful. Let him know how up for it you are.'

'Well, that won't be too much of a problem,' laughed Emma. 'We're about as up for it as two needy young wives could be.'

'Excellent. Now, underwear. No bras, as it's a strappy dress. And thongs, not knickers, of course.'

'Of course,' agreed Jayne. 'Knickers would ruin the look of a well cut evening dress.'

Emma giggled. 'I was going to suggest wearing nothing at all under the dress. But bearing in mind the essential nature of the assignment, that might not be too good an idea.'

'If you want to be bare under the dress, you could always carry a thong in your handbag to put on for the journey home,' said Tracie.

'True.'

'Stockings and suspenders,' continued Tracie. 'Never tights.'

'Of course not. They're so sexless...'

'And high heels, needless to say. At least three inches. But as both of you girls are tall you needn't wear anything higher than that. When you strip off, ask him if he wants you to keep your suspenders and stockings on. Most of them do.'

'Fine.'

'For daytime work, short skirts and close-fitting tops and jackets. Sexy, but smart. Not tarty. And again, high heels.'

'Right.'

'Talking of daytime work, let me tell you of an amusing little episode which carries a moral warning. Nickie, one of our several young housewives who're in it for the money more than the sex, accepted an assignment in a high rise office block. Mr Peterson, a sales director, was interviewing potential saleswomen for a position with his company. Her task was to provide him with a little light relief during the course of the interviews. She was to pretend to be one of the interviewees, and then fuck him during the "interview". This went well. She played along with the part, then started coming on to him, and finally ended up having sex with him on top of his desk. It was only when he was admiring her bottom as she retrieved her skirt and knickers from the top of the filing cabinet, that she began to suspect she'd made a mistake.'

'Why? What happened?'

'He offered her the job. He told her that anyone who was prepared to give a third party an occasional slice of such a beautiful bottom would be bound to collect additional contracts and must therefore be worthy of the position. After quite a bit of confusion she eventually discovered that the Mr Peterson who'd made the booking worked for a similar sounding firm on the floor below. And the moral of the story is... always double-check you have the right address, because accidental freebies do not help to swell the bank balance - not yours, nor ours.'

The two would-be escorts collapsed onto the tabletop in fits of girlie laughter.

'But Nickie did well in the end,' continued Tracie. 'Less than ten minutes later she was screwing the right Mr Peterson. The only trouble was he kept complimenting her on how beautifully lubricated she was. This made her giggle when she should have been displaying rather different emotions.'

'Oh dear!'

'When she walked through her front door an hour later, even wetter below the suspender belt, the first thing her husband did was to insist on having her, bottoms-up, over the back of the settee. With exactly the same result. The same compliments, I mean. Not the same unstoppable giggles of mirth. She was far too petrified that he'd realise what she'd been up to.'

'Oh crumbs!'

'Fortunately he never suspected the truth. He just assumed she was pleased to have been jumped on like that. But enough of Nickie. I see you've brought a suitcase, so I assume you've got all your party gear?'

'Yes. An evening dress each, stockings and suspenders and so on.'

'Good. It's for the photo shoot, of course. We'll take a video of you in a moment. Then we'll use the best of the stills for the website, as I explained to Emma on the phone. Titillation. That's what the clients need to see. Something to encourage them to come onboard and make a booking.'

'You're certain no one will be able to recognise us?'

'Quite certain. You can rest assured about that. We are professionals, after all.'

'Yes, we realise that.'

'We're completely revising our "Doubles" pages on our website. You two will be ideal for that. One blonde coming on to one brunette, and vice versa. Have you looked at those pages?'

'Yes.'

'So you understand the sort of thing I'm talking about?'

'Yes.'

'Would you be happy to help out?'

'I don't see why not,' Emma said, after a short pause.

Tracie took a sip of coffee. 'On that sort of subject, you realise that any double dating will often involve a spot of actual lesbianism? The men love that sort of thing.'

The girls coloured slightly. 'Yes, we understand,' murmured Jayne.

'You can handle that sort of thing without showing embarrassment, can you? It's vital that the clients don't think you have a problem with what you have to do. Are you sure you can manage that all right?'

'Yes...'

'So you're happy to do double dates, as well as singles? Bearing in mind what you'll probably be asked to do?'

'Yes. But we'd like to be with each other, rather than with a girl we don't know.'

'Yes, I can understand that.'

'It's odd,' mused Emma. 'We're both happy to go to bed with a man we've never seen before, but not a girl.'

'Basically, it's because you're both much more heterosexual than bisexual,' explained Tracie. 'Have either of you ever done it with a girl before?'

'I had an affair with a girl when Jayne and I were at boarding school,' replied Emma. 'It was lovely. We had a lot of fun. But it seemed quite different to what I was doing with my boyfriend at the time. I mean, it didn't really feel like sex. More like an expression of appreciation of the female qualities of the other girl.'

'Emma and I have done it once,' said Jayne, remembering the pleasure she'd experienced making love to her best friend the night before. 'But as Em just said, it didn't seem like sex as such, even though we made each other come.'

'We certainly did,' agreed Emma, smiling at the thought of what they'd done. 'Several times, in fact.'

'I'll make sure that all the double dates you have are with each other, then. There'll probably be quite a few of those. Especially after we show you starring in the "Doubles" section.'

'Thank you.'

'Very occasionally we have clients who are real lesbians. Women who want to fuck you with a dildo. How would you feel about that?'

'I suppose we could manage it,' said Emma. 'I suppose it might even be fun. Especially if she's pretty.'

'Good. Now, the spanking. You saw we offer that as well?'

'Yes, but we'd rather not go in for that,' Emma said quickly.

'She's had a few bad experiences,' Jayne giggled into her hands.

'The last one wasn't so bad,' Emma said with a hint of a grin, recalling the penthouse suite capers. 'But we definitely don't want to go in for that.'

'A pity, but never mind. We'll include some CP shots of you on the "Doubles" page anyway. We can always explain to the client, if he queries it, that it's for titillation only, and that CP is offered by some of the others.

'One final point,' she continued. 'You've seen from our site that you can refuse a client if you don't like the look of him?'

'Yes. That's a bit of a relief, I must say.'

'If you do that you'll be responsible for refunding his hotel expenses.'

'That's fair enough.'

'And if it happens more than twice in six months, then you're off our books.'

'Okay. That's understood.'

'Well, I think that's about all we need to discuss at the moment. Follow me through to the back of the café. I've arranged for us to borrow a couple of rooms for the photo shoot. We have a good understanding with several places like this. We need to, because we don't have an office. For obvious reasons.'

'For obvious reasons?'

'In case the boys in blue decide to take an interest in our business. It is against the law, as I'm sure you know. Not what you're doing, of course. That's perfectly legal. It's the soliciting bit that could land us - not you - in court.'

Chris was almost back to his office block. It had been a truly spectacular sight, he thought. His wife's bare bottom draped submissively over his knee. So big and shapely and inviting. And so dark crimson in colour by the time he'd let her go. He'd gone straight up to bed when he finally finished with her, expecting she'd stay well out of the way downstairs.

But within less than a minute he heard Jayne's car driving away and, seconds later, Emma slid into bed beside him and started to make love - wordlessly, and in the most ferocious way he'd ever known. And he responded appropriately, his penis engorged with every spare drop of blood in his body. He'd never known such an erection. It ached painfully at the way it stretched and strained at the leash. The mental images of her being fucked by another man, coupled with the way in which he'd just spanked her so severely, added inches to his normal size.

So they made love fiercely and silently, with Emma lying on top of him, her mouth glued to his and the rest of her body almost as hot as the sexy little bottom he'd so thoroughly set ablaze. The lovemaking seemed to last forever. She wriggled and writhed and squirmed and squealed with pleasure, while he in turn had lain there, semi-motionless, letting her work frantically on him, wondering whether his enormous erection might do her some sort of harm.

Next morning, Saturday morning, he'd found her in the kitchen, sipping a cup of coffee whilst perched prettily on the edge of a stool. A soft cushion from the lounge had been tucked underneath her and she'd been wearing nothing apart from the angry-red aftermath of the spanking. They hadn't really spoken since she'd slid off his knee the night before, although she'd made love to him again early that morning, just as urgently as she had a few hours before.

'I'm sorry,' she'd whispered, a single teardrop sliding slowly down her lovely face.

'I'm sorry I hurt you,' he choked, wrapping both arms round her shoulders and pulling her to him. God, how much he loved her, he could remember groaning to himself.

'Don't be silly. I thoroughly deserved it. I've hurt you even more, I know.'

'I shouldn't have done it though.'

'It's nothing,' she replied, half laughing and half crying. 'A sore bottom is nothing compared with what you've had to endure. And anyway,' she giggled, tears still in her eyes, 'I can still sit down... just about... provided there's a cushion...'

'I still shouldn't have done it.'

She looked at him earnestly. 'Let me tell you about Jonathan. Let me tell you about last night.'

'Em, I don't think...'

'Please, Chrissy. Please let me tell you. I'll feel better about things if I do. And that way there won't be any secrets between us, will there?'

'Okay,' he sighed.

'It just happened... I never meant it to... I don't even fancy him, really... well, not that much at least. We were in the photocopying room... and he was pretending to be cross with me because I'd lost one of his files. He was trying to slap my bottom... just playfully... actually, he had every reason to be cross. It was an urgent file and I should never have mislaid it. So I let him smack me... through my skirt, of course... just for a joke. Five or six times... quite hard, really, because he thought I deserved it. Which I guess I did. Then he pulled me back against him and jammed his groin into my bottom. I could feel how huge and hard he was... it made me go all weak and funny... next thing I knew I was bent forward over the copying machine letting him give it to me from behind. I'm sorry. It'll never happen again... never...'

Once again he'd felt that peculiar sense of sexual excitement. The thought of someone else taking his wife from behind in that manner had, inexplicably, turned him on.

'So we did it over the photocopier,' she continued. 'Really hard. He was just fascinated by my bare bottom. So I agreed to go back to his flat so he could have some more of it. He only lives round the corner. We went to bed and I let him do it twice more. I'm sorry...'

'Em, I don't really want to hear any more. I accept it was just one of those one off things that can sometimes happen.'

'There's something else I have to tell you. It makes me feel so ashamed, but I have to tell you.'

'What is it?'

'You know when I phoned you last night?'

'Yes.'

'Well, when I was speaking to you on my mobile, we'd only just finished doing it. I was still bending over the photocopier, full of his come...' She started to cry in earnest. 'I'm so ashamed, Chrissy. I was talking to you on the phone less than a minute after his prick had been jammed all the way up inside me! I was lying to you over the phone while he was groping my bare bottom with both hands and urging me to take it back to his place so he could romp with it in his bed. I'm so sorry...'

'I've forgiven you already, Em.'

'I don't deserve to be forgiven. I don't deserve a husband like you. I'll give up the job straightaway. I won't go in on Monday.'

'There's no need for that. Go back for a couple of months or so, and then leave. Just make it clear to him on Monday that it won't happen again.'

'But I'll never be able to keep his hands off me. I've told you before what he's like. He'll be even worse now. There'll be even more finger-marks on my bottom for me to explain to you.'

He'd laughed, not at all unkindly. 'I don't mind him grabbing the occasional handful of bottom, provided the aforesaid bottom reverts to its former habit of staying safely under wraps. I want you to go back to work. I want to show you that I still trust you, despite what happened yesterday.'

'I love you!' she'd gasped, hugging him tightly. 'Let's go back to bed and fuck as hard as we can.'

So he'd followed her upstairs, his eyes glued to the discoloured cheeks that wiggled sexily from side to side in front of him. This was going to be yet another fuck of the century, he realised, reaching out and clamping his hand around her gracefully undulating right buttock. She glanced back at him over her shoulder with a look of such mischievous sensuality that his dick stretched even further up towards his ribcage. Yes indeed, this was going to be yet another fuck they'd never forget, he said to himself, squeezing fiercely and making her squawk - and all of it starting with the way in which her boss, Jonathan Crowe, had been granted permission to trespass upon these parts.

First of all Jonathan had been given leave to take his fill of this gorgeous bottom - three times in a row. Then, such a short while later, and with much of the other man's sperm still inside her, the same naughty bottom had been made to pay in full for its infidelity. And now, because of all that had occurred, here it was, still steeped in recent adultery yet once again inciting him to service his wife in a manner he'd never quite been able to achieve before.

Chris sighed as he stepped into the lift that led to his floor. If he had to be brutally honest with himself, if the whole sordid truth had to be told, he'd been more than a little intrigued with the thought. With the thought of his wife having to return her lovely bottom to its place of work, for it to be ogled lecherously by all the men in the know, and groped by the very person with whom it had been romping so freely. It had given him a perverse thrill to anticipate how it was going to be leered at and manhandled.

On the one hand, he'd hated the idea. On the other, he'd found it inexplicably stimulating from a sexual point of view. He told Emma about some of these feelings. And she seemed to understand.

Emma had remained at the job for a further two months, during which time there'd been no lack of leering or manhandling. The men in her department constantly cracked jokes about photocopying machines and asked her whether she'd care to lose one of their files for them. And Jonathan's hands had roamed all over her bountiful buttocks, squeezing and gripping until she eventually managed to swat them away. In order to tease him further she'd taken to wearing a thong under her lightweight skirts so he could have an even better feel of that which he'd once had but which he was subsequently being denied - making him increasingly bemused and frustrated at his failure to engage her in a repeat performance over the copying machine or in his bed.

For the next year and a bit their sex life had been incredible. Utterly incredible. The one off fuck with Jonathan Crowe had, as it turned out, actually managed to strengthen their marriage. They'd made love in one way or another several times every day. But then, of course, twelve months ago, he'd got his promotion and everything in the matrimonial bed department had suddenly and dramatically changed. And now it had come to this. Now here he was, dreading the thought that, through sexual frustration, she might become emotionally involved with someone else.

Part Six

'This is Max,' said Tracie, ushering the girls into a small room at the rear of the café. 'He's our photographer.'

'Hi girls,' grinned the middle-aged man busily adjusting a video camera and tripod. Behind him was a white screen and a chair facing a set of spotlights, and beside him lay a smaller video camera on a table. This was for use by hand, not tripod.

'Hi,' they both replied.

'Have you ever done any glam modelling before?'

'No. Never.'

'Well, there's nothing to it. Just be yourselves, doing whatever Tracie or I ask you to do. Take your suitcase through that door into the side room and get changed into your glad rags.'

Five minutes later the girls reappeared, wearing their full length evening dresses, stockings and high heels.

'Ravishing!' whistled Max.

'I agree,' said Tracie.

'Thank you,' said the girls.

'Okay,' Tracie said in a businesslike manner. 'Jayne first. Stand over there in front of the screen, facing Max, and listen to what he has to say.

Max peered into the back of the camera. 'Hands on hips. Don't smile, just look straight at me. Fine. Now, hands by your sides and look at me again. Fine. Fine. Now turn your back to me and look at me over your shoulder. Turn your head a bit more. And push your bottom out a bit. No, don't smile. Just look at me normally. Perhaps a little quizzically. Fine. You're done.'

Emma was dealt with in much the same manner.

'Back into the side room,' ordered Tracie. 'You've seen our website, so you know what comes next. Strip down to your stockings, suspenders and high heels. I know it's cheesy, but the clients absolutely love that sort of thing.'

The girls recalled the events of the previous night, and silently concurred.

Emma and Jayne stood together in the side room, stripped in the manner demanded. 'Your bottom still looks really sore,' observed Emma.

'And yours, Em. Whatever are we going to say to them?'

'The truth, I suppose. That we were both soundly spanked last night. We don't have to go into all the gory details.'

'How embarrassing!'

'Yes, it is a bit. I suppose...'

'Come on. Let's go and face the music. Or whatever.'

'Don't forget this might be some sort of test to check we really are suitable for the job,' Emma said thoughtfully. 'So we'd better not act too modestly. We don't want Tracie deciding we're too prim and proper, do we?'

'We'd hardly be here if we were.'

'No, but you know what I mean. She's looking for girls who're definitely up for a bit of hanky-panky, and who act that way. Not girls who're shy enough to put off the clients. It doesn't matter if Tracie has a few porny photos of us. After all, she has no idea who we are.'

Blushing prettily they trooped back into the adjoining room, boobs, pubes, and slim waists now nicely on display.

'Fuck a duck! I wish I had a couple of thousand pounds in my pocket right now!' sighed Max. But only to himself.

'Okay,' said Tracie, as the girls stood with their backs carefully positioned away from view. 'This time we want you standing side by side facing Max.'

'Just as before to start with,' continued Max. 'Hands on hips and look at me without smiling. Then hands by your sides and look at me. Fine. Fine. Fine. Now, move right up close together and look at each other. Turn towards each other a bit more - an arm round each other's waist with your hand on each other's bottom. That's it. Emma, press one breast against Jayne's. Good. Fine. Now smile sexily into her face. Yes. Great. Jayne, do the same. Remember, you both fancy each other and you're going to do something about it. Good. Good. Now, a fingertip on each other's clit and rub gently and slowly. Keep smiling into each other's eyes and keep fondling bums while you rub each other up. Good. Now, a gentle kiss on the lips. Yes. Great. Show me some tongue now. Lots of it. Yes, just like that. Plenty of tongue while you keep on rubbing and squeezing and rubbing and squeezing. Great. Show me how much you're enjoying it...'

'We are,' breathed Jayne, savouring the feel of Emma's loving hand all over her bottom and her sweetly stimulating finger on her clitoris.

'I know. I can tell. That's really good. More kissing please. And more mutual masturbation. Good. Good. Okay, that's fine. That's more than enough. I can get plenty of good stills from that.'

'Do we have to stop?' giggled Emma.

'Yes,' replied Tracie. 'We need to move on.'

'Such a shame,' murmured Jayne, taking a step away from her friend.

Max was back in control. 'Okay. Now, turn round and look back at me over your shoulders. Just like you did when you were dressed.'

The girls glanced apprehensively at each other, but then slowly did as they were bid.

'Oh, I say!' whistled Tracie, her eyes, like those of Max, greedily devouring the sight of two shapely female bottoms, both sullenly discoloured as they pouted petulantly back at the camera on its stand. 'I thought you said you don't go in for spanking?'

'We don't,' confirmed Emma. 'But unfortunately that wasn't enough to save our hides last night.'

'There's nothing unfortunate about it,' enthused Tracie. 'It will look great on our "Doubles" page. It will add a degree of authenticity to the CP shots we always show there. It will really get the punters interested. I don't know why I didn't think of using the real thing earlier. Rosy-red, genuinely spanked bottoms will go down a treat. How often have you girls been spanked?'

'Four times altogether,' Emma replied ruefully.

'Just once before last night,' said Jayne. 'That's how I met my husband, actually.'

'Oh? Do tell me about it.'

'It was during a wild party at someone's house. My then boyfriend was drunk and took exception to something I did. He put me over his knee in front of everyone else. Martin, my husband, was so smitten with the sight of my bottom being beaten raw that he asked me out later that night. And I was so furious at what my boyfriend had done that I said "yes" immediately. A few weeks later I swapped that boyfriend for Martin, and we got engaged almost at once.'

'A fascinating tale. That, in a way, is how we managed to sign up Angela James, one of our five-star housewives. After she had her backside beaten mercilessly by her husband she joined us in order to get her own back on him. Now she's learnt to enjoy being spanked. Are you sure you can't be tempted to follow her example?'

'Yes. Very sure.'

'Then there's Leanne Howlet, a friend of mine. Somehow she managed to save her marriage by getting herself caned by her husband.'

'That's fine for her,' said Emma. 'But I think we'll try to keep ours free from hurt.'

'And another friend of mine makes a fortune out of that sort of thing. Alison North. She writes books about it. Have you heard of her?'

'Yes, we know her. We were at school together.'

'Well, she's ended up with severely burnt buttocks more times than she cares to remember. Just like her close friend, Pauline Peach. So now she writes about what's happened to her and her friend Pauline, and makes money. You might do the same?'

'No, we don't think so. Thanks very much.'

'Oh well. Never mind. Max, let's press on.'

'Right then, girls. Same sort of thing as before. Stand against each other, side by side. A hand feeling each other's bottom, and a finger on each other's clit. Look back at me over your shoulders and stare into the camera. Let everyone see what fun you're having. Good. Fine. Fine. Now kiss each other again. Plenty of tongue once more. That's great! Keep on kissing and feeling and rubbing. Now turn towards each other, boobs against boobs. But don't stop what you're doing. That's excellent. Just keep doing all that kissing and petting for a bit, while I move around you with the other camera. Okay, now squeeze bottoms as hard as you like. Really make a meal of it. I want some close-ups of those gorgeous spanked cheeks being kneaded and massaged with gusto. Great! Now stop kissing and stare over each other's shoulder so I can capture the pleasure on your faces while you rub clits and massage bums. Fabulous!'

'You feel incredibly wet,' whispered Emma.

'So do you.'

'I could easily come.'

'Ditto.'

'Let's go for it. Push your finger right up my fanny. I'll do the same for you...'

'Ohhh...' sighed both women as they shuddered in delight at the deliciously slow, soft, gentle sort of orgasm that only a girl can give to another girl.

'Wonderful!' murmured Max, managing to record both their faces while the two friends climaxed sweetly and dreamily together in each other's arms...

'Spanking next,' said Tracie.

'Hey!' complained both girls.

'Don't worry. Just a few slaps are all we need. Max can use the two cameras and some clever editing to make six slaps look like six hundred. We can then split the film of the spanking from the rest of the footage to make two separate ones, and add both films to the DVDs we sell on totally different websites. And yes, don't worry. As I said, we'll make sure your faces are suitably obscured.' Mentally she crossed her fingers. The films she was intending to sell would be far better if the girls' faces remained untouched. After all, the chances of anyone they knew buying them and recognising them were remote. On the Housewives, Inc. web pages she would make sure their features were suitably changed. Those pages got hundreds of hits every day, and it wouldn't be fair to risk anyone they knew realising they were prepared to sell pussy for money.

'We'll start in the traditional way,' announced Tracie. 'A dark-haired girl spanking a blonde. Then we'll reverse the roles. Emma, sit down on that chair. And Jayne, fold yourself over her knee.'

Reluctantly Jayne obeyed. 'Just a few slaps?' she asked Tracie to confirm, hands and toes resting on the carpet and her blonde hair touching the floor.

'Yes. Just six good hard ones.'

'I suppose that's not too bad...'

'Six on each cheek. Then six more across the middle of both.'

'Hey!' Jayne repeated, lifting her head in order to look up at Tracie instead of the floor directly below her nose.

'Don't be a baby, Jayne. Judging by what I can see you took a great deal more than that last night.'

'That's why it's going to sting a damn sight more than it should.'

Emma gazed down with pleasure at the sore bottom now at her mercy. She could definitely see the appeal this sort of thing might hold for a man. That cheeky bare bottom looked so attractive; those beautifully dimpled cheeks so helpless and inviting, and so ready to be hurt even more. Already she was starting to lubricate once again. Surely she was quite wrong in thinking she was going to enjoy what Tracie had instructed her to do to her closest friend?

'Ouch!' gasped Jayne, as Emma's hand splattered loudly across the centre of her bouncy right cheek, instantly turning the sullen pink hue of the flesh a marked degree angrier. 'Ouch!' she gasped twice more in rapid succession.

No, thought Emma, she wasn't wrong at all. Those three hard slaps had proved most enthralling. Exhilarating, even...

So she slapped three times more, as hard as she could, darkening the same cheek even more. Of course she was feeling sorry for the way her friend was beginning to suffer, but that wasn't going to stop her doing what she now had firmly in mind. The fascination of hurting that saucy bare bottom was simply too great. Now she fully understood how her line manager at the bank, Lisa Browne, had got such enjoyment from welting her poor bottom with that heavy ruler three years before.

'Hey!' squawked Jayne, as Emma's palm cracked down again and then again on the same buttock, and then again and again after that. 'You're only supposed to do six on that side!'

Emma said nothing, but continued to slap, tight-lipped and full of grim determination. This really was great fun.

'Emma!' yelled Jayne, unable to do anything to avoid the ringing smacks on her right cheek because of the way Emma's left hand was holding her down. 'What are you doing?'

'Don't worry,' breathed Tracie, admiring the view with enthusiasm. 'We'll let you do the same to her when she's finished.'

'That's not the point,' squealed Jayne, still squirming her hips in a vain attempt to break free. 'This is really starting to hurt like hell.'

'As I said before, don't be a baby. You'll get your revenge in a while. In the meantime this is making a splendid movie.'

'You're just going to have to put up with it,' confirmed Emma, still assaulting the same mound of pretty red flesh. 'This is so much fun.'

'Ouch!' Jayne yelped unhappily. 'Oh! Owww! Ouch!' Then she began to cry, sobbing softly but profusely as blow after blow struck home on her sore right cheek.

Despite Jayne's tears and continued struggles and protests, Emma held her firmly down across her lap and spanked on and on, delighting in the way Jayne's plump right buttock was bouncing and darkening so rapidly. Delighted, also, at the weeping and wailing produced. She felt ashamed of the pain she was inflicting, but was incapable of holding back. It was just so exciting. Now she could fully understand the fun a man obtained from giving this sort of treatment. It was all to do with domination.

Emma began a full-scale assault on the left cheek, slowly colouring it up to the same degree as the right. It took over a hundred swats, but eventually it was just as inflamed as its long-suffering twin. Then she turned her attention to the high point of each blistered buttock, welting her hand down across the centre of both with all her strength. 'I'm sorry, Jayne,' she whispered at length, still smacking long and lustily while Jayne cried buckets of tears. 'I can't help it. I just can't stop. You'll see what I mean when it's your turn...'

As indeed she did. The positions were reversed and Jayne began laying into her friend with equal intensity, making her yip and yelp and cry real tears to the same or even greater degree. For Jayne was now doubly motivated. Not only was she relishing the newly-found delight of flaying a sexy female bottom, she was also getting her own back for the gross mistreatment of hers. One stinging slap followed another, echoing around the room and making both girls as wet as could be at the join of their legs.

Tracie produced a leather tawse from a bag that lay on the floor beside the camera and tripod. 'Try this,' she suggested helpfully, holding it out for Jayne.

'Thank you,' she panted, grasping it gleefully and immediately putting it to work with great effect.

'Try it across the tops of her thighs,' Tracie suggested. 'You'll be amazed how quickly they'll redden up.'

Jayne was more than happy to oblige. Emma continued to howl, but made no real effort to escape, feeling her juices starting to trickle down her legs.

And throughout both spankings the static video camera heroically performed its silent duty, while Max skilfully ducked and weaved back and forth, using the handheld camera to maximum effect on tearstained faces and red, bouncing bottoms.

'Right,' announced Tracie, when the girls were finally done, 'that's enough foreplay. Now for the real thing. It's dildo time, girls. Who's going to fuck who?'

'I'll fuck Jayne,' Emma declared at once. 'I've always wanted to do it to another girl.'

'I've never even thought about being fucked by a girl,' confessed Jayne. 'But if someone's going to do it to me, I suppose it might as well be Em.'

'Plus,' continued Emma, 'I owe you for the way you've just spanked my poor bum so hard.'

'You started it. You were the one who couldn't stop hurting mine.'

'Totally irrelevant,' grinned Emma. 'Fucked to a frazzle you're going to be. I shall make sure of it, believe me.'

Tracie pulled a huge pink dildo from the same bag as the tawse.

'Jesus!' gasped Jayne. 'You expect me to take all that?'

'Yes indeed. If you're wet enough there won't be a problem.'

'She'll be wet enough,' said Emma, staring greedily at the mammoth rubber penis Tracie had begun to strap onto her. This was going to be just as much fun as hurting Jayne's sexy little behind! Enough false prick here to screw her to the point of total insensibility, just as she so richly deserved.

'Now listen,' Tracie said to Emma. 'Use this little strap here to make sure this pad is directly against your clitoris.'

'Why's that?'

'Because there's a lever and two springs inside this contraption. If you adjust it just right the pad will rub back and forth over your clit each time you push in and pull out.'

'You're joking. You must be.'

'No. It's perfectly true.'

'It's ingenious.'

'Yes, it is. And Jane, see how the top length of this giant dick is ribbed?'

'Yes.'

'If you get the correct angle, then the ribbing will do the same thing for you.'

'Wow!'

'Best of luck. Max will use both cameras for maximum effect. Take as long as you like. I want you both to have fun.'

'We will,' the girls said as one.

Jane sat on the wooden chair, facing the mounted camera at a slight angle, while Emma knelt on the floor between her outstretched legs, the long thick appendage pointing proudly up at the ceiling. Carefully the two lovers adjusted their positions until Jayne was able to slip the tip of the dildo a fraction of an inch inside. Then without any further ado Emma thrust, spearing her friend and filling her to a seemingly impossible degree - in less time than it takes to recount.

'Owww!' Jayne squealed in shocked surprise. 'Do you have to be so rough?'

'Yes,' growled Emma, taking a deep breath and savouring the moment. 'I'm going to fuck you so hard you'll remember every moment for the rest of you life.'

And sad though it is to relate, she was entirely true to her word. For the next forty minutes the girls proceeded to copulate with a frenzy that amazed the two seasoned professionals who'd thought they'd already seen everything there was to see - several times over.

Part Seven

Three days later Emma and Jayne were heading for their first assignment, in full-length gowns and finery as instructed to wear.

'It's a very special client,' Tracie had advised them. 'A very, very special one. He'll send a limousine to collect you from the Savoy Hotel at nine o'clock tomorrow night. Be waiting in the reception lounge. I trust you'll be well and truly up for it?'

'I think Jayne should be able to walk again by then,' Emma had replied down the phone. 'Just about.'

The white limousine stopped at the wrought iron gates of the large secluded house in the most expensive part of Hampstead, and the chauffeur wound down his window. He punched four digits into the control panel on the wall beside the gates and they instantly swung apart.

The fully liveried butler ushered the girls into the wood-panelled hall and then threw open a pair of double doors to display the brightly lit room that lay beyond.

'Mrs Brampton and Mrs Jamieson!' Sir Roland Rayke cried in delight, before turning expansively to the sixteen young men who stood behind him, all of them attired - as was he - in dinner suits and black bow ties. Both girls instantly recognised all of them as Sir Roland's most trusted personal assistants. 'Gentlemen,' he announced with evident enthusiasm, 'here are the real life stars of the films we've been watching so avidly. Don't they look superb, even fully dressed? Don't they live up to their screen images one hundred and ten per cent? Gentlemen, may I present Mrs Emma Brampton and Mrs Jayne Jamieson - for your pleasure and entertainment. They are to be treated with the utmost disrespect!'

Emma and Jayne stared in horror at the long whippy cane he grasped in his hand, and at the six giant TV screens that ran along three sides of the room. Two of the screens were depicting varying scenes of the girls bringing each other to orgasm in the back room of the café near Covent Garden. One was showing Emma mercilessly spanking Jayne, while another showed the situation reversed. And the two final screens showed different scenes from the film that Max had made of Emma kneeling between Jayne's widespread legs and shafting her with an enormous dildo. Shafting her with such vigour and enthusiasm it was clear she was having the time of her life. And the look of ecstasy on Jayne's face told everyone that she too was up for all that Emma could give her, and maybe a little more on top.

Emma took a step backwards. 'We've changed our minds about this assignment,' she said without hesitation. 'We're entitled to do that.'

'Indeed you are,' Sir Roland agreed at once. 'But I wonder exactly how Christopher and Martin would regard these rather delightful DVDs? And what, do you imagine, would be their opinion of your willingness to sign up for Housewives, Inc. and fuck the rest of the world for money? I shall be fascinated to listen to your views.'

'Oh, my God!'

'I don't think that even he will be able to save you from what lies in store. It's time to teach you a much needed lesson in humility. Or rather, several much needed lessons. To start with bend over that table, both of you. Side by side, if you please. Legs straight and elbows and foreheads on the tabletop.'

Sir Roland flexed the cane in both hands. It was over five feet in length, with a curved handle. 'Yes, side by side and close together, just like that. I said don't bend your knees. Yes, that's better. Now then, errant housewives, this little beauty in my hands is going to deal with both of you at one and the very same time. It's more than up to the job, as you will shortly discover.'

He turned to address his personal assistants. 'Very well, gentlemen. Prepare these wayward young ladies for the first part of the evening's frivolities. Remove their dresses, bras and thongs, and then stand well back while I impress them with the quality of this exceedingly fine instrument of torture. Twelve of the very best, right across them. Right across their impudent little behinds. Delivered with all my strength. Enough to ensure they remain on their feet for a week. Afterwards, all of you can have both of them as often as you please. The more times the better, because they have a very important lesson to learn.'

Five minutes later two of the prettiest bare bottoms imaginable were pouting painfully up at the men, writhing uncomfortably from side to side as if to cool themselves. Twelve times the cane had landed across them with a crack like a shot from a rifle, provoking screams of anguish and floods of tears, and raising twelve evil red welts so long and thick they were a joy for all to behold. Twelve times Sir Roland had punished those pretty bare bottoms for their insolent perfection, as well as their previous insolence in having refused to allow themselves to be bared for him of their own free will. Refusals he'd found impossible to bear. Twelve times the girls had felt the fire being laid across them, howling up at the ceiling as it burned right down into the fulsome fleshiness they were being obliged to offer up to their tormentor. Twelve times the cane had branded them so excruciatingly, while they stood side by side, bent forward over the table, clasping hands in an effort to comfort each other. Twelve times did they learn that Sir Roland was a man who couldn't even contemplate the idea of refusal, let alone tolerate it. Twelve times did the cane hiss viciously through the air before biting deeply into the delightful pair of twin peaks that had no option but to accept the punishment being bestowed upon them. Twelve times did the cane perform with an excellence above and beyond the call of duty, making all the onlookers as erect as ever they'd been in their lives. Twelve times did the burning, blistering heat ensure that the escorts were as wet as the Pacific Ocean at the join of their legs.

Now it was time for the next stage of the evening's entertainment. Sir Roland was in charge of the proceedings, but disdained to take part personally. He'd exacted the first part of his revenge already, and was pleased to allow his underlings to have their fill of the girls on their own. He had no intention of sullying himself with what was to follow. No intention of dignifying the occasion by participating in person - except to direct operations.

Once again he offered a prayer of thanks for the way Tracie had, only yesterday, rushed round to his office armed with a folio of photographs of her latest recruits. Two girls who would more than grace his next offering of corporate hospitality, she'd said excitedly. His astonishment and delight had been plain for her to see. But they wouldn't be used for corporate hospitality, he told her. That would be far too easy for them - eminently suitable though they were for such an occasion. No, these girls would be employed to pleasure his entire personal staff instead. He wanted to ensure they were worked as hard as possible. The relatively genteel business of corporate hospitality would mean letting them off far too lightly. He wanted to be certain that they received the maximum amount of yardage it was possible to pack into them over the course of just one evening. Then he'd explained why he was so keen to have them used and abused in that way...

Sir Roland began to outline his plan of campaign to his sixteen personal assistants, all of whom listened with eager enthusiasm. There was to be a mammoth topping and tailing party, he announced, much to male delight and even greater female misgivings.

So, at his instructions, the men spread the escorts out across the tabletop, bottoms up but facing in opposite directions. There they lay, side by side, legs down at right angles, toes touching the floor. There they lay waiting, Emma's prettily striped bottom beside Jayne's head, Jayne's equally pretty bottom nestling nicely beside the head of her friend. There they lay close beside each other, attired in just their lace-topped stockings, frothy suspenders that matched, and high-heeled shoes. There they lay in fear and apprehension, not daring to contemplate any part of what lay in store for them. The epic topping and tailing of two bored young housewives was about to begin...

At Sir Roland's command the men rushed to form queues on either side of the table, jostling good-naturedly for prime position. Eventually four semi-orderly queues were formed, four deep, two behind upturned bottoms and two in front of pretty young mouths. Sir Roland continued to explain how matters would proceed. Once the fucking and sucking had started the persons at the front would move clockwise every three minutes, from mouth to pussy and so on. Or more accurately, from mouth or pussy to pussy or mouth, then on to mouth or pussy, then on again to pussy or mouth. In that way each would have a total of twelve minutes to finish themselves off, before recouping for another go. Plenty of time, said Sir Roland, bearing in mind the added stimulus of so much variety; two girls, two mouths, two pussies, and two freshly caned bottoms on which to feast their eyes. If they didn't, then that was just tough luck. Back they'd go to the start of the queue, where they'd have to bide their time until they were able to work their way to the front again.

Finally, anyone not hard enough to penetrate from behind would be allowed to swap places with anyone fully erect in front. Brownie points would, however, be lost.

Finally again, early-comers would not be a problem. They'd be welcome, in fact, since they'd help to keep the queues moving.

But first, in order to start the party with a bang - or rather, with several - Sir Roland declared that quick introductions all round were essential. All those present would be introduced into one or other of the girls in the space of only a few minutes, he announced. Just so everyone could get acquainted. Everyone would have just one minute in just one of the four openings on offer. And then, once the introductions had been effected, it would be down to the serious business he'd already described; the twelve minute slot.

The introductions were successfully completed Everyone had poked something, if only for a mere sixty seconds. The mood had been set. The men were upright and hard, the escorts had been opened up and made ready for their marathon ordeal, and Sir Roland was happy that the rehabilitation process for the two wayward young women who'd dared to spurn his advances was now well and truly on course. Everyone was instructed not to hold back. 'Fuck 'em fast' was the order of the day.

Off they went like rats up a drainpipe. While the girls lay on their fronts, stock-still and passive, wide open fore and aft, four overstretched penises began to race back and forth inside them, almost as if they were in competition with each other. Groins slapped hard into bouncy buttocks that pulsed with the pain of the caning, while mouths gaped open wide as length after length slithered in and out at speed. Fat little female bottoms began to wriggle with the early onset of desire, despite themselves, and the onlookers fervently prayed for their turn. There was no giving of head - just the taking of it.

Three minutes were up and the men switched positions clockwise; Jayne's lower opening being exchanged for Emma's mouth, Emma's mouth for her own lower opening, Emma's lower opening for Jayne's mouth, and finally Jayne's mouth for her own lower opening. Now each girl was able to savour the taste of the other, and savour it they certainly did. The men instantly adjusted to the delights of the new orifice and continued to shaft as before.

Then it was all change once more. Almost immediately one of the finance assistants was the first casualty of the evening. Having withdrawn from Emma's mouth and then re-entered her from behind, he glanced down at the multitude of fiery-red welts that adorned every part of her pouting bare bottom, and immediately started to spurt.

'Oh!' gasped Emma, feeling herself being flooded with a ferocity she found hard to believe. 'Oh...' she sighed a moment later as he continued to vent stream after stream of her favourite substance deep into her womb. 'Oh, that's not so bad I suppose... rather the opposite, in fact...'

The assistant with special responsibilities for credit control, Julian Root, was next in line behind the unfortunate finance man. 'What a feeble performance,' he muttered, pushing hard into Emma the very second she was vacated. 'But then again, all finance guys are poofs, apart from those of us up at the sharp end of credit control.'

Julian made the same mistake of staring in fascination at the cruelly caned bottom, instantly suffering the fate of his predecessor. 'Fuck it!' he cried at the top of his voice.

'I intend to,' replied the man in the queue behind him, elbowing him out of the way.

The men swapped over for the third time. Almost at once both girls were swallowing sperm. Then Emma was implanted below the waist yet again. Seconds later, so was Jayne.

Another three minute spell was over, and another casualty recorded. New recruits began to come forward frequently and fast, happily hammering in and out of the sweet little passage or mouth that had become vacant. More minutes ticked by. The assistant in charge of company takeovers was replaced in Jayne's mouth by his second in command, just as the PA mounted on Emma's bottom began to gush.

Very soon one of the loans assistants had run all the way through Jayne, his place being taken by the floatations man, whose penis would very shortly be in Emma's mouth. Jayne began to gobble and swallow again, just as the man

94

behind Emma started to squirt. Seconds after the floatations PA had slid out of Jayne and into Emma, Emma's insides were splattered and splashed once more. And then, when the floatations man was subsequently inside there, two of the finance PAs simultaneously spermed Jayne - top and tail.

The floatations man was in Jayne's mouth, and he knew his twelve minutes were almost up. He lifted his gaze from her bouncing bottom and turned to watch Emma at work. He'd fallen head over heels for her the first time he'd set eyes on her, three months previously. That did the trick. Staring intently at the thick organs servicing her front and rear he erupted straight into Jayne's face and mouth. Greedily, she started to swallow.

Now most of the early-comers were recovered and up and ready for more, eagerly awaiting a second helping of all that was on offer.

Emma groaned aloud, despite the fact that her mouth was full of one of the loans assistants. Oh crumbs! A truly monstrous weapon was forcing itself into her poor pussy. He was already stretching her further than she'd comfortably go, and he still wasn't all the way home! He still had more to provide! But at least she was more than adequately lubricated, thanks to all that had come and come. What was it she'd said to herself in bed the other night? About wanting lots of cock? Cock without any other sort of involvement? Well, it seemed that someone had been listening rather too well. And she somewhat suspected this was only the start of the evening's frivolities...

A few minutes later one of the finance men was in trouble. He was running desperately short of time. Try as he might he just couldn't bring himself off in Emma. Any second now he'd be relegated to the back of the queue. 'I'm sorry,' he gasped to her. 'But I don't have any other option. I hope you don't mind?'

Of course, Emma couldn't reply; she had penis right down her throat. 'Arrgghhh...' she tried to shriek a few seconds later, but couldn't, the man having vacated pussy in favour of tight little bum.

'Gotcha at last!' he cried triumphantly, searing her anal passage with squirt after squirt of hot seed.

'Ohhh...' sighed Emma, her insides starting to spasm with orgasm...

Five minutes later Jayne, although securely mounted from behind, found her mouth momentarily unoccupied as a result of a mild dispute as to whose turn it was to be in there. Seizing the unexpected opportunity, she took several deep breaths and cleaned her face as best she could, licking her fingers and savouring the salty taste. Then she glanced sideways at Emma and grinned. What a sexy sight! Emma spread across the table facedown, one gleaming dick thrashing away between the cheeks of her bottom, another sliding smoothly in and out of her mouth. And more waiting patiently in line, both in front and behind.

Oh dear! Whatever would Martin think if he could see her now? If he could see for himself how quickly she'd adjusted to her unfortunate plight? If he could see how she was wallowing in the luxury of the situation, in the way she was being poked and prodded and implanted time and time again? What on earth would he make of all that? Martin, her ever-loving husband who doted on her every move. Martin, who steadfastly refused to believe she was capable of perpetrating even the tiniest misdemeanour. What in God's name would he think if he were here and watching her now?

Poor Martin! How devastated he'd be! He'd never be able to come to terms with the fact that she was capable of behaving this way. She'd never been unfaithful to him until four nights ago, and now she had no idea how many times she'd done it...

Jayne returned her attention to the two young men standing naked and rampant in front of her. 'Haven't you sorted it out yet?' she asked with mock disapproval. 'Surely you can agree on who's next?'

'Not really,' muttered the one to her left.

Jayne reached forward with both hands, at the same time grimacing at a particularly violent thrust from behind. 'Look here,' she murmured helpfully, taking one urgently throbbing tool in each hand. 'Move forward a bit more and I'll do both of you at the same time. That will save any further argument.'

'How the hell can you manage that?'

'Just watch me,' she laughed, sucking powerfully at one and then the other. 'I don't think it'll be too difficult. Do you want to bet I can't?'

'Not me,' groaned the first one, closing his eyes and pulling back his head as she sucked again.

'Nor me,' croaked the other, doing exactly the same.

She tugged them a little nearer to her face. 'The waiting must have done you good,' she giggled wickedly. 'You're both as stiff as a board. I can hardly wiggle you at all.'

It was as well for the men that they'd declined to wager their money. Her tousled blonde head flew from one to the other, causing both to gasp and grimace. So fast did she work that before either of them had the chance to realise he'd been abandoned, her hot mouth was back in place. Back and forth she beavered between them, sucking and squeezing for all she was worth, making both of them moan with pleasure, despite the fact that they had to share. At last, just as a new recruit was settling onto her upturned buttocks, she felt both men in front of her start to stiffen and jerk. Not very long now, she thought to herself, her head flying even faster than ever between them. Using her hands she brought the two of them as close to each other as they could get, the two swollen, purplish tips stretching eagerly at her face. Then she set to work with a vengeance, her mouth enveloping one and then the other every half second or so.

'Eureka!' she gasped happily some thirty seconds later, as two piping hot effusions suddenly burst upon her, swamping her face before she was finally able to direct the double deluge into her mouth and begin swallowing as fast as she could.

On and on went the topping and tailing: the men erupting first here, then there, penis after penis taking its turn to plunder and poke, the men dispatching one load after another from front and back, taking their turns one after the other, while the girls wriggled and giggled and enjoyed every squirt and spurt. And still the men piled into Emma and Jayne with an unfailing energy. Groins slapped noisily against bottoms, pricks fucked and were lustily sucked, sperm flew in profusion, and the girls climaxed time and again. Time and time again, one orgasm following another as they wriggled and writhed and squirmed and wormed with the pleasure of their gross excess. Emma's bottom was trespassed on once more. Then Jayne suffered the same fate, twice in a row, as the idea gained support.

'Not you again,' gasped Emma, staring at the enormous weapon that had stretched her and Jayne to capacity more than once already. 'It only seems five minutes since your last go.'

'Time passes quickly when you're enjoying yourself,' the PA replied.

She stroked him with both hands. 'You're sure you're not queue jumping?'

'If I tried something like that I'd be torn apart by the angry mob.'

'Do me a favour and try to finish off before you get round behind me?'

'Hey!' said the credit control man standing immediately behind. 'Is this meant to be a blowjob or a parliamentary debate?'

'Point taken,' mumbled Emma, guiding the oversized organ into her mouth, with some difficulty, just as she felt the onset of yet another spasm, prompted by the brisk pace being set by whoever was currently mounting her from behind.

Emma gasped as she was once again splattered simultaneously from front and rear. The men seemed to be gaining in strength rather than losing their power. They seemed to ejaculate harder and in greater volume as time ticked by. And it also seemed to take less time for them to make it. She was sure this was the third time she'd been implanted from behind in the last five minutes. She wasn't keeping an eye on the clock, but she was sure she was right, nevertheless. And she could tell from the way the newcomer was jabbing her that he wouldn't hang around for long. You could always sense when a man was coming to the boil. Something just told you so. It had nothing to do with the speed of the coupling, it was just some sixth sense that told you he was about to blow.

And the lad in her mouth wouldn't be long either. Perhaps she'd be treated to yet another double discharge. That had proved great fun...

But eventually a halt had to be called. The girls had really worked wonders, but even for two bored - and previously sex-starved - young housewives, enough was at long last enough. The sheer physical strain had taken its toll. Wearily they staggered away, escorted by the liveried butler, who closed the door of the side room behind them. Bathrobes and towels were instantly provided.

'Oh, my God,' Emma groaned painfully, flopping down onto an armchair and closing her eyes. 'I think I could sleep for a week...'

'Yes indeed,' Jayne croaked in agreement, following suit. 'Good grief, I'm absolutely smothered from head to toe.'

Emma licked her lips and squeezed her thighs together. 'Jesus, all those men...'

'It was your idea to join Housewives, Inc. and improve your sex life.'

'I know. But I didn't expect my wish to be granted in quite this way.'

'I'll instruct the maids to run your baths,' said the butler. 'Will you bathe together or separately?'

'Together, please,' replied Jayne.

At that moment the door flew open and in strode Sir Roland. The girls looked up at him apprehensively, involuntarily wriggling their caned bottoms, but he was smiling broadly and appeared in the very best of moods.

'You young ladies have done exceptionally well,' he enthused. 'I'm very pleased with you. Full rehabilitation has been achieved. You have repaid your dues many times over.'

'Thank you.'

'You have more than redeemed yourselves. I think I may have been a little harsh in my judgement and treatment of you. But now I will show you that sometimes I can be a generous man.'

'Oh?'

'I shall instruct Tracie to ensure that no hint of your nocturnal activities could ever reach the eyes or ears of your husbands. I shall instruct her that she is to take the very utmost care to ensure that your security is never breached, either over tonight or in the future. I shall, of course, do exactly the same myself.'

'That's very kind of you,' murmured Jayne.

'Yes, it is,' agreed Emma. 'Very kind indeed. But I don't think either of us will be working as escorts again after tonight. I think we've both had enough of that to last us a lifetime.'

'Really? A great loss for the agency, I have to say. And for my future hospitality gatherings, as well.'

'Could we ask you for one other favour?' Emma continued. 'One other favour, apart from making sure no one else hears about what we've done?'

'What is it?'

'We never see our husbands. They spend all their time working for you. Night after night, and every weekend too. It's ruining our marriages.'

'Go on.'

'We'd like to have them back. Couldn't you take your legal work to a different law firm, please? It would be wonderful if you would.'

'Are you sure that's what you want me to do?'

'Yes, positive,' Emma replied at once. 'Absolutely positive. The extra money is lovely, of course, but we don't really need it. We were fine beforehand... and a lot happier too. We'd much rather have our husband's back, Sir Roland. We do love them, you see. Very much. I know it's asking a lot, but couldn't you do that for us, please?'

Sir Roland smiled in an almost fatherly manner. 'Well then, my dear young persons, consider it already done.'

CHAPTER THREE - GIRLS BOARDING SCHOOL

Emma and Jayne were best friends since kindergarten, and at boarding school together in Hampshire. Both of them had boyfriends from the local market town, and both of them had recently started experimenting with sex. Jayne giggled naughtily. 'Do you know something, Emma?' she asked.

'What's that?'

'I'm sure Annie really fancies you,' she replied, referring to the beautiful, red-haired head girl.

'Why do you say that?'

'Oh, just the way she looks at you when she's talking to you. And the way she keeps touching you. Particularly your bottom.'

'Lots of people do that. You do sometimes.'

'Not in the same way as Annie. She doesn't just pat your bum, she fondles it. Haven't you ever thought she might be after you?

'Well yes, sort of...'

'Think of the way she's made you captain of the tennis and swimming teams, when you're not even in the sixth form yet.'

'But I'm better than anyone else. Look at all the shields I've won.'

'I wonder what it's like with a girl,' mused Jayne. 'Alison says it can be really good fun.'

'I think I'll stick with Mike. His dick gives me all the fun I can manage at the moment... and more besides.' Emma grinned mischievously and ran a hand through her short black hair. 'I've agreed to spend the night with him on Friday, instead of going back home for the whole weekend.'

'Make sure you don't get found out,' warned Jayne.

Annie followed Emma into the almost deserted library, her eyes riveted to the lateral swing of Emma's bouncy buttocks, clearly discernible through her navy blue school uniform. 'Do you mind if I sit next to you?' she asked.

'Of course not,' Emma replied, feeling pleased.

'Let's sit at that desk over there, behind the bookcase.'

The girls sat down, with Annie on Emma's right. Annie looked down at Emma's lap. 'Have you shortened your gymslip?' she asked with a knowing grin.

'Yes. And tightened it round the hips.'

'You're not supposed to do that, you know.'

'I know. But it was so long and unattractive before.'

'That's how it's supposed to be,' giggled Annie. 'Foolish child!'

'I don't see why it has to be like that.'

Annie placed a hand on the other girl's thigh, just below the hem of the item in question. 'Because sexy bottoms and bare legs like these can incite lust in other people. In other girls, as well as boys.'

'Oh...'

'And lust is one of the seven deadly sins.'

'Oh.'

'It can make them want to do this to you,' she whispered, smiling sexily into Emma's face as she slid her hand up between smooth warm thighs until it was almost lost from sight. Emma blushed, but parted her legs to allow easier access to the trespassing hand. 'And it can make them want to do this,' she added, her hand sliding up even further.

'Oh,' Emma gulped again, feeling Annie's fingertips brushing lightly against the plumply filled crotch of her small, non-regulation panties, and instantly starting to lubricate, despite herself.

Slowly and gently Annie began to massage the rapidly dampening knicker-crotch. 'It can make them want to do this, as well.'

'Oh...'

'And this.'

Emma closed her eyes and allowed herself to enjoy the delicious sensation Annie was provoking at the join of her legs. Somehow it was even nicer than when her boyfriend touched her there. She supposed it was because this was even more illicit...

Now Annie's fingertips were inside the petite panties, stroking and petting the parted lips; lips now bare to her touch, because there was no longer any material to act as an obstruction. 'I do like boys, you know,' whispered Annie. 'As well as girls, I mean. 'But I think I like you more than anyone else.'

'Thank you...'

'Do you have sex with your boyfriend?'

'Yes, occasionally...'

'I hope you're on the pill?'

'Yes, of course.'

'I've dumped my boyfriend. He thought he owned me just because I let him fuck me a few times. Some men are like that, Emma.'

'Oh...'

'Open you eyes,' Annie coaxed her softly. 'I want you to look at me when I do this to you.'

Emma stared into the other girl's loving face. 'When you do what?' she asked.

'This,' murmured Annie, slowly pushing a slim finger all the way into Emma. 'How does that feel?'

'Lovely,' she sighed truthfully. 'Really lovely. You're so much gentler than Mike...'

'Girls are. And they know exactly what another girl wants, as I'm going to show you. Try to keep looking at me for as long as you can.'

'I'll try.'

'You're incredibly wet.'

'I know...'

'Are you always like this?'

'Not always...'

Annie leant forward and kissed her, using her tongue very lightly. 'Would you like me to do this?' she asked, slowly withdrawing her finger before making the next long, slow, easy insertion. 'Would you like me to finger-fuck you?'

'Oh, yes please.'

'Shall I see if I can make you come?'

'That would be lovely, Annie.'

Red-faced and breathing heavily, Emma continued to gaze into Annie's eyes as her finger worked steadily in and out. 'I love you,' whispered Annie. 'I think I always have.'

'I love you too...'

'Sweet little hole,' cooed Annie, fingering as slowly and gently as ever. 'Sweet little, hot little, wet little hole.' She began to use her thumb to brush back and forth over the other girl's swollen clitoris in time with each push and pull of her finger.

'Oh, that's so good!' groaned Emma, having to close her eyes at long last because she felt the need to concentrate her whole being on the way she was being so delightfully aroused. Each long, loving incursion stoked up the feeling of desire to ever greater heights, until she thought she couldn't stand any more. 'Ohhh...' moaned Emma. 'Oh Annie, that's just so lovely... oh God!' she squealed suddenly. 'Oh God, you're making me come already!'

She climaxed with a rush, very powerfully indeed, clapping her hands over her mouth in order to stifle the sounds of her happiness.

'Come to my bedroom tonight,' breathed Annie. 'Dawn won't mind. I've had a girl in there before. And she once smuggled her boyfriend in for the night.'

In fact, Dawn was happy to sleep in Emma's own bed, so that the two girls could be on their own. Emma slipped into the bedroom, wearing an ankle length dressing gown and only her brief non-regulation knickers underneath. The brief non-regulation knickers which Annie had successfully invaded with her fingers earlier that day.

Annie lay naked on top of the bed, smiling warmly at her new lover. 'Why don't you take off your dressing gown?' she suggested.

Emma complied, dropping the gown to the floor and blushing sweetly as she stood at the foot of the bed in just her knickers. 'You have a beautiful body,' enthused the older girl.

'So do you.'

'Take off your knickers and then turn round... oh, what a charming little bum! So perfectly shaped. So plump and inviting. I hope Mike appreciates what he has here?'

Emma giggled back over her shoulder. 'He certainly gives every impression of doing so.'

'Has anyone else had it bare?'

'No. He's my only boyfriend. But everyone seems to want to touch it. Particularly you, Annie.'

Annie cocked her head to one side as she gazed in approval at the pretty bare bottom that seemed to blush back at her so appealingly. 'It's so sweet it makes me want to smack it really hard.'

'You can, if you like...'

'No, I like you far too much to hurt you.'

'Thank you.'

'It's just the sweetest, prettiest, most delightful thing I've ever seen. So full and plump in exactly the right places. And so impishly dimpled, too. It looks as if it's smiling cheekily at me. It's just the sauciest little bottom imaginable.'

'Thank you...'

'I bet Mike can't keep his hands off it.'

Emma turned her head and giggled naughtily over her shoulder. 'Last week he covered both cheeks in love bites. Quite hard ones, actually. Enough to make me squawk.'

'I shall do that to you later, but much more gently. In the meantime, come and lie down here so we can kiss. Then I'll show you how good it can really be with a girl.'

'That sounds like a nice idea.'

Two weeks later the Headmistress, Miss Amelia Stricton, sat at her large oak desk glaring balefully at Annie and Emma as they stood side by side in front of her, nervously waiting to learn their fate.

'This morning you two girls were found in bed together, administering oral sex to each other.'

'Yes, Miss Stricton,' said Annie.

'A disgrace! A positive disgrace! Such disgusting conduct in my school can never be tolerated.'

'We love each other,' Emma objected.

'How old are you? What can you know of such things.'

'It was my fault,' Annie said calmly.

'It most certainly was. As Head Girl you are supposed to set an example to everyone else. Instead, you led this girl astray.'

'Yes, Miss Stricton. I'm sorry.'

'You will be expelled forthwith.'

'Yes, Miss Stricton.'

'And both of you will be caned, here and now. Six of the best across your bare bottoms. And I mean *the best*.'

'Yes, Miss Stricton.'

'Annie, you're to be first. Remove your kilt and knickers, and then bend over the side of the desk. Emma, you stand over there so you can watch and understand what is shortly going to happen to you. You will be allowed to stay at this school, because of your tender years, but let this be a lesson to you.'

'Yes, Miss Stricton.'

The cane whistled through the air and landed with a loud, evil crack across the very fleshiest part of Annie's enticingly upturned bottom. She jerked back her head at the sudden streak of seemingly unendurable pain that seared right across her, howling pitifully up at the ceiling in dire distress.

Tears of dismay trickled down Emma's face. 'Stop it!' she cried. 'You're hurting her far too much.'

'Be silent, girl! Otherwise I shall double her punishment. And yours, as well.'

The Headmistress stared in satisfaction at the contusion she'd raised. The pale, sensitive skin of the red-headed girl meant that the welt was almost twice the size and colour it would normally have been. A most promising start, she thought. And more than enough bottom, like she knew Emma would have, to accommodate all six strokes very adequately.

'I'm all right, Emma,' gasped Annie. 'Don't worry about me.'

'Be silent too, young lady! If you know what's best for you.'

Emma put a hand over her mouth to ensure there was no risk of her causing Miss Stricton to prolong her friend's chastisement. Miss Stricton, on the other hand, would have been delighted to be given the opportunity to do so. Never had she felt so outraged. Sexual activity amongst the girls was anathema to her. Sexual activity, full stop, was anathema to her. It might have been different, however, had she possessed a sex life of her own...

Crack! The cane landed again, producing more shrieks of agonised anguish and a second red-hot swelling to match the first. And then *crack!* again. Another savage swelling, and yet more screams of outrage. Now both girls were weeping. Annie because of the pain across her soft white buttocks, and Emma because of the other girl's obvious suffering. Emma had no concern at all for her own bottom. She would willingly have taken all the remaining strokes herself if it could have meant that Annie would escape further hurt.

But it was not to be. Three more cruel welts were added. Three more blistering welts were added to those poor bouncing cheeks, before it was time for Emma to lift her gymslip, lower her panties and take Annie's place over the Headmistress' desk.

Mike's throbbing erection demanded urgent and immediate attention. He'd just finished administering Emma's second severe punishment of the day, and had thoroughly enjoyed himself. Each vicious red welt on her cheeks had been spanked dozens and dozens of times. Spanked with all the strength he could muster.

'You can get off my lap now,' he muttered thickly, much to her relief.

Less than sixty seconds later the tears had stopped and Emma was goggling in astonished disbelief at the giant penis that speared up in front of her boyfriend's T-shirt. 'I don't know if I'll be able to get all of that inside me,' she gulped, her tight blue denim jeans still round her ankles.

'Maybe not, but it'll be fun trying,' he replied.

She squeezed her thighs together, relishing the glorious feeling of warm wet juices where they joined. 'I guess you might be right,' she giggled mischievously.

CHAPTER FOUR - EMMA BENDS THE RULES

The Fleet Street branch of Barclays Bank was quiet that Christmas Eve. Lisa stared, yet again, at the superbly filled seat of Emma's short skirt as it swished impishly from side to side down the corridor ahead. Did all girls, she wondered for the thousandth time or more, feel this way? Did all girls gaze in fascination at a shapely female bottom and fantasise about how they'd like to treat it? She rather suspected they didn't. It wasn't as if she was lesbian, or even truly bisexual, although she'd twice had sex with a girl. Yet she'd dreamed about what she would like to do to a beautiful girl like Emma. A beautiful girl like Emma with a really cheeky, inviting arse. Twelve months earlier she'd even gone to the extremes of purchasing and secreting the XT3 in her office, in the hope that one day it might be put to good use.

Lisa caught up with Emma and patted her firmly across the fullest part of her bottom. Something she made sure she did at least once every working day. 'That skirt's a bit tiny for work, isn't it?' she said.

'Do you think so? It is Christmas, after all. Do you want me to change it? I've got a longer one upstairs.'

Lisa patted her again, savouring the warm springiness of deliciously bouncy buttocks through the lightweight material of the other girl's snug-fitting skirt. 'No, that's okay. As you say, it's Christmas. When you've finished at the counter I've got some title deeds that need to be checked against the computer and then returned to the depository. I'll be in my office.'

'Okay. I'll see you in an hour, Mrs Browne.'

'Lisa, please. I've told you before. After all, I'm only a couple of years older than you.'

'Sorry, Lisa.'

In truth, Emma was a ravishing twenty-five year old, and Lisa a stunning thirty-three.

Emma smiled to herself. Why was it that so few of the staff could keep their hands off her bottom? Particularly Mrs Browne. Sorry, she meant Lisa. Why were the women as well as the men always so keen to touch her there? Was it just because she was quite a nice shape down there? Not that she really minded too much. It was rather nice, in a way. Sort of comforting and reassuring. And she'd grown used to the practice over the years. She'd had to, she supposed. Her rear end had always been a constant source of interest to other people. Not just to her boyfriends, of course. Almost everyone. Mind you, her boyfriends had really displayed enthusiasm for the item in question. Particularly when they'd had to chance to manhandle it bare.

And Chris, her husband. How fond he was of that particular part of her person! The number of times he'd laid her facedown on the bed and given her a love bite in the middle of each cheek. The number of times he'd then sprayed sperm all over the love-bitten cheeks!

Ninety minutes later Emma tapped the entry code into the door of the deeds depository and stepped inside.

'Hello, Gorgeous!' exclaimed George Franks from promotions, looking up from one of the computer screens along the opposite wall and grinning widely at the attractive young woman who seemed to be all legs, boobs and bum, topped with the cropped black hair that always gave her such an impish look. 'I was hoping I might bump into you here.'

'Were you indeed?'

'I like the skirt you're almost wearing.'

'It's a Christmas special, approved by Lisa this morning.'

George gave her a knowing grin. 'And I can guess why she approved it.'

'Pardon?'

'Come on, Ems. She's happy to let you parade around in such a saucy little scrap of skirt because she can't keep her eyes off it herself.'

'I don't know what you mean. She's married, isn't she?'

'Haven't you ever heard of a married woman having the hots for another bit of skirt? Particularly another bit of skirt that's filled as splendidly as that.'

'Well, yes. But I don't think it's like that with her.'

'And changing the subject a fraction, there's a bunch of mistletoe right above where you're standing.'

Emma giggled. 'What could it be doing there, I wonder?'

'It's waiting for you. I need a Christmas kiss.'

'You can have that, but nothing else.'

'One thing can lead to another, Emma. As I'm sure you know very well.'

'It can't now I'm married, George. Just a kiss, and nothing more.'

'You might change your mind in a moment.'

'I can assure you I won't.'

George stood up and started to approach her. Then he stopped. 'Damn! I'd forgotten about the new security camera over there. Have you got anything in your handbag we could hang over it?'

'I haven't even got my handbag.'

'Buggeration! And the red light's on as well.'

Emma giggled wickedly. 'Now don't go getting any ideas, George. But I could slip out of my knickers and hang them over the camera for a couple of minutes, I suppose.'

George admired the very briefest glimpse of bare lower cheeks as Emma stretched up with both hands and dropped a tiny pair of filmy black knickers over the security camera that was threatening to expose them. A split second later the hem of her miniskirt dropped back into place, much to his regret...

Emma was beginning to wonder whether this knickerless state might have been a mistake. With George's tongue down her throat and his hands all over her bare buttocks, not only could she feel it was making him incredibly erect, but she knew it was making her more and more wet by the second. More and more wet, and more and more randy, too. She must maintain her earlier resolve, she warned herself urgently. She must maintain her resolve to remain faithful to Chris, despite the messages emanating from below the suspender belt. Not that she was wearing one...

Crumbs, his dick felt enormous against her tummy! Perhaps all the rumours were true.

'Come on, Ems,' breathed George. 'Just a fuck for Christmas. Just a very quick Christmas fuck?'

She wriggled against his groin, despite herself. 'No George. I told you. Just a kiss and nothing more.'

'But I'm bursting apart at the seams. And it is Christmas, after all. Christmas doesn't really count, does it? Everyone's at it if they get the chance.'

'Well I'm not.'

'Your husband will never know.'

'That's not the point at all.'

'Oh, Ems,' he groaned plaintively. 'Please. You've made me so hard it hurts...'

With a sigh of resignation she stepped back and then knelt on the floor in front of him, reaching for his belt buckle. 'Okay, I'll offer you a compromise.'

'Thank God for that.'

'Gosh, you are hard, aren't you? I can't even waggle you at all, let alone move you towards me.'

'I know...'

'I'll have to stand up and then come down on you sideways. It's the only way to get you right into my mouth.'

'There's another problem with the camera in the deeds depository, Mrs Browne,' said the security man.

Lisa stared at the row of monitors on the wall in front of her, one of which was dark grey. 'Why isn't it completely blank?' she asked.

'I don't know. It's rather odd.'

'Is there a back-up camera in there?'

'Yes, on the far side of the room. Shall I activate it?'

'Yes, please. Some of the title deeds in there are unregistered, and therefore irreplaceable.'

'This should bring the screen back to life,' he murmured, pressing two buttons and then flicking down a switch. 'Good grief!' he gasped, as the two of them stared in surprise and disbelief at the tabloid thus revealed.

Emma was standing on the depository floor, bending down straight-legged, the lowest part of the cheekiest part of her bare bottom peeking naughtily out from under the hem of her skirt as she worked her head up and down on the half naked man standing in front of her. Suddenly the man jerked violently and sperm began to spurt all over her pretty face, despite her struggles to direct it into her mouth. At last she succeeded in doing so, and started to swallow with evident relish. The man cupped her head in his hands and lifted his face to the ceiling, groaning with delight.

'Mark that section of the tape,' said Lisa, when the fellatio had finally finished. 'Then remove it and put it in storage. I may need to refer to it later.'

As the security man began a third rerun of the tape, surrounded by four other gleeful colleagues, Emma stood in front of Lisa's desk, head bowed and knickers back in situ.

'You realise this is a case of instant dismissal?' asked Lisa, not unkindly. 'The bank's rules are very specific.'

'Yes, I know...'

'I ought to send a full report to our legal department right now, so they can prepare the necessary paperwork.'

'I know...'

'But your husband works there, so I won't.'

'Oh thank you, Mrs Browne. I mean, Lisa...'

'I shall deal with this particular disciplinary matter myself.'

'I'm really very grateful.'

'I shouldn't be too grateful if I were you, Emma. I do have my own agenda, you see.'

'Oh...'

Lisa stood up and moved behind her subordinate, leaving Emma facing the now empty desk. 'Actually, I'm the one who should be grateful,' said Lisa, her right hand commencing a thorough exploration of Emma's fulsome bottom through the lightweight material of her skirt. 'Grateful for this opportunity,' she continued.

Emma gulped but said nothing, feeling Lisa's other hand joining the first. It was beginning to seem that George Franks might well have been right about Lisa, after all. Not that this was particularly unpleasant. Slightly embarrassing, yes. But not particularly unpleasant. Almost the opposite, in fact. Lisa's gently roaming hands were starting to make her wet between the legs. Nearly as wet as she'd been when sucking George's magnificent erection.

'Take off your skirt and put it on the desk,' Lisa said softly. 'That's right... and now those charming little knickers as well... thank you.'

Lisa's hands returned to their intimate examination of buttocks that were now very bare indeed. An intimate and extremely searching examination. 'Do you know what I've always wanted to do to this beautiful bottom of yours, Emma?'

'No...'

'Try to guess.'

'Erm, stroke it bare, like you're doing now, I suppose...?'

'And what else, do you think?'

'I don't know...'

'Have another guess.'

'I can't really imagine...'

'I've always wanted to hurt it, of course. Really, really hurt it, I mean. It's so saucily sweet and pretty that I want to flay it alive.'

'Oh...'

'And that's exactly what I'm going to do, Emma my love. Flay it alive. Turn it all shades of red. Beat it with a heavy ruler until it burns like a bonfire on November the fifth.'

'Surely you don't mean it, Lisa...?'

'Yes, I'm afraid I do.'

Emma glanced back over her shoulder at the other girl. 'Couldn't you settle for just fondling it a bit more? I don't mind you doing that. I don't mind it at all...'

'No. I'm going to do just what I said; welt it with a long, heavy ruler until it's dark red and hotter than a furnace at an iron foundry.'

'Oh, grief!'

'I'm not going to do it to you because I'm angry with you, or because I don't like you. In fact, I like you very much indeed. I'm going to do it precisely because I do like you - and because, at long last, I can. Do you understand what I'm saying, sweetheart?'

'Yes...'

'Good. Now bend right forward over the back of that typist's chair. Keep your legs straight and rest your elbows on the desktop beyond. Then put your head down on the desk as well, so it's below the level of your hips.'

As demurely as circumstances would permit Emma did as she'd been told, blushing fiercely. She supposed a lot of people must feel the same as Lisa about wanting to punish her poor little bum. She supposed many of the people who showed an interest in that part of her anatomy would like to hurt it in the way Lisa was proposing. She knew the way men felt about that sort of thing, of course. But where was the pleasure for a girl in doing it to another girl? Why would they want to make you suffer so? She'd never had the slightest inclination to do it to someone else. What would she feel like, she wondered, if she ever did get the chance?

Lisa stared hungrily at the beautifully turned bottom being offered up to her so enticingly. The beautifully turned bottom displayed to perfection below the smart white blouse that ended tightly but elegantly around the slimmest part of Emma's waist. From there down to her high heels not a single stitch adorned her. Mouth-wateringly plump buttocks reared up right in front of her. Mouth-wateringly plump buttocks, the spectacular swell of which was making her lubricate more and more. All her adult life she'd waited for this moment; a really beautiful girl with a really cheeky bottom that had no option but to submit to the kind of torture she was proposing to inflict upon it. And no bottom could possibly come any cheekier than this one! It was so perfectly plump that the fullest part of each cheek seemed to vie for space with its counterpart...

Lisa went to a cupboard and collected the ruler she'd purchased three days after Emma had started to work at the bank. It was a plastic architect's ruler, XT3 variety, one meter in length and over half a kilo in weight. A truly formidable weapon. She swished it through the air, causing Emma to look back over her shoulder and gulp once again.

Oh Mary, Mother and Father, had she ever been in such trouble as this? Just look at the size of that ruler! And yet, strangely, she still liked Lisa a lot...

Slowly and lovingly Lisa ran the flat of the ruler over the bent-over bottom that confronted her so appetisingly, making Emma quiver with fright. 'This is going to hurt you, Emma. It's going to hurt you a lot. But with every slap of the ruler I shall love you a little bit more.'

'I'm not sure that's going to be much help...'

'It might be, if you think about it enough.'

'I'll try...'

'You're to count each stroke out loud. If you're a good girl I'll stop when the count gets to two hundred. If you forget to count one, then you'll get it again.'

Thwack! The ruler seared itself right across the centre of both cheeks with all the strength Lisa could muster, making Emma lift her head and howl in shocked surprise. Oh God! She'd been mortally wounded! A sudden flash of fire had seemed to burn her all the way down to the bone. And it was still continuing to burn, even though she'd only received one single stroke. How on earth was she ever going to be able to get through all the rest?

Lisa gazed with pleasure at the perfect red print, five centimetres in width, that the ruler had painted across the saucy bare bottom she had at her mercy. The saucy bare bottom that was pouting up at her so nervously. Very gently she ran the back of her hand along the ruler-print, savouring the heat as well as the sleek smoothness of the flesh. 'You can't believe how beautiful that looks and feels,' she enthused.

'Oh, good...' muttered Emma, with considerably less enthusiasm.

Thwack! The ruler kissed her again, almost exactly along the same line, making her howl and her cheeks bounce and redden just as before.

Thwack! It did so again.

Thwack! It did so for a fourth time.

'You haven't been counting, silly girl,' Lisa said softly. 'But never mind, I'll overlook it this time. You can start from five.'

Thwack! 'Five!' yelped Emma.

Thwack! 'Six!'

Thwack! 'Seven!'

Thwack! 'Eight!'

Thwack! 'Nine!'

Thwack! 'Ten!'

Tears were squeezing out of her eyes and running freely down her face. 'Eleven! Twelve! Thirteen!' She yelped, yelped, and yelped again. 'Fourteen! Fifteen! Sixteen! Seventeen! Eighteen! Nineteen! Twenty!

'Ooooohh!' Emma sobbed unhappily. 'Oh, Lisa, that really hurts...'

Lisa ran a caring hand lightly over the afflicted area. 'Poor little, sore little bottom,' she cooed. 'Poor little, sore little bum.'

Emma yelped out the next ten numbers in scarcely more than the same number of seconds, the ruler splattering across wildly bouncing cheeks with consummate ease. Then she lay the side of her face on the desktop as if it was a pillow and began sobbing quietly but uncontrollably, an endless stream of teardrops pouring onto the wooden surface.

A pause of two or three minutes followed, in order to allow Emma to regain some composure. Then it was time for the ruler to be wielded again. Emma no longer had the strength to yelp, so numbers thirty-one to fifty were mutedly sobbed instead. Now the weeping was even more pitiful than ever. Something that made Lisa love her, and want to hurt her even more.

'How many are we up to, honey?' asked Lisa, after another composure break.

'Fifty,' snuffled Emma.

'Well, you can have a couple more minutes to get yourself ready for the rest.'

'Thank you...'

'Just think how wet and womanly this is making you feel.'

'I don't think that's much consolation right now.'

Lisa's loving hand returned to stroke and soothe the buttocks she was blistering so thoroughly. 'But it will be when we're finished,' she purred. 'Then my tongue will give you the most magnificent pussy-petting you've ever had in your life.'

'Couldn't we just stop and do that now?'

'I'm afraid not, baby. I want to love you with the ruler a lot, lot more before then. Just keep thinking about how much I'm going to make you come when the time arrives.'

Lisa sighed happily. This incredibly cheeky young lady hadn't just bent the strict rules of the bank, she'd well and truly broken them. She'd broken them with George Franks in the deeds depository. So now, here she was, bending the heavy rule she held in her hand. Bending it as far as it would go, time after time after time. And she was going to continue to bend it until that sexy bare bottom was an even more glorious hue. And what a sexy bare bottom it was, to be sure! And what a great deal more beating it was going to have to endure before it would be allowed back into its knickers and skirt and sent on its way in disgrace. Could anything, anywhere, ever be so sweet?

Twenty more strokes were savagely delivered, causing Emma to squirm her hips from side to side in the very gravest of grave discomfort.

'Seventy,' gasped Emma, teardrops rolling down both cheeks in ever-increasing abundance.

'Yes, seventy,' Lisa murmured proudly, after a short pause. 'From now on I'll do the counting, so you can just concentrate on crying in peace. That might help you a bit.'

'Yes, that would be nice...' sniffed Emma, tears still flowing.

Ruler in hand, Lisa stared down at the bright red bottom she'd already managed to incinerate so well. The delightful high-points of each cheek, which had so far taken the brunt of the punishment, were turning crimson, while the rest of the bent-over bottom was a most pleasing shade of scarlet. The six strokes she'd laid across the tops of the thighs were an added embellishment.

'Your spanked bottom is so unbelievably pretty,' she breathed, after a lengthy pause.

'And sore,' Emma muttered ruefully.

Lisa laughed, but not at all unkindly. 'But it deserves to be that way. No one with a gorgeous, juicy-ripe bum like yours should expect anyone else to want to treat it in any other way.'

'I'm beginning to realise that now.'

'Haven't you ever been spanked before?'

'Once. When I was still at school. I was caned by the headmistress and, two hours later, found myself over my boyfriend's knee.'

'So your husband's never done it to you?'

'No,' replied Emma, her little misadventure with Jonathan Crowe still over twelve months in the future.

'Well, I'm surprised. Jim has roasted my bottom several times. I rather enjoy it.'

'I have to confess that I don't.'

Very tenderly and lovingly, Lisa squeezed the burning flesh. 'You'll feel differently when we're finished, Em.'

'I hope so,' she said with feeling. 'Did you mean what you said about using your tongue on me?'

'Yes, of course I meant it. I do love you, you know.'

Emma sensed the ruler being lifted on high and braced herself for the onslaught soon to be renewed. So, then. Lisa still insisted that she loved her. Surely she, Emma, didn't really feel something similar towards Lisa? Towards the woman who was intending to add a further one hundred and thirty searing slaps to the mere seventy that had already succeeded in setting her poor bottom so fiercely ablaze? But it rather seemed that she might...

CHAPTER FIVE - DESPERATE HOUSEWIFE
Introduction by Mary Alice

In the total scheme of life it didn't take long for Crystal to conclude that the man she'd married was really a bit of a prat. Benny had been her first boyfriend, and they'd pledged their troth when she was just eighteen years and thirteen days - mainly because of her mother's unending insistence that they shouldn't. Their daughter, Cheryl, was born twenty months later, and shortly after that Crystal began to grow up. As she did so she started to realise that, in a way, Benny was indeed the man of her dreams. Unfortunately for Crystal, it was only her bad dreams in which he was the star. In her good dreams she listened to her mother's advice and flushed Benny down the hole where her mother felt he so rightfully belonged.

But it was her bad dreams that were the reality. It was her bad dreams with which she was hoist. As Crystal grew into maturity Benny seemed to travel down the opposite road, becoming childlike and sulky towards his blossoming young wife, and displaying a deep-seated jealousy that was as irrational as it was counterproductive. Crystal could now see quite clearly that she'd made a profound mistake. But with an infant daughter and no means of self-support - and not wanting to concede that her mother's opinion, but not her tactics, had been right all along - this was a mistake scheduled to take the rest of the decade to rectify. Of course, at that time she was quite unaware how long the rectification process would take, or indeed whether there'd be any rectification at all.

And so, as the next few years slipped slowly by, Crystal came to discover that one way of helping to tolerate the mistake she'd made was by granting herself the luxury - just every now and again - of living the sort of life she should have lived before ever considering the possibility of settling down and tying the nuptial knot.

Cold Store

Crystal Langley - slim, fair-haired, and as saucily sexy as the polar day is long - was leaning forward over one of the stack of green trays that housed the vegetables, her forearms resting on the top as she gazed attentively at the plastic inner door of the cold store, directly ahead of where she stood. She sighed to herself. It was now four whole days since Benny had stopped talking to her. He'd taken offence because she hadn't instantly agreed with some totally trivial point he'd been trying, but failing, to make. A point so unimportant that, for the life of her, she couldn't remember what it was. Which meant, of course, that it was going to be difficult to pacify him. How could she acknowledge, albeit belatedly, that he must have been right after all, when she had no idea what it was that the prat had been wrong about in the first place? But pacify him she must. By Sunday morning at the latest. Otherwise he'd refuse to drive her and Cheryl to the zoo. And how upset that would make their four-year-old daughter. How upset that, once again, Benny was being sulky and stupid over some utterly unimportant disagreement that had arisen between Mummy and Daddy, and consequently refusing to cooperate in matters appertaining to the family.

Oh well, there was always the sex option, she supposed. There was always the sex method of making up with her dear husband, and thereby achieving whatever the desired result might be. It had proved very reliable since she'd started using it two years ago. Benny was so pathetically predictable. He wouldn't speak to her for days on end, but if she were to let him catch a quick glimpse of her in just her tiny knickers, and then, half an hour later, suggest that he might want to re-establish conjugal relations, the outcome was always the same. She'd end up on her back, enthusiastically expressing what a fantastic time she was having, Benny would be talking again and, afterwards, Benny would be perfectly happy to do whatever it was that Crystal wanted him to do...

Crumbs, those tomatoes looked a bit overripe. She needed to get them out on the shelves today if there was going to be any chance of selling them. How had they ripened so quickly? She was sure the temperature had been maintained at a constant minus two degrees. Unless, of course, the thermostat was faulty again. Why did this branch always get the oldest of the old equipment? It wasn't as if...

Oh crikey! What on earth was she doing? However could she have been so lax as to have been staring down at the tomatoes instead of keeping a vigilant watch on the plastic door? It was no use expecting Stephen to be any help there. She couldn't trust him to keep a proper lookout even at the best of times. And she most certainly couldn't expect him to do so now that he'd stepped up a couple of gears. Nine months' not-so-bitter experience had taught her that he was rapidly approaching the vinegar strokes. If she didn't keep her own eyes glued to the door she could well expect another near disaster, like last week's. Or even worse...

Despite the ever-mounting pleasure induced by the rhythmic beating of groin against soft buttocks, Crystal kept her gaze riveted to the semi-transparent plastic door. Notwithstanding the chilly temperature, no one could accuse this of being any sort of frigid affair, she told herself happily. Indeed, Stephen was a red-hot lover, even in the extremes of cold. For ten months now he'd been jumping on her during some of the frequent visits her part-time job required her to make to the cold store. And for the last nine of those months she'd been prepared to let him jump all the way, as opposed to pushing him off after a quick grip, grope and a giggle. But regrettable though it was in many ways, the end of their fuck-in-the-fridge affair was now very much in sight.

Stephen's seduction technique had been both clever and very, very sweet, she thought to herself, as the bludgeoning from behind started to build towards a crescendo, lifting her up onto her toes with the power of each forward thrust. Ten month's ago he'd known she was a married virgin - meaning that only Benny had ever been up there. So he'd overcome her natural feelings of trepidation with tender consideration, gently taking just a single step at a time.

'There is life after marriage!' she'd exclaimed to herself, when Stephen had first started to stalk her in the cold store and touch her bottom and boobs. She was married with a kid, but someone else actually fancied her, she'd been sufficiently naive to think to herself in surprise. Over the course of the next few days the touching and kissing had begun to include the encouraging of her hand into his clothing, in search of the one-eyed trouser snake that constantly seemed to uncoil itself at the slightest provocation. In turn this led, after a couple of successful finds, to the happy release of the rampant reptile so it could be rubbed intimately against her from behind, her shop uniform hitched up and her tiny knickers hitched down. All eyes of course, except Stephen's, being focused warily on the plastic door.

After a further few such outings, the not-so-cold-blooded creature in question had tentatively been allowed to inveigle itself all the way up to the top of the warm, welcoming nest it had always known was waiting for it inside her - on Stephen's promise that it definitely wouldn't be permitted to spit forth any of its venom in there. And the promise had been kept during that and the next three visitations, although it did once have to spit into his hand after becoming particularly aggressive...

'You can finish off in there, if you like,' Crystal had whispered over her shoulder during the fifth deep incursion; sincerely hoping that the idea would hold as much appeal to him as it did to her.

And the rest was just history now, Crystal mused to herself, as groin smacked harder and faster against smooth bare bottom. Most workdays during the past nine months had seen her pretty little knickers wet and sticky well before it was time to start the ten minute bike ride home. And cycling back had simply made matters worse, each downward push on the pedals seeming to release more fluid into the already over-burdened panty crotch.

She'd always been careful with semen-soaked knickers, of course. She'd never allowed them to dwell in the dirty linen basket, just in case. She'd always kept them safely, and tightly, in situ until she was able to pop them into the washing machine. Her view had always been that discretion was definitely the greater part of valour so far as her newfound pastime was concerned. And anyway, she never minded the dampness; it made her feel, well, sort of naughty and nice.

How wet they'd been last month! That Wednesday afternoon when they'd managed to do it twice. Stephen had been feeling particularly randy that day. And the food store had been really quiet. There'd hardly been any customers at all. So they'd been able to indulge. Yes, how sopping wet and sticky her knicker crotch had been by the time she'd squelched through her front door en route to the washing machine.

'Ohhh! Ohhh! Ohhh!' gasped Crystal, her vaginal muscles starting a series of violent contractions as the sudden surge of hot sperm brought her to the boil as well. But even so, she made sure she kept half an eye on the door.

'Lovely fuck,' she murmured back over her shoulder, when both of them were finally through.

Half an hour later Crystal glanced up at her next customer. Oh God! It was Benny's mother. And here she was, sitting at the till in a puddle of warehouseman's come! Perhaps, just at that particular moment, the dampness of her knickers was suddenly not quite so nice.

'Hello, Crystal. How are you?'

'It's been a bit frantic,' she replied, starting to blush when she thought of the reason why she'd had to be in such a rush to get the fresh produce out onto the shelves before it was time for her to take her turn on the till. It had been kind of Robert to help out, particularly as he must have been well aware why she'd got so far behind with her work.

'Well, being busy will help to keep you out of mischief.'

'I suppose so,' she murmured, blushing even more.

'I expect you're upset about tomorrow night?'

'How do you mean?'

'About Benny having to spend a night in London because of his new job.'

'Oh, that. Um, yes. Very upset...'

'You and Cheryl could always sleep at our house, if you think you're going to feel too lonely.'

'That's very kind, but I expect I'll be okay.'

'Well, let me know if you want to come round for the night. I'm sure Benny would like you to do so.'

Crystal was sure of it, too.

At seven o'clock that evening Crystal began changing into her jeans in readiness for her evening job. She was wearing a fresh pair of almost non-existent knickers identical to those that had earlier seen the light of the working day in the cold store, but nothing else except a forced smile. 'You're off to London in the morning, Benny. I shall miss you terribly. We really ought to make things up before you go.'

He stared at the reflection of her knickered bottom in the bedroom mirror. 'You shouldn't have said what you did,' he muttered, but his mind was clearly elsewhere.

'I was just being silly,' she started. 'And anyway, you know how girls can often... oh!' she suddenly gasped, Benny having propelled her backwards onto the bed and then landed heavily on top of her. 'Oh, this is a nice surprise...'

Pulling More Than a Pint

Crystal placed the freshly pulled pint of bitter onto the bar counter and reached out to give the change to the young man who sat on the stool in front of her. He took hold of her hand instead of the money, and she made no effort to make him release it.

'So you don't have a boyfriend?' he asked, smiling sexily into her eyes.

'Not at the moment, Pete,' she replied, not entirely truthfully, because she'd not yet had the heart to tell Stephen that the shag in the cold store earlier that day had been their last. That decision had been due, in no small way, to the mortal existence of her current customer.

'Why's that?'

'Because I have a husband.' Again this wasn't strictly the whole of the truth. The continued existence of Benny at home had never curtailed her extra-curricula coitus in the cold store. Rather the opposite, in fact. But Crystal had come to learn that withholding part of the truth was an essential element of being able to get her end away with someone other than Benny.

'A husband?' he gasped in dismay.

'Yes. I'm married to Benny.'

'Benny?'

'Yes. You know. Benny who works here at the bar two evenings a week when I don't.'

'Benny? You're married to him? You're married to that prat?'

'Yes.'

Pete coloured. 'I didn't mean to be rude. I'm sorry.'

'There's no need to be. You're quite right, he is a prat.'

'Why aren't you wearing a ring?'

'I can't at the moment. This finger's still a bit inflamed and sore. I cut it in the cold store at work last month.' She blushed when she recalled the exact circumstances of the minor mishap. She couldn't really blame Stephen for the violent thrusting that had caused the pile of crates to crash to the floor all around them. After all, she'd been encouraging him to give it everything he'd got...

'I wouldn't have spent the last three weeks pestering to see you if I'd known you were married.'

'Wouldn't you? In that case I'm very glad you didn't know.'

'You mean you don't mind the way I've been pestering to see you?'

'No, I don't mind it at all. In fact I'd rather like you to see me. And I'd certainly like to see more of you.'

'Oh...'

She squeezed his hand. 'Benny's away from home all night tomorrow. His new employers are sending him on a training course for two days. Why don't you come round and we can both do lots of seeing together?'

He'd stay for a second pint, Pete decided. Well, actually, if the whole sordid truth had to be told, he'd stay so he could continue to study the delightful contours of Crystal's buttocks in those skin-tight blue jeans. That was nothing new, of course. He did it every time he was perched on this stool and she was working on the far side of the counter. Just the sight of that pretty little denim-encased bum as she stretched up to the optics on tiptoes was always enough to make him as hard as granite. And he felt even harder tonight, after the invitation she'd just given him. It was lucky he was wearing a long baggy T-shirt. Otherwise she might think he was being a trifle presumptuous.

Crystal stooped, straight-legged, to retrieve the pile of beer mats that she'd knocked to the floor, accidentally on purpose. She was well aware of the nature, and consequence, of the interest she aroused in Pete. She sighed. Men! Men and their willies! Just because her bottom was quite a nice shape.

Oh dear! It was as well that Pete couldn't get into her mind as easily as Stephen had been able to get into her hot little hole these past few months! Otherwise he might be a little surprised to learn what the aforementioned bottom had been up to over the course of the last four hours. On the other hand, maybe he wouldn't...

'Can I have a slice of that?' asked a newcomer to the bar, perched on the stool beside Pete and sipping a gin and tonic.

'Another slice of lemon?'

'No. A slice of your sweet little arse,' he replied, somewhat coarsely.

She smiled politely. 'I'm afraid that's only on sale to our regular customers.'

'I could soon become one of those.'

'Piss off, mate!' said Pete, judging that the guy was probably non-violent. 'She's with me.'

Crystal felt a warm glow in a rather familiar place...

Crystal lifted her head. 'Let's go upstairs and do it in bed,' she murmured, kicking her minuscule pink knickers off her left ankle and away from the sofa on which she was lying, thereby divesting herself of her last remaining item of clothing.

'But what about your daughter?' Pete asked dubiously. 'At least down here we can hear if she gets up and comes down the stairs.'

'She's fast asleep, and she'll stay that way. She never gets up in the night.'

'But supposing she does? Supposing she comes through to your room while we're at it like knives?'

'Then I expect you'll have trouble maintaining this rather handsome erection,' she replied, using a fingertip to flick the stiff object in question, before returning it to the warmth of her mouth.

'I'll jam a chair against the bedroom door,' she mumbled two minutes later - rather indistinctly because he was a very considerable size.

'Okay, you win,' he breathed. 'Come on, I'll follow you upstairs.'

She lifted her head from his groin once again and gave him a knowing grin. 'You just want to stare at my bare bum,' she said accusingly.

'Too bloody right I do!'

'Will it give you inspiration?'

'Let's put it this way; you might find it uncomfortable cycling to work for the next few days.'

'Mmm... that's the sort of discomfort I wouldn't mind at all.'

'And you might find you don't want to shag Benny when he comes home tomorrow night.'

'I find that all the while.'

Fortunately for everyone Crystal had been quite correct about Cheryl's sleeping habits, because Pete stayed until seven-thirty the following morning, having been too exhausted to get out of the matrimonial bed and make his way home at an earlier hour. Four highly charged bouts of sexual congress, lasting well into the small hours, had taken their toll, and both of them had slept soundly after such a marathon performance.

On his long-unawaited return from London later that evening Benny failed to notice the sea of semen stains on the bed sheets. This was largely due to Crystal's clever forward planning. The existing sheets had been replaced with fresh ones a few hours before Pete's visit, and the following day these no-longer-very-fresh ones had been in the washing machine and the originals back on the bed, well before Benny walked through the front door.

Despite the rigours of the previous night, Pete's prediction was proved wrong. Crystal was quite happy to cycle to and from work that day. Although she was significantly less happy to accommodate Benny's carnal desires on his triumphal return home, but did so anyway, basically because at that stage of her marriage she harboured the idea that a young wife should never refuse her husband, even if he was unfortunate enough to be Benny.

No Bra Too Far

One warm September morning two days later Crystal woke up in the spare bedroom, still wearing the tiny pair of knickers that had served her so well the previous evening. Benny had reached the absolute zenith of his prattishness, she sighed to herself. Last night he'd managed to get his wife fucked by someone else because of his nonsensical objection to the outfit she'd chosen to wear. An outfit entirely respectable and right for the party they were attending on one of the few balmy summer nights you were lucky enough to get in England. It was such a shame he couldn't be made aware of the consequences of his crass stupidity. It was such a shame she couldn't speak her thoughts by saying, 'Hey,

Benny, guess what I've been up to while you were sitting at home sulking.'

How stupid, Crystal asked herself in despair, could one man be? Think of the very maximum, quadruple it, and her husband was still a hundred times worse. If only her wretched mother hadn't made such a diabolical and constant fuss, she'd now have been happily married to someone as gorgeous as Pete. Benny would have had more than his fair share of her, she'd have moved on - two or three times - and finally she'd have married someone she could truly love and respect.

It had been the dungaree-suit that caused last night's argument. The burgundy coloured, needle-cord suit she'd bought for last night's end of season party at Leslie's house in the country. The one Benny had helped her choose earlier yesterday, and of which he'd thoroughly approved.

She'd driven to the holiday camp bar at which they both worked during the summer months. Benny was working that evening and she'd come to pick him up and take him to the party, together with another young couple who also worked at the camp. Almost at once she knew there was a problem. She knew it from the long black looks Benny gave her from the far side of the counter whilst serving other customers.

At last there was an opportunity to speak. 'We're not going,' he said morosely.

'Why not?' she asked, genuinely bemused.

'You're not wearing a bra.'

'What does that matter? I'm fully covered up. This suit is high-sided. You can't see anything you shouldn't.' It was true. The suit didn't display a glimpse of any part of her boobs, not even the sides. And the comfort and freedom she gained from dressing like that on a humid summer night was unbelievably good. Apart from her sandals she was wearing only two items of clothing - her dungaree-suit, and knickers of the very flimsiest kind. Knickers so small she could have folded them up and fitted them into a matchbox three times over - and still have room for all the matches. But as she'd just told herself, she was perfectly respectable. And her breasts, although of generous proportions, were firm and in no need of support.

'I'm not taking you to a party looking like that,' he said stubbornly. 'I'm not having my wife dressed up like some sort of tart.'

'Don't be stupid, Benny.' That was a mistake, she realised the second she said it. Calling him stupid always made him more stupid than ever. If such a thing was possible.

'We're not going,' he repeated.

'Well I am. And I'm taking Jim and Beth as well. It's up to you whether you come along.'

'I'm not going anywhere with you dressed like that.'

'Fine. Suit yourself. But are you quite sure you want to stay behind?'

'I've told you, I'm not taking you anywhere when you look like that.'

'Okay. Have it your way then.'

With that she rounded up the teenage couple to whom she'd promised a lift and drove off, knowing full well that Benny was expecting her to circle the block and then collect him, ready to go home with him after dropping the two youngsters off at the party.

'Well bugger that!' she said to herself. Why should she always go along with his stupid ways? Life was too short. And anyway, Pete would be at the party...

For Crystal the party was a rip-roaring success, with no Benny to scowl at her if she spoke to another man for more than thirty seconds. Everyone loved the story of why she was there on her own.

'What a prat!' she heard more than one person exclaim, referring to Benny, of course. For once she was able to act like all the other young wives whose husband's possessed a modicum of common sense; sitting on various laps and flirting innocently but outrageously. Something unthinkable if Benny had been there. Three times in the past he'd dragged her away from a party because he thought she was getting too much attention.

Just after two o'clock in the morning she was dancing with Pete. A slow smoochy dance to a slow smoochy number. She smiled impishly into his face. 'Have you recovered from the other night?' she asked, not at all innocently.

He squeezed her neatly-trousered bottom with the hand already cupped round one cheek, and then pressed his groin against hers. 'What do you think?'

She pushed back firmly, and then wriggled her hips. 'Mmm... I think I'll take that as a definite "yes".'

'Did you have any problems with Benny?'

'Only the fact that he came back.'

'Shall we shag?'

'You've just talked me into it, you silver-tongued serpent!'

'Whoops, sorry!' muttered Pete, having switched on the light in the spare bedroom only to find the bed was occupied by the young couple Crystal had brought to the party. Although still dressed it was clear they were starting to get it all together. 'But never mind. If you budge over a bit Crystal and I can join you.'

'I'm not so sure about that,' murmured Beth.

'We can turn the light off again and share the bed, can't we? I wasn't meaning we should share anything else as well.'

'Well it would be a bit embarrassing, wouldn't it?' she asked. 'What do you think, Crystal?'

'It would be just about okay, I suppose. But if it bothers you Pete and I can use Benny's car.'

'It's a deal,' said Pete. He turned back to the teenagers on the bed. 'Not a word to Benny, of course. Or anyone else.'

Beth, who lived with her parents in the same road as Crystal and Benny, wondered if she should say something to Benny before things went too far. But fortunately she didn't.

The sex in the back of Benny's car was just as torrid as the sex that had taken place in his bed earlier that week. The removal of the dungaree suit and knickers was achieved in a trice, leaving Crystal naked and naughty on the back seat. But the passion thus aroused caused a problem. In Pete's anxiety to exit his seriously overstretched trouser-fronts, the top button tore itself loose and proceeded to hide itself somewhere in the car. A fact that escaped their attention at the time.

As Pete sat facing the front of the car Crystal climbed nimbly on top of him, her knees pressing into the upholstery on either side of his lap. She reached down to his groin.

'You're an exceptionally upstanding young man,' she whispered naughtily, making final adjustments to his rigidly upright stance, before slowly lowering her tail-end onto him. Seconds later she buried him root-deep in warm, willing, wet flesh. 'Oh, yes...' she purred, lifting her head and savouring the way in which he'd opened her up so extensively. Keeping him stock-still inside her she pulled his T-shirt up over his head and tossed it onto the front seat. Then she leant forward, allowing her firm young breasts to snuggle comfortably into his chest.

He could feel the hard, pointed nipples boring hotly into him as he slid a hand round each silky-smooth buttock and squeezed. His erection seemed to gain even more strength as he sat there, patiently waiting for her to start to move. Eventually she began to lift her hips - further and further, and further still, until she'd voided him completely.

After a long pause, in order to tease him as much as she dared, she sank back down, inch by inch, enveloping him once more in the glorious pliability and wet warmth she harboured inside. But no sooner was he fully ensconced than she began to withdraw once again, very slowly, all the way, until he was exposed for the second time, to the relative cool of the night air.

'How long are you going to make me wait this time?' he croaked, his hands still exploring the firm cheeks of her bottom and his penis seeming to stretch and strain even more.

'Patience is a virtue,' she murmured, before kissing him.

Then she began frigging the tip in and out. Very gently. Just an inch or less at a time, making him groan with frustration. 'Don't you dare push up,' she warned him softly. 'Otherwise I'm going home to shag Benny and make things up with him.'

Pete decided not to take the risk - just in case. He rather suspected that Crystal's highly mischievous sense of humour could, at times, lead her to extremes. So he sat motionless on the back seat, penis aching painfully, allowing her to tease and tantalise the very end as much as she liked. Was she ever going to relent, he asked himself plaintively, and bear down on him?

Less than five minutes later everything had changed; both Crystal and Pete were pumping each other with increasing vigour. 'This is lovely,' Crystal panted. 'But at this rate we'll never make it last.'

Pete's hands were still clamped round her tight little bottom. 'Well never mind,' he muttered breathlessly. 'If this finishes too soon we can get started on the next instalment.'

'Sounds good enough to me...'

Pete sighed happily. This was a fantastic way to have her; Crystal riding him on top. Everything was available to him. Everything she possessed. He was pigging himself on every last square centimetre of her; her fanny, her bum, her boobs, and her mouth. All at the same time, if he wanted. He was shagging her as extensively as it was possible to shag a girl. Nothing was being withheld from him. Nothing was denied. And didn't she just love it. Already she'd climaxed really fiercely. What a donkey of a husband she had! What a twat! If he'd been in Benny's position he'd have treated her like a goddess. He'd have put her on a pedestal so high she'd need an oxygen mask to breathe.

Pete kneaded her neat buttocks in both hands, pressing his chest into her breasts and then pushing his tongue deep into her mouth. Now it was time to show her how strongly he felt about her...

'Hold on tight, Mrs Langley,' he growled, 'I'm moving to wharp factor five!'

Faster and harder he pumped her, seeming never to tire. Faster and harder he thrust, pounding her and bouncing her up and down on his lap, while she squeaked and squawked and squirmed. He was voiding her completely at the end of each withdrawal, then plunging back with an audible squelch. The pace was quite phenomenal and the degree of athleticism required was high. Nevertheless he continued to shaft with all his strength, thrusting into her up to the root, and then out and back again at electrifying speed. He knew he ought to be providing her with a far more varied and sophisticated service, but he just couldn't slow down. All he wanted was to fuck her harder than she'd ever been fucked before.

Crystal had no objections. He was driving her into a delightful state of oblivion with the speed and strength of the coupling. The sex was becoming slightly painful, but that simply added to the delicious feeling gathering momentum in her loins. As she allowed herself to sink down into the happy abyss that awaited her, her one negative thought was that she should never be having to get her own back on Benny this way. Why had she been so daft as to allow herself to marry him, simply to escape the diametrically opposed pressure he and her mother were exerting upon her? Six years ago, why hadn't she moved to live with her aunt hundreds of miles away, and given herself time to reflect on everything? If she'd done that Pete might even have been her husband by now.

Crystal started to spasm sharply as Pete continued to plough into her with gusto, ramming one stroke after another as ferociously as he could. And still he showed no sign of tiring or coming to the boil. With his face buried in fine firm breasts and his hands clasping silky firm buttocks he shagged on and on and on, quite unable to get anything like enough of the hot little pussy he was stretching as tight as a drum.

She closed her eyes and groaned with pleasure as the long thick pole of Pete's manhood continued to tear all the way in and out at pace. All the way up to the neck of her womb, and then all the way out of her lower lips. Again and again and again. 'Ohhh...' she moaned breathlessly, starting to push forcefully down against the power of his incoming erection, thus ensuring that with each thrust he was embedding himself in her to the absolute maximum. Then she wrapped her arms round his neck and hungrily sucked his tongue into her mouth, at the same time savouring the sensation of one monumental thrust after another slamming violently into the tightness of her overflowing vagina.

After a while she had to break the kiss and fight to regain some breath. If at all possible the thrusting then seemed to become even more violent. Crystal, in response, groaned longer and louder and wriggled her hips in delight. His fingers were buried deep into the fleshiness of her buttocks, but the discomfort only added to the pleasure she felt.

Another five, ten, fifteen minutes flew happily by, yet there was no relent. No respite for the desperate young housewife being pillaged and pummelled so mercilessly in the back of her husband's car. Not that she was the least bit interested in being shown anything remotely like mercy. She'd willingly spend the whole night being subjected to this sort of assault and battery, even though she might be a bit tender afterwards. Oh crumbs! He was making her come all over again...!

Pete's hands were still clenched round the cheeks of her bottom, damp and slippery with her juices. He was reminded of the delightful sight he'd been given of those self-same cheeks a couple of nights earlier, as they'd snaked their way across her bedroom floor less than two minutes after the conclusion of their third bout of lovemaking. Pert, plump, and excruciatingly pretty they'd been, and as naked as nature intended. And, to add just that touch of piquancy, liberally daubed with streaks of freshly shot semen. Thick white streaks smeared decoratively across the glossy pink cheeks of a posterior so perfectly moulded and formed that his over-used penis started to stiffen and stir there and then.

There and then as he laid on the dishevelled bed-sheets watching her sticky bottom wiggle and jiggle and wink at him from six feet or so away.

'You'd better get back into bed,' he'd croaked. 'Something's just come up!'

She'd looked back at him over her shoulder. 'Surely not another matter arising?' she asked with a quizzical stare.

Still fixed on the mental image of those saucy sperm-laced buttocks sliding so mischievously from side to side as she crossed the room, Pete gasped, then moaned, then groaned, and then began to vent himself violently inside her.

For the fifth time that week she felt him start to implant her. She felt his thick juices spilling copiously into her womb, the ferocity of each burst flooding her insides within seconds. Almost instantly her climax was renewed. She gasped with delight as her vaginal muscles proceeded to contract in a series of vicelike grips around the iron-hard shaft forced against the top of her channel, instilling her with wave after wave of boiling seed. 'Oh, Pete...' she groaned. 'That just feels just so good...'

Some ten minutes later Crystal was curled up on the back seat in Pete's arms, as naked as before but now happily full of his fluid. Suddenly there came the sound of a hand banging on the car roof, followed by a male voice calling, 'Pete, are you coming in now? Leslie's starting to lock up.'

Pete was intending to doss down in the house overnight.

'That didn't sound like Jim,' said Pete.

Crystal sat up and peered out into the gloom, fingertips demurely covering her nipples. 'No, it didn't. I hope he hasn't been telling everyone what we're up to.'

She rummaged hurriedly through her handbag. 'Damn! I don't have any tissues in here. And I'm absolutely awash. Do you have any?'

'I haven't got my handbag with me.'

'Ha, ha... I'll just have to use my knickers to make running repairs, I suppose. If I can ever find where you threw them. Oh God, I'm really and truly swamped...'

'Bugger it! The top button's missing from my trousers.'

'You shouldn't have been in such a red-hot hurry to get out of them and into me.'

'Are you complaining, woman?'

'Not in the least. But I can't let Benny find a man's trouser button in the back of his car, can I? Particularly the day after I leave him behind and go to a party on my own. I'll have to pull up under a streetlight on the way home and search for it.'

'I'd quite like it back. My mother could sew it back on.'

'I'd quite like it out of Benny's car. That's all I'm concerned about. Otherwise your mother might have to sew my arms and legs back on.'

Crystal stood naked in her kitchen, feeding the previous night's crusty knickers into the washing machine. Benny hadn't locked her out last night, as she'd half expected. Probably because he'd needed the car to get to work and had concluded, correctly for once, that it wouldn't have been there if he'd denied her access to the house.

She shook her head sadly. 'Benny, you berk,' she muttered to herself. 'You refuse to take your wife to a party because she's not wearing a bra, and as a result she ends up on the back seat of your car not wearing anything at all. What in God's name happened to the man I thought I was marrying?'

Epilogue - Joining the Queue

'Get in the queue?' Julian gasped in surprise. 'What the hell do you mean, I'll have to get in the queue?'

'Exactly what I said,' Crystal replied mischievously. 'You'll have to get in the queue.'

'What sort of fucking queue is this?'

'Just that. A queue for those who want to fuck me. You'll have to wait your turn.'

Julian couldn't believe what he was hearing. He'd never had this sort of trouble before. She was only a slip of a girl, more than twelve years his junior. And clearly pissed off with her terminal tit of a husband. Which anyone could readily understand; even Tony, after his fifteenth triple pernod, ice, and water. 'And just how many men are there in this queue of yours?' he asked eventually.

'Only Pete. You don't know him. He's divorced, with a bachelor flat on the other side of town. Although technically, I suppose he's not actually in the queue at all, because he's already been well and truly in me - lots and lots of times. But he may not be available for that sort of thing much longer. Very unfortunately. He's looking for a job away from here. Perhaps I should have told you to form a queue, not join one? Would that have been better, do you think? Would that have been expressing myself more clearly? Would that have been easier for you to get your head around?'

'You cheeky little morsel! I ought to put you over my knee and spank the living daylights out of you.'

'Perhaps you'll get the chance to do it, if you ever manage to fight your way out of the queue. Pete has told me several times I'm such a saucy cow that it must be my ultimate destiny to get myself soundly spanked one day.'

Eight months later, Julian did manage to fight his way out of the one-man queue. And a while after that, following her umpteenth mischievous remark or minor misdemeanour, he helped her to fulfil her ultimate destiny. Not that the punishment made any difference to the sauciness of her subsequent conduct, even though it was almost forty-eight hours before she dared let Benny catch sight of her still slightly blushing cheeks. Despite the incredible sex that followed, she asked herself at the time, had the pain and discomfort been worthwhile? Yes, she decided, five years later - Benny having made his long overdue departure and Jonathan having become the full-time partner she'd always wanted to be able to love, honour, cherish... and fuck till the spunk flew out of her ears.

CHAPTER SIX - ANGELA UNCOVERED

Angela was bent right forward across the mahogany writing table, red-faced and very bare-bottomed. Her boldly patterned summer dress and frilly white petticoat had been pushed right up her back, and a tiny pair of filmy white knickers clung saucily to her nicely rounded thighs, just below the tops of her stockings. She stood straight-legged, elbows and forehead resting on the surface of the desk, her buttocks several inches above the level of her head. Her long black hair had fallen in front of her eyes, and was spread out on the desktop in an almost exact semicircle.

Her husband, Keith, stood directly behind the perfect full moon of her bottom, gazing down with mixed feelings at that which she was offering so invitingly. The cheeks were delightfully dimpled and resembled an inverted heart, plump but firm and pert, the cleft between deep. The texture of those dearly cherished cheeks, he knew, was impeccable; silk and cream combined. As he stood admiring her rounded buttocks they gleamed proudly up at him, reflecting the overhead light in the centre of each pouting cheek. And while they gleamed, they also shivered very slightly.

Keith stared intently at the pale twin peaks that had afforded him such pleasure during six years of marriage and two years of courtship before. They were the pride and joy of his conjugal collection. Even after all that time he could still scarcely keep his eyes and hands off them, even in public. Big, bare, beautifully shaped buttocks they were. Buttocks that, six years ago, she'd vowed to keep only unto him. Buttocks so smooth and vibrantly lubricant that, in their present stance, they simply sucked his breath away. Buttocks so prettily turned up towards him that they brought teardrops to his eyes, as well...

He could almost imagine they were blushing demurely at their present unfortunate predicament. There seemed to be a slightly pinker hue to the fullest parts, just as if they were expressing the discomfort they felt as they pouted up at him, so exposed and helpless in their plight. Just as if they were embarrassed by the current situation.

Keith swallowed hard. What a poignant spectacle she made. White slip, white knickers, white suspenders, and that classically sculpted bottom pointing up at him betwixt frothy suspender belt and matching stocking-tops. A spectacle so misleadingly virginal in appearance. He was strongly reminded of their wedding day, when he'd fucked her in her full wedding regalia before the reception had even started.

He was hugely tempted to manhandle that rump. But it would be totally amiss, given the prevailing circumstances. Instead he'd just feast his eyes upon it for a little longer. He'd savour, with the same mixed feelings as before, the perfectly formed cheeks that reared up directly ahead of him. They were such an appealing shape that women, as well as men, turned their heads in the street to stare after them, particularly when she was in her tight denim jeans...

Were many women, he wondered, turned on by the sight of a shapely female bottom? Angela freely admitted that her best friend, Tracie Trix, still found it difficult to keep her hands to herself when the two of them were alone together. But that was Tracie for you. She just fancied anything that moved, male or female. He had to confess that sometimes it was quite exciting to recall how his own wife had once been seduced by her closest female friend. The thought of another woman bringing Angela to orgasm by finger-fucking that gorgeous bottom was really rather erotic. He'd have felt very differently, however, had it been done by a man.

At length he spoke. 'Five minutes ago you say, Mr Harris?' he murmured thoughtfully, turning towards the pinstriped managing director who stood at his side.

'Yes, no more than that. I summoned you at once, knowing that you worked on the next floor. I trust I did the right thing?'

'Indeed you did, Mr Harris. Indeed you did. She was in this very pose, is that right?'

'Yes, Mr James. Partially unclothed and bent forward across my desk, exactly as you see her now. I ordered her to remain in that position until you arrived, of course.'

'I'm very much obliged to you. You've acted impeccably, I must say.'

'Thank you. I assumed that was what you'd desire.'

'You were entirely correct. So, at your instruction, she's retained this position over your office desk ever since you interrupted matters a few minutes ago?'

'Exactly so. I told her she was to stay in situ until you answered my call. I felt it was for the best, so you could perceive all matters for yourself in order to know all that had transpired and thereby form a properly balanced judgement.'

'And the other man? This marketing consultant? This Jonathan Crowe?'

'He was, of course, removed from the scene the very second he'd got back into his clothes.'

'He was mounted on her back?'

'I'm afraid that is the case.'

'And they were actually fornicating when you arrived on the scene?'

'Yes indeed, Mr James. I'm sorry.'

Keith looked back at his wife's upthrust buttocks, deep in thought. 'They were still fornicating, you say? In which case,' he said slowly, 'it would seem that the full act of coitus was never actually completed?'

Mr Harris coughed apologetically into his hand. 'I questioned the man, of course. While he was making himself decent. Since they believed I'd be away from the office for the rest of the day, it does appear that the sexual congress started some while ago. When I disturbed them it would seem that it was, um, how should I put it? Second helpings...'

'I see.'

'I'm sorry, Mr James. But I feel you should be in possession of all material facts.'

'Yes, of course. Thank you, Mr Harris. That is exactly as I would wish. Shall we now proceed along the lines you have already suggested? I think the time is right.'

'Indeed it is, Mr James.' He looked across to the youngest of his two personal assistants, both of whom were standing stiffly to attention by the window to his left. 'Jason!'

'Yes Sir?'

'Ask my secretary to arrange for those items I mentioned earlier to be brought up here from the gentlemen's cloakroom as soon as possible, if you please.'

'Certainly, Sir,' he replied, reaching for the nearby phone.

'Now then, Mr James. As you say, the time is certainly very right indeed. This young lady has not only broken the terms of her engagement with my company, but she has also breached the even more serious contract of matrimony into which she entered with you. The time could not be more right, in fact. Examples have to be made, and erring wives have to be discouraged, as do errant employees. This wayward young woman has to be shown the folly of her ways, as do her female work colleagues, in a bid to discourage any similarly disgraceful behaviour on their part. Let justice be done! And even more importantly, let justice be seen, heard, and *felt* to be done!'

The two men assumed their positions behind and to either side of her. Keith, who was right-handed, stood to her left, while Mr Harris, who was conveniently left-handed, stood to her right. They looked at each other gravely, and after a pause Mr Harris nodded his head.

Crack! The heavy palm of her husband's right hand welted her bare left cheek, sending a sound like a report from a pistol echoing throughout the office, instantly followed by a high-pitched squawk of pain.

In the adjoining partitioned rooms the men grinned broadly, while the girls giggled and blushed. Due retribution, they knew, was now being taken for the manner in which the boss' desk had been so improperly defiled.

As her left cheek coloured and bounced Mr Harris struck with all his force. *Crack!* His left hand splattered her right cheek just as noisily as Keith's had blasted the left. She yelped again, her right cheek quickly beginning to emulate the left. While those listening in the neighbouring rooms held their breath the two men adjusted their stance and readied themselves to proceed at pace.

Crack! Keith again landed his right hand on her left buttock as forcefully as he could, making her squeal again.

Crack! Mr Harris landed his left on her right.

Crack! Keith splattered her left.

Crack! Mr Harris splattered her right.

Crack! Keith on her left.

Crack! Mr Harris on her right. Mr Harris was left-handed, she remembered. Which was why he was able to make such a joint and equal contribution to her suffering.

Crack! Keith on her left.

Crack! Mr Harris on her right.

127

Crack! Keith again on her left.

'Wretched girl!' hissed Mr Harris, once again welting her right buttock with all his might.

'Yes indeed!' snarled Keith, blasting her equally powerfully on her left.

'Take that!' hissed Mr Harris. 'And that! And that! And that!'

'And that, and that, and that!' Keith snarled with equal venom.

And so on and so on for ages, her stricken bottom bouncing vigorously up and down and starting to glow as brightly as a beacon at night.

'Wretched, wretched, wretched girl!' Mr Harris walloped her six times in a row on her right cheek, heightening her distress.

'Wretched, wanton hussy!' Keith repeated the treatment on her left.

'Wretched, wretched, wretched girl!'

'Wretched, wretched, wanton hussy!'

On and on and on went the chastisement, their weighty male hands relentless and without mercy as one blow after another landed loudly across rapidly overheating cheeks, while tears ran steadily down her face at the severity of the unremitting punishment.

After some considerable while the men turned their attention to the tops of her thighs, painting them to the same vivid hue as the bountiful buttocks above. Now she was a sea of colour from a point just below the small of her back all the way down to her lacy white stocking-tops.

At last the men stepped back to scrutinise their handiwork. Keith had always been proud of her bottom, but now it was even more breathtaking than usual. And in a strange way he appreciated the fact that he'd been able to share such beauty with somebody else. Somebody, he said to himself, grinding his teeth, other than that so-and-so of a marketing consultant whose seminal fluid would, at that very moment, be dribbling slowly but surely down her legs...

His resolve was strengthened and his eyes settled on the two matching clothes brushes that had by now arrived from the gentlemen's cloakroom. Two heavy, wooden, long-handled clothes brushes that looked to have been made for the occasion.

Mr Harris followed his gaze. 'Yes. Thank you for bringing these to me so promptly, Miss Talbot,' he said to his secretary as she stood near the filing cabinet, surreptitiously admiring the view.

'It's my pleasure, sir.'

'Yes. Quite.' He turned to Keith. 'Shall we?' he enquired politely.

'Why not?' came the response.

Angela glanced back over her shoulder, observing the men, each with a clothes brush in hand. Her bottom already felt swollen and bruised, as well as incredibly hot. She longed to be able to rub it with both hands, but realised she'd have to wait. She also realised that the unyielding clothes brushes would inflict yet more swelling, bruising, and heat before her torment was over...

At long length the four other persons present concurred with Mr Harris that justice had been done, and Angela was allowed into an upright stance. Not before time, she thought ruefully, the front of her dress soaked with her tears.

Then with her dress still rolled above her waist, and her knickers strung tautly across her thighs, she was directed to stand in the corner, facing the wall in disgrace. There she would have to stay, her hands well away from her blistered cheeks, until released back to the typing pool, tearstained and red in the face - but much redder elsewhere.

Mr Harris handed one of the clothes brushes to Keith with a sympathetic smile. 'Take it home, my dear fellow. Take it home and use it on her as often and hard as you like. It's the least I can do in the circumstances. It's the ideal implement for use on a straying wife. Take it home and use it on her as you will. Use it on her with my compliments, please do. At least once a day, I suggest.'

'Thank you, Mr Harris. You've been most understanding. Keep the other one here in your office and feel free to use it in exactly the same way, I beg you.'

Chapter Seven - Alison and the Pre-emptive Strike

Hi, I'm Alison North. Perhaps you read my last book, *Painful Consequences*? If you did, then you might like to hear a little more about my own personal experiences OTK or, indeed, elsewhere. If you didn't, then perhaps you might like to anyway. So here we go...

My recommendation to all respectably married young ladies attending an intimate dinner party for four at a friend's house is this: do not wear a short cocktail dress for the occasion. Alternatively, if you do, make sure you're wearing a heavy-duty pair of high-waisted tights, as opposed to stockings and suspenders. And if all this excellent advice still falls on deaf ears, then you should at least salve some of the guilty conscience from which you will later suffer by enduring a pre-emptive strike at the hands of your long-suffering husband.

'A pre-emptive strike?' do I hear you ask?

Yes, a pre-emptive strike, I reply.

You know what I mean, don't you? Or at least you can surely guess? Being soundly spanked in advance, of course. Suffering your girlie bottom being severely punished before you've actually committed the crime.

Believe me, the painfully unpleasant experience really does help with the pangs of guilt.

Believe me, because I know. And you'll know too, if you allow me to tell you all about the disastrous Saturday evening Michael and I spent at Jonathan and Rosalind's house last week...

The day started badly, although it got better before it got worse again. Without thinking, I was insensitive enough to make some sort of stupidly flippant remark to Michael about the way he'd caught me misbehaving myself with George Franks at that boozy party the previous month. I realised my mistake at once, but it was too late. Next moment I was over his knee and undergoing the same sort of really hard hand-spanking I'd had to endure as soon as he'd got me home from the party. Then the spanking was concluded with three of the very best from the vicious cane he'd bought from a sex shop the morning after the party.

But we made it up in bed almost immediately afterwards. I told him - as we fucked like fiends - that I was really sorry about what had happened at the party. And that it would never happen again. And that I should never have made a silly joke about it, because I understood how he felt and how he was entitled to be so cross. And he said he was really sorry for hurting my bottom again and making me cry, because I'd previously suffered enough for my indiscretion with George. I have to admit though, that the lovemaking was considerably enhanced for both of us by the way he'd just dealt with me over his knee. It's strange how that can work, isn't it?

So, by the time I slid off the bed the pain was virtually forgotten and had been replaced by that lovely 'fucked and floating' feeling that most young wives will understand.

Anyway, soon it was Saturday evening. I'd just finished dressing and applying my makeup. 'How do I look?' I asked him, twirling round in a circle so my sexy little dress spun up to reveal lace-topped stockings and skimpy knickers that matched.

'So fuckable I can hardly keep my hands off you,' he growled, advancing on me even as he spoke. 'In fact, so fuckable I can't keep my hands off you.'

'Michael!' I squealed in protest as he bent me right forward across the dressing table. 'Don't you dare! I've spent ages getting ready for tonight! And we're horribly late as it is...'

But he took not the slightest notice. Not that I'd really expected he would. He's a raging animal whenever the urge is suddenly visited upon him. I'm totally delighted to say. Before I could object any further my dress was above my waist and my pink panties around my thighs, just an inch or so below the tops of my stockings. I could feel his eyes all over the cheeks of my bottom. And I just knew he was admiring the way they were still lined and blushing fiercely from his earlier mistreatment of them.

I gasped as he thrust into me from behind. I was already wet in anticipation. It doesn't take a lot to turn me on; as you might just possibly have gathered from my previous quality work of art. But I knew the shagging wouldn't last very long. It never does when the mood takes him like that. All of a sudden, out of the blue, I mean.

Gripping me tightly round the waist his hard stomach muscles and groin began beating vigorously against me. Very quickly I heard him gasp, then moan, then groan, and then I felt his creamy fluid pumping powerfully into my womb. 'That's lovely,' I whispered over my shoulder.

Five minutes later we were on our way to the dinner party, and I was learning to live with the combination of sticky knickers and a red-hot bum. We'd known Jonathan and Rosalind for years. Jonathan and Rosalind, our hosts for the evening. I liked them both, even though Jonathan was a really cheeky young devil who'd been trying - but failing - to get me outside my knickers ever since

Ros had introduced me to her new boyfriend five years earlier.

So there we were, one hour after dinner had finally finished. Just the four of us, as Tommy and Jillie had called off at the last minute. Michael and Ros in one corner of the living room, smooching to the sexy music from the hi-fi. And me perched warmly on Jonathan's lap as he sprawled back in a large armchair. Perched high on his unmistakably masculine lap, and my short flared cocktail dress - whilst protecting my modesty from the eye - meant I was, in effect, sitting on him in nothing more than my tiny silk knickers. There was no other protection between me and his bulging trousers. No other layer of clothing. The seat of my dress was around but not underneath me. A fact of which Jonathan obviously approved, since inside his jeans I could feel his erection jammed happily against the fleshiest part of my bottom, pulsing with life. Hidden from view in this way he began to flex his penile muscles, grinning knowingly at me as he did so.

'Now you can feel exactly what I think of you,' he murmured, far too quietly for Michael and Rosalind to hear above the music.

'I've felt it before,' I giggled. 'Almost every time I dance with you, in fact.' I looked across the room to where the others were locked together in each other's arms. 'And I'm sure Ros can feel much the same sort of thing right now.'

For the next ten minutes I remained comfortably curled up on top of him, enjoying the way his manly presence was making me lubricate so nicely. It was only a bit of fun, after all. Jonathan knew I had no intention of letting him have his way. I'd lost count of the number of times I'd made that perfectly clear to him.

Then disaster struck our small party. The booze ran out! So the men hastened on foot to the nearest pub, for a quick couple of pints and to return with fresh supplies.

'Let's dance?' suggested Ros, holding out a hand to guide me up from the armchair. We slipped easily into each other's arms and began to move to the wafting tones from the CD. Within seconds I could feel both her hands exploring the cheeks of my bottom, slowly and lovingly. I reciprocated at once, liking the feel of her round rump in lieu of the usual bony male buttocks.

'It's been so long,' she sighed, before sliding a hot tongue deep into my mouth and making me gush.

I knew what she meant. We'd been best friends all our lives, and had spent many a delightful time petting each other to the point of orgasm. But not in recent times. Not since Ros had married Jonathan and I'd got serious with Mikey. We simply hadn't got round to doing it. Not that we regarded it as wrong. We just hadn't found, or made, the opportunity. That's all. I don't think of it as being unfaithful. I don't think of it as being sex. Not really. More like an expression of your appreciation of the female qualities of the other girl. Mind you, I'm not absolutely sure that Michael would see it that way.

Our hands were now in the crotch of each others' knickers, pampering and pleasing in the way a girl can so please another girl.

Eventually Ros broke our kiss and stared urgently into my face. 'Let me do it to you, Allie,' she whispered. 'Let me do it to you right now.'

'Anytime for you,' I replied with feeling, allowing her to ease my damp panties down my thighs until they fluttered silently to the floor in sweet surrender. Then, with my dress around my waist, I sank back into the armchair and Ros knelt between my silk-stockinged legs, gazing with affection at the shaven pink opening that was so glisteningly wet and ready to be taken.

'I love your bare pussy,' she giggled wickedly. 'She looks good enough to eat...'

I began to groan with a mixture of desire and frustration as she ran the tip of her tongue lightly round and round the outer lips.

'Oh, Ros...' I gasped, writhing my head from side to side while she continued to tease and torment.

'Sweet little pussy,' she cooed, gently kissing the wet flesh. 'Sweet little, hot little pussy...'

I tried to encourage her deeper inside me, but she refused to rush anything. Once again she kissed me where I yearned and burned for her to probe. 'Sweet little, wet little cunt...'

At last she began to lick inside with her tongue. Slowly and deliberately. Gradually she probed deeper, making me climax so sweetly. The sort of soft, gentle orgasm a girl can only have with another girl. Eventually she was able to remain patient no longer and began to eat me with the appetite I knew she possessed. I parted my legs as far as I could and moaned pitifully as she forced her tongue and lips in to the depths. And the more she gobbled the stronger my climax became, causing me to squeal with delight while her head worked between my bare upper thighs. I wriggled my hips from side to side and pushed down with my hands on the back of her head, hoping she might penetrate me even further.

Ros came up for air, her mouth and chin glistening with the honey-sweet elixir of my loins. 'You taste beautiful,' she breathed hotly. 'Sort of spunky? Am I right?'

'Yes. Mikey and I had a bit of a session just before we came out. Just very quickly. You know how it is.'

She slipped her hands under my bare bottom. 'Christ, your bum's hot. Did he have a go at that as well?'

'Yes. This morning.'

'So you've been spanked as well as spunked?'

'That's right.'

'Actually, Jonathan bought a video in Amsterdam last week called something very much like that. *Spunked and Spanked*, I think that was the title. Or maybe it was a little bit longer?

'Oh...'

'He thought it would be a bit of a laugh for all of us to watch it later tonight.'

'Oh...'

'But he can't find it anywhere. Silly bugger must have left it on the ferry.'

'Oh,' I said again, this time with relief.

Slowly and gently she slid her hands back and forth underneath me. 'You've been caned as well?'

'Yes.'

'I can feel the ridges. Three of them. They feel enormous. Does it hurt very much?'

'Quite a lot. But it's bearable, just about.'

'Why did he do it?'

'Do you remember that wild party I told you about? At Keith and Angela's? Well, I made some stupid joke about tumble dryers. You know, referring to the way he'd caught me with George Franks, bending forward over that tumble dryer.'

'Oh, I see.'

'It wasn't totally my fault. With George, I mean. I'd had far too much vodka and tonic. And Mikey had spent ages dancing and canoodling with his ex-fiancée, Jennie Jamieson.'

'You said he spanked you afterwards?'

'Yes. Very hard indeed. He was furious. Then next morning he went out and bought a cane and used it on me with all his strength. I could hardly sit down for two days.'

'I wish Jonathan would do something like that to me,' she sighed. 'The idea really appeals.'

'I can't think why. It hurts like hell.'

'Doesn't it make you feel extra randy afterwards?'

'Not the cane, no.'

'I'd love Jonathan to do that to me. But I don't quite like to mention it.'

'It is difficult, I suppose.'

'Anyway,' she laughed, 'now you can be as naughty as you like, as you've already paid the price earlier today.'

'Eh?'

'You can be as naughty with me as you like, because you've already been punished in advance.'

'But that was because of what happened at last month's party.'

'Yes, but he'd previously spanked you and caned you for that, hadn't he?'

'True...'

'So now you're licensed to have a bit of fun. You've paid for it in advance.'

'I hadn't thought of it like that, I must say.'

'Well you should.'

'Perhaps you're right. After all, George only had his dick inside me for about ten seconds when Michael interrupted us. So I'd only been a teeny-bit unfaithful.'

'Why was Michael coming into the utility room in the first place? Was he taking Jennie in there to fuck her?'

'I don't think so. I didn't see her anywhere. But on the other hand I was rather busy trying to disengage myself from George. He hadn't heard Michael come through the door, you see. So he didn't want to stop. There I was, bare-bottomed and jammed over the top of the dryer, desperately trying to dislodge him while he kept pumping away from behind and asking what was wrong. It was hideously embarrassing.'

'I bet.'

I blushed and giggled. 'Michael eventually pulled him off me and punched him on the jaw. Then he dragged me off home with my knickers still round my knees! He was livid!'

'What about George?'

'Oh, Ros, I know it's awful, but he looked so funny! The last I saw of him he was sitting on the floor, groaning and clutching his face, but with his dick still hard and pointing up at the ceiling! I think the sight of that must have made Michael even angrier. You could see it was dripping wet with my juices.'

'Well as I've just said, he's already dealt with you for all that. He shouldn't have done it to you again this morning.'

'Maybe not. But he was pretty upset about that stupid joke.'

'Did you fuck afterwards? This morning, I mean?'

'Yes. Like crazy.'

'It was extra good because of what he'd just done to your bottom?'

'Yes, I suppose that's true.'

'Wouldn't you like him to do it again sometime?'

'I don't know, Ros. As I said, it hurts like hell at the time.'

'I've had my bum beaten once. By a girl in my car. Then she made love to me. I've never enjoyed anything so much in my life. But I've never seen her again. I must try to get Jonathan to do it.'

'You'd better let him catch you having it off with someone else,' I laughed. 'I was only joking,' I added quickly.

'I know. Now then, let's both of us share the taste of your pussy,' she suggested, before kissing me passionately.

Then her face was between my thighs once again, her mouth pleasuring me even more than before. Eagerly I unzipped my dress, pulling down the top and unclipping my front-loading half-cup bra. Big, firm breasts burst happily into view, tipped with nipples so erect and sharply pointed that they felt they were about to burst. These I began to rub between forefinger and thumb, adopting the same rhythm as Ros' tongue inside me.

'Oh Ros,' I groaned, shuddering more wildly than ever. Her hands were gripping my bottom quite painfully and her tongue was spearing me so powerfully I thought I'd simply die. I squeezed my boobs and nipples even harder, gasping uncontrollably at the sharp pangs of desire racing back and forth between breasts and groin. Suddenly I could tell Ros was climaxing too. I could feel it pulsing through her. Like an electric charge. I remembered she'd always enjoyed the giving of pleasure almost as much as its receipt. Which was just as well, I can recall thinking. Since there wouldn't be the time for me to repay her in kind.

I was just about seen-to when we heard the sound of a key in the lock. Ros stood up quickly, licking her lips in appreciation. 'Don't forget your knickers,' she giggled, stooping to retrieve them from the middle of the carpet.

I got to my feet, rather unsteadily, boobs back under cover. 'That was good,' I croaked as she pressed the pink flimsies into my hand. 'Really, really good...'

Alcohol began to flow once more. Michael and Ros were dancing again and I was back on Jonathan's lap, his over-stretched penis pressed powerfully into the plumpness of my knickered behind, just as before. The wretched thing seemed to have a life of its own as it wriggled and writhed against me under cover of my short dress. But at least it was safely tucked away inside his trousers, I reflected, unable to prevent myself returning the compliment by wriggling back. As unobtrusively as I could, of course. Michael might well have guessed exactly what I was sitting on, but it just wouldn't have been right for me to have been seen to be enjoying it too blatantly.

I didn't object when Jonathan surreptitiously slid his hand underneath my bottom. After all, it's a fairly standard ploy in that sort of situation, whether on the dance floor or elsewhere, isn't it? The fact that it had accidentally slipped inside my knickers was neither here nor there. At least, that was what I was easily able to persuade myself as he started to stroke. Now I had two reasons for lubricating into the crotch of my panties. Both his penis and palm were moving firmly against the cheekiest part of my person. But it was only a bit of harmless fun. And anyway, Michael was clearly enjoying himself too. His arms were wrapped right around Ros as the two of them danced slowly and closely together. And I could see her groin was pressed enthusiastically into his. Again, a perfectly normal occurrence between friends after such a boatload of booze. I nibbled the lobe of Jonathan's ear, relaxed and happy with the way the evening was passing.

'I understand you've been spanked as well as caned,' he murmured into my ear. 'Do you?'

'Yes. Ros told me when we were in the kitchen together. She knows how much I fancy your sweet little arse. I think she decided to try to frustrate me with the thought of it all swollen and sore and striped by the cane.'

'Do you indeed?' I asked, raising my eyebrows in mock surprise. Ros had obviously made a start on getting him to put her across his lap.

'Three of the best,' he enthused. 'I can feel the lines across you.'

'Don't squeeze,' I warned him anxiously.

'I'd love to do that to Ros. But she's never given me cause.'

'Maybe you don't need cause?'

'How do you mean?'

'You'd better talk to her about it. I have a very strong feeling she'd like the idea.'

'Do you think so?' he enquired excitedly. 'Has she said so?'

'More or less,' I confirmed.

'Great!' he breathed happily, at the same time saucily moving his hand downward, thereby drawing the rather insubstantial seat of my flimsy knickers down to the tops of my thighs. But of course this was all out of sight. So I wasn't really concerned, even though my bottom was now totally bare on his lap. Short

135

though the cocktail dress might have been, it was more than adequately concealing my bareness from our partners. Actually, to be honest, it felt rather nice. Naughty but rather nice, sitting in front of the others with my naked rear being appreciated by another man.

I leant forward, briefly lifting the aforesaid part of my person a few inches off his lap, and took a refreshing sip from the glass of vodka and tonic resting on the coffee table in front of me. But instead of following my very vulnerable posterior with his hand, as I'd fully expected, Jonathan seemed to be fiddling with his crotch. Adjusting himself, I decided. Making his overgrown member a little more comfortable inside those tight blue jeans. And who could have blamed him for that? I'd been able to gauge its size and power for myself. Space must have been very restricted inside his underwear, I thought, visualising the scene in there, a mental image of his fiercely erect penis making me even wetter than ever between the tops of my legs.

Oh well, I sighed to myself, taking another glug of my drink before replacing the glass on the table and then starting to lower my bottom back towards his lap. This wasn't meant to be taken seriously. It was only a bit of a giggle. Nothing more than a spot of harmless fun. Even though the shortness of my dress had probably just given him a glimpse of the handiwork the cane had woven upon me. And at least Michael and Ros couldn't see what he was fiddling with. They were dancing in the corner of the room directly in front of me, with the result that I was obscuring Jonathan's mid-section from their view...

As I eased myself down onto his lap I felt his hand underneath me once more. But strangely, and somewhat uncomfortably, it seemed to be bunched into a fist. Then he wrapped his left arm round my waist from behind and hoisted me even further back towards him. Suddenly I perceived the terrible truth. Suddenly I realised that his zip was undone and in the palm of his right hand he was holding something hot, hard, and horribly familiar! I could feel the bulbous end of his scalding organ as he thrust it up between my legs - just above the spot where my displaced panties were strung uselessly across my thighs.

'Jonathan!' I hissed in alarm, understanding only too well his evil intent. 'Jonathan! Stop that at once!'

Desperately I tried to wriggle away but his arm held me fast. Then he pulled back with his hand and pushed his groin hard against me again. 'Oh, Jesus,' I groaned in dismay, feeling several inches of thick cock sliding into me with consummate ease. Sliding into my far-too-welcoming wet channel, and stretching me with its girth. I twisted and turned on his lap in the hope of dislodging him, but he was already too well ensconced. Anxiously I peered across the room, and was hugely relieved to see that neither of the other two was taking any notice of the silent struggle on the armchair.

Despite my fiercely whispered protests Jonathan pressed forward against me once more, and another two or three inches forced its way inside, opening me even wider...

'Stop it,' I gasped helplessly, but without any real expectation that he would.

He no longer needed his hand to guide himself in. As a result both arms were locked round my waist, pinning me down on his lap and making it quite impossible for me to get away from his intrusive presence. And the more I struggled the deeper he sank. The more I struggled the more he forced a deeper invasion into the yielding privacy of my sopping person, poking harder and harder against the neck of my womb. 'Stop it,' I said again, but all to no avail.

By now it was a fait accompli and I was obliged to give up and sit still on his lap, his swollen pole of penis firmly embedded in me right up to the root. It felt as if it ought to be reaching the back of my throat...

He loosened his hold on my waist. After all, he'd nothing to fear. I was so comprehensively hooked that I could scarcely have escaped if I'd tried. And anyway, how could I possibly have tried? How could I have stood up? How could I have stood up and left that huge swathe of bone-hard flesh waggling wetly in the air for all to see? I had no option but to sit there on his lap while he skewered me all the way up to the top of my over-poked hole. He felt incredibly big inside me, partly enhanced I suppose because of the angle at which he was impaling me. He was like a steel bar riveting my insides together. Then he bore up against the ample springiness of my buttocks, at the same time pushing me down onto his groin, thereby forcing every last living centimetre deep inside.

'Isn't that nice?' he breathed hotly and happily, buried right up to the hilt in warm, wet tightness.

I tried to disagree, but slowly and surely I could feel his sheer bulk starting to make me come.

I looked anxiously down at my lap to ensure that everything was still hidden from view. The front hem of my dress was an inch or so above the tops of my stockings, but everything else was safely concealed. And I could tell that the seat was just about doing its duty, albeit it with nothing to spare. I couldn't help envisaging the scene had that little dress not existed. There I'd have been, sitting on Jonathan's groin, his flies wide open and the base of his over-grown cock disappearing into me between the cheeks of my knicker-free bottom. What a picture that would have presented! As it was the dress was a perfect curtain, screening the bare essentials of our coital embrace, but nothing more. Literally nothing more. Had it been any shorter the tautly stretched line of displaced knicker material would have been visible just below the junction of buttocks and thighs.

Jonathan shifted position slightly, making me gasp at the power of the movement inside me. He was implanted so deeply and tightly that there seemed not a millimetre of space left unoccupied.

To my horror Ros turned down the music and then she and Michael flopped down onto the settee opposite us. 'Would you like me to top up your drink, Al?' Michael asked politely, while I was sure I was coming apart at the seams.

As I opened my mouth to reply the despicable Jonathan flexed his dick inside me. Quite deliberately, I'm sure. 'N-no, thank you,' I only just managed to stammer. 'I think I've had more than enough...'

'Really?' Jonathan asked innocently, flexing himself really hard again. I was crammed so full of him that it made me want to close my eyes and faint away.

'Surely you've had this much before?' he enquired.

'You do look rather flushed,' said Michael, leaning forward to peer into my face in concern. 'Would you like to go for a stroll in the fresh air?'

I shook my head, not trusting myself to formulate the words I needed.

Michael looked more than a trifle worried, making me colour even more deeply as he continued to stare. 'Perhaps I should take you home to bed,' he said at last.

I made a supreme effort to control myself. It wasn't easy, of course. I mean, how many of you girls would like to have been sitting there just a couple of feet or so away from your husband, with somebody else's prick rammed all the way up inside you? 'I'm all right, Michael. Thank you. Just a bit tired. I'll just sit here for a while longer. Why don't you and Ros have another dance? I'm perfectly okay. Really I am.'

I reached forward for my drink in an effort to convince him, wincing inwardly at the discomfort it caused.

'Well, if you're sure?'

'Y-yes, Mikey. P-p-perfectly sure...'

Ros chipped in next. 'Go up to the bathroom and splash some cold water on your face. I always find that helps. I'll come with you, if you like?'

Jonathan flexed again. 'I-I'm fine,' I gulped weakly.

'Jonathan,' she said, 'go and get her some of that hangover stuff you brought back from Munich. That will do the trick.'

'No. Really, I'm quite okay...'

'Are you sure you don't want me to get you some?' the cheeky sod asked with apparent concern, laying the back of his hand against the side of my face. 'You do seem rather hot and bothered. Are you sure there's nothing up?'

Piss off! I wanted to tell him. 'I'm feeling better already,' I replied instead.

At long last Michael and Ros decided to return to their vertical expression of a horizontal desire, leaving me to my own devices, speared from middle to mouth, it seemed, on Jonathan's lap.

'You bastard!' I hissed angrily into his ear.

'I know,' he chuckled, wriggling his groin underneath me when he was sure he wasn't being observed.

'Don't do that!' I protested in a fierce whisper, momentarily closing my eyes at the scouring effect it produced.

As the music began to play I gripped Jonathan as hard as I could with my vaginal muscles and started to squeeze and squeeze and squeeze. It was my only means of salvation. My only way out from under. Unless I could make him shoot his lot, and then wither away, I'd have been obliged to spend the rest of my life sitting there on Jonathan's huge horn of plenty, hiding it from view. There was simply no other way to get free from him.

Surreptitiously I also began to wriggle my hips against him, as well as squeeze, getting a sort of rhythm going. That would help, I decided. That would help to speed him on his way. To bring him to the point of no return. And once I'd made him spout like a fountain inside me he'd be able to tuck himself back in his trousers, hidden from view behind my back, and I'd be free to stand up and hobble upstairs to the loo But how long it might take I'd no idea. All I could do was wriggle gently, squeeze, and hope...

After what seemed an age I eventually won the battle, and he started to implant me just as hotly and profusely as I'd expected from the size of his tackle. Stream followed stream, swamping me within seconds and making me shiver with pleasure, notwithstanding the close proximity of my husband. As Jonathan continued to squirt I glanced up apprehensively and was appalled to catch Michael's eye and see him wink at me. Somehow I managed to smile back, despite the way I was being spunked right in front of him!

And still he was spurting forth, with a force I found hard to believe. I closed my eyes, dreading that one of the others might be able to read in my face what was happening to me below the suspender belt. And I knew with shame that Jonathan could feel the effect his climax was having on me. But there was nothing I could do about it. I just had to sit there, curled up on his lap, and accept his seed. I just had to sit there and submit to the duty that was imposed on all womankind at the very dawn of creation.

At long last he made himself decent and I was able to haul myself back to my feet, almost instantly feeling his sticky juices starting to trickle down inside me.

'Do hurry back,' grinned Jonathan, stretching out in the chair so smugly that I had to resist the very real temptation to plant my toe right in the middle of the area where my bottom had so recently sat. I squelched my way past Michael and Rosalind, trying to appear as normal as possible, but knowing how red I was in the face.

'Are you feeling any better?' asked Michael.

'Yes,' I replied truthfully, squeezing my thighs together to celebrate my relief at being my own person once again. 'Yes, a bit more myself at last...'

As I came out of the bathroom a short while later I saw Jonathan's huge Alsatian dog lying across the landing, apparently waiting for me. *Woof!* he cried excitedly, jumping to his feet with alacrity and thumping his tail back and forth against the wall.

'I'm sorry,' I told him. 'I know everyone else has, but I do have to draw the line somewhere, don't I? Even if I have already paid the price in advance.'

CHAPTER EIGHT - ALISON THE MOVIE

Hi, it's Alison again. Can you remember when I spoke to you at the end of my last book, *Painful Consequences*? I asked you several questions about the spanking/blue movie to which Sylvia's ancient computer had accidentally assigned me. I asked you whether you thought I'd got up and staggered home after the spanking was over, or whether I'd stayed to make the rest of the film by fucking my screen husband. However, I forgot to ask you whether or not you thought I'd returned to the studio one week later to film the first part of the movie, due to the fact that my screen lover, John, was not available until then.

Well, if you go into one of the sex shops in Amsterdam and buy a DVD entitled - rather crudely - *Spunked, Spanked, and Spunked Again*, then you might discover some of the answers. Alternatively, you could try reading the next few pages...

'I think you'll like this,' Pete said smugly, holding up the luridly illustrated front cover to the full view of his three mates who were spread out on comfortable armchairs in front of the TV set, cans of lager in hand. 'I got it last week from that little shop in Canal Strasse. It's a real stormer. Just see what you think of this.'

'The female lead certainly looks the business,' enthused one of the young men, gazing with interest at the tall, strikingly attractive girl in the minuscule blue miniskirt, curly hair twisting and twining almost half the way down to her waist. 'Just look at the state of that!'

'Jesus, she's stalky!' whistled another. 'Look at the body on it! I wonder how much they had to pay her to take part in something like this? A fucking fortune, I guess.'

'Almost literally, I'm sure.'

'I love the title,' laughed the fourth of the friends. 'Does the film live up to it, Pete?'

'You'll have to wait and see.'

There came a rap on the door.

'Come in,' called the girl on the TV screen. 'The door isn't locked.'

'I thought I'd take you up on your offer,' said her visitor, closing the door after himself.

'Hello, John. What offer is that?'

'Your offer of a cup of coffee this morning.'

'I can't remember saying that.'

'No. But you did say that Tony was safely away in Manchester all day today on business.'

'I didn't say anything about *safely*, I'm sure.'

'Maybe not. But he is safely away, isn't he?'

'Yes...'

'So I just assumed you forgot to add the bit about me popping round here for a coffee while he's away.'

'I see...'

'I thought you might fancy me a bit? After that kiss and cuddle at Paul's party last night, I mean.'

'Well...'

'More of a good long grip and grope really, I suppose.'

'Er...'

'I hoped you might fancy me half as much as I fancy you. That would still be a hell of a lot.'

He walked up slowly and slid both arms around her.

'Oh crumbs,' she gulped, but not making any real effort to get away from him.

'Tony may be my best mate,' he murmured, easing her against him, 'but I can't help the fact that I'm absolutely crazy about his wife, can I?'

'Well...'

'Don't you fancy me at all?'

'Yes,' she whispered, as his hands roamed back and forth across the superbly filled seat of her skirt, seeking and exploring every curve and contour. 'You know I do, John...'

'Let's do it then. Just the once, and never again. What do you say to that?'

She lifted her face towards his. 'OK,' she replied softly, before opening her mouth to accept his tongue. At that same moment his hands whipped the seat of her short skirt up past her waist. There was no sign of any objection on her behalf...

'Oh, yeah!' the four young men in the sitting room groaned as one, goggling in delight at the pretty pink cheeks, entirely knickerless and bare, that pouted back at them so saucily from the giant TV screen.

'What an arse!' one of them croaked in admiration, the camera having panned in to fill the screen with acres of shapely round bottom, as creamy-smooth and perfect as anyone could possibly have asked. 'What a beautiful arse!'

'You can say that again,' agreed Pete.

'Do we actually get to see it spanked?'

'You'll have to wait, won't you.'

'If we do I'll bet it's just a few gentle taps.'

'Like I've said twice already, you'll simply have to wait and see.'

Now the four of them were greedily devouring the sight of a large male hand painstakingly exploring every millimetre of those mouth-wateringly plump bare cheeks. For a good three minutes he stroked, moulded and kneaded each gorgeous twin orb in turn, clearly relishing his labour of love. The boys stared appreciatively as the man's fingers and palm continued to savour the firm, satin-like flesh to the full. Now he was running his fingertips slowly up and down the deep divide between her buttocks, before pressing gently inside until they were hidden from view. Then he was fondling and squashing the very ripest part of both cheeks in the same one-handed hold. Then, once again, he was caressing the plumpness of each individual cheek in turn, the buttery-smooth, pearly-pink flesh sliding sweetly back and forth through his outspread fingers, very slowly and deliberately, for all to see and enjoy in vivid close-up.

'Christ, that's horny!' breathed one of the voyeurs, surreptitiously adjusting the front of his jeans as he spoke.

'What couldn't I do to that lovely bare bum!' growled the lad sitting next to Pete.

'Nothing that hasn't been done to it at least a thousand times already,' that worthy replied with a knowing air.

'Surely you weren't expecting me?' asked the man on the screen, squeezing her delightfully dimpled left buttock firmly enough to leave a row of fleeting white finger-marks behind, before repeating the treatment on the right. 'Wearing no knickers, I mean.'

With her skirt hitched up round her waist she dropped to her knees in front of him. 'I'm not going to say,' she giggled as she reached for his zip. Seconds later she was pressing his smooth penis against the side of her face. 'You're incredibly hot!' she breathed appreciatively, brushing her lips lightly over the iron-hard flesh.

'Who wouldn't be?' he gulped, looking down as she opened her mouth and started to swallow him inch by inch.

The four occupants of the sitting room stared in fascination as the whole of his handsome cock slowly vanished into her lovely mouth, only to reappear and disappear again at regular intervals. 'I think I'm going to shoot my load!' gasped one.

'Me too!' chorused the rest.

The man on the screen was clearly in the same plight. Less than thirty seconds later the girl on her knees jerked back her head and allowed stream after stream of seed to splatter her face and then gush into her open mouth.

'Let's go to bed,' she whispered, when John was finally spent. 'I'll soon be able to revive you with my mouth.'

'Oh yes!' croaked one of the young men on the settee, the scene on the TV set having changed to the bedroom, where the girl was lying, naked and wide-legged on her back, while John's recently re-erected organ was slithering slowly and wetly in and out. The camera closed in and for several long seconds there was nothing but penis and pussy on view. Then it drew back, showing first her spectacularly upthrust breasts, and then the look of ecstasy on her pretty face. Then the camera returned to her groin. Then slowly back to her face. Then penis and pussy again, then boobs and beautiful face.

On and on went the lovemaking, the couple swapping positions every now and again so that sometimes she was wriggling and writhing on top of him, and sometimes - as now - she was on elbows and knees while he plundered her from behind.

'His dick looks bigger than ever,' commented the young man to the left of Pete.

'Wouldn't yours?' responded the latter. 'Taking her in that position, I mean? Banging your groin into that lovely pert bum while you probe her all the way up to her tonsils?'

'Look how wet she is!' commented one of the others. 'Look at the oil dripping down her legs. She's obviously having a whale of a time.'

'You can see that much from the look on her face,' agreed Pete. 'And from the way she's wriggling that fabulous arse from side to side as if there's no tomorrow. Go on! Go to it, my son! Give her as much as you can!'

Advice for which the man on the screen had absolutely no need whatsoever.

He was now dishing it out for all he was worth. Groin slapped loudly against uptilted buttocks, while penis stretched wide-open pussy as tight as a drum.

'I've always dreamt about giving it to you this way,' panted John, his hands gripping her tightly round the waist as he continued to pile lustily into the hot little cunt which still dripped with lubrication. 'Ever since I first caught sight of this horny little bum in a pair of tight blue jeans. I hope your good husband appreciates what he has here?'

'He certainly seems to,' puffed the girl on the bed, momentarily raising her head from the pillow into which her face had become buried, and then grimacing up at the ceiling at the strength and speed of the coupling.

'Who wouldn't?' groaned Pete, sounding more than a trifle envious. 'Imagine sliding into bed every night beside something as pretty as that bum!'

'If she was my wife,' said the lad to his right, 'I'd shoot my lot all over it at least once a day.'

'Inside it is where I'd come,' said another. 'All the way up inside it.'

'You bugger!' Pete replied pleasantly.

'I'd just beat it with whatever was handy,' announced the fourth voyeur. 'Until it was as red as a beetroot.'

'Oh!' gasped the young lady whose bare buttocks were the subject of such wide-ranging appreciation. 'Oh God! You're making me come all over again...'

'It's the blowjob he got earlier,' Pete announced with authority. 'That's why he's able to keep it going so long. Lucky sod!'

Slap! Slap! Slap! went groin against bouncy buttocks as he impaled her with all his power. *Slurp! Slurp! Slurp!* went penis inside warm wet pussy, as he probed and opened her as wide as she'd comfortably go. The four friends stared at the gleaming wet stalk that pumped in and out at pace.

'I don't know how much longer I can put up with this,' muttered the young man on the end of the sofa. 'It's so fucking frustrating!'

'Don't worry,' said Pete. 'Relief will soon be at hand.'

'Speak for yourself, you tosser!' came the instant retort.

But Pete was right. A few seconds later John's seminal fluid began to spurt for the second time during the course of the video, graphically depicted on the screen thanks to the skill of the cameraman and the cooperation of the copulating couple.

Then John was up and gone, leaving the beautiful girl lying on her back on the bed. She reached down to her groin, and the camera followed the fingers of her hand as they checked the seepage of creamy-white sperm from between the tops of her legs. Having ascertained the substantial extent of the leakage she gave a long drawn-out sigh of contentment and then extracted a miniature pair of black knickers from the drawer beside the bed. Still sitting on the satin sheets she eased the filmy little panties over her feet and then wriggled them up into position. Then she turned on her front, writhing her hips slowly and luxuriously from side to side, and groaning softly at the pleasure of the oh-so-recent lovemaking.

'Caught you!' bellowed a voice on the screen. 'Bloody well caught you right in the act!'

'This next bit is what I meant when I said that relief was at hand,' explained Pete. 'You're going to enjoy it a lot. The horny little baggage is about to get her just desserts. Sexual frustration is now a thing of the past. I promise.'

And Pete was entirely right once more. Less than thirty seconds later the four friends goggled in delight and fascination as a huge male hand cracked down noisily across her bare-again left buttock, causing her to shriek in distress as well as leaving a clearly defined handprint across the centre of her wildly bouncing cheek. The hand cracked down again, blurring the edges of the handprint whilst darkening the hue. And then it cracked down again. Momentarily her face filled the screen, displaying the anguish she so clearly felt. Her howls of outrage increased as one blow after another rained down on her unprotected cheek. Tears rolled down her cheeks, but scream and struggle as she might the spanking proceeded at a truly blistering power and pace. Then it was the turn of her right buttock to be dealt with exactly the same.

'I'll teach you to have it off behind my back!' growled her screen husband, starting to lay into one bright-red cheek after the other as hard as he could. Despite her vociferous protests the punishment continued to be meted out with ever increasing gusto.

Then after a while a wooden coat hanger was brandished and put to good use, laying one crimson stripe after another across the sea of glorious scarlet, much to the delight of the audience.

'Is that any better?' Pete enquired of his pal on the sofa, the sound of the howling and yowling combined with the crack of wood on fleshy bare buttocks filling the room.

'Yes, much, much better!' he breathed slowly, feasting his gaze on the most satisfying sight it had ever been his privilege to encounter. 'She certainly deserves all she's getting, and more besides. Shagging his best friend like that...'

'It's only a film. It isn't real.'

'Yeah, well, I know that, but well, you know, I mean to say...'

The young man to his left looked round at Pete. 'I hope he gives her plenty of cock once he's finished with her arse?' he asked anxiously.

'You'll have to be patient and find out.'

But of course, he did. Yard after yard of it, while she remained in the submissionary position on elbows and knees, just as she'd done for much of her time with John. The audience fell silent in fascination as the yardage continued to mount up.

'Now he's teaching her a second lesson,' muttered the lad on the sofa - groin continuing to smack merrily into the discoloured cheeks of her bottom while she wriggled and sighed. 'He's even bigger than the first bloke. And just look at the state of that bum! You could flash-fry a steak on the middle of each of those cheeks!'